CHAPTER ONE
BODHI

"**R**oses are red, pickles are green. I like your legs, and what's in between!"

Ledger Dayne leads the team in a fit of laughter as I step onto the ice for our last preseason practice wearing a pair of light blue pajama pants with bright green pickles of assorted sizes all over them. The peculiar gift from Griffin Ollenberg was waiting for me when I walked in this morning along with a note explaining that it's a team tradition to wear goofy pajama pants for our last preseason practice and that since he forgot to tell me earlier, he took the liberty of buying me a pair.

I had a feeling it was all a joke.

Somehow I knew I would be the only one on the ice today with these Godforsaken pickle pants on, but a tiny part of me wondered if Griffin was being honest with me since he seems to wear pants like this a lot around the arena. It's what he's known for, really. He has this fascination with pajama pants that I don't understand but hey...the fans get a kick out of it so more power to him, I guess.

I could've been my regular asshole self about this whole thing.

I could've refused to wear these ridiculous pants.

But I know if I want the respect of my teammates, I have to earn it, so, pickle pants it is.

"Hey, Kid." Harrison gestures with the tip of his chin. "That a pickle in your pocket or are you just happy to see me?"

More laughter from the guys.

Har, har, har.

"Guess I fell for that one, huh?" I chuckle skating over to the guys who clearly all got here early so they could stand here and wait for me to show up. I survived much of preseason practice without too much stress in the form of hazing from the guys, but definitely was on the receiving end of a few harmless pranks. They turned off the hot water to the showers during my first week and while I was in said cold shower, someone switched out my underwear in my locker for a pair of granny panties. Last week, before one of our practices, I went to grab some stick tape out of my bag only to find it gone. Lo and behold, the only stick tape that just happened to be lying around everywhere was pink sparkly tape with unicorns and rainbows all over it.

Yeah. That was a colorful practice.

I suppose it could be worse.

They could be giving me swirlies in the locker room toilets.

I may not have gotten the warmest reception from the team but they haven't been cold either. What's a little fun among teammates anyway? Stopping in front of the guys I gesture to my new pants with a smirk.

"You guys want to stare at my pickle all day or are we going to get to work?"

August gives my pickles a once over and then meets Griffin's amused glance. With a shrug of his shoulder, he asks, "Depends, Roche. You got a perky pickle worth looking at?"

Griffin twists his mouth and shakes his head trying not to

laugh. "Nah. He's young. He's got to pump his pickle first to make it perky."

August laughs. "Dude did you just say this kid pumps his pickle?"

"What?" I scowl. "I'm not a—"

"He's a pickle pumper?" Ledger asks.

"Hell yeah!" Griffin says with a smile. "All the way to Perky Pickle Palace."

"What the hell is Perky Pick—"

"Alright, alright," Coach Hicks rallies with a slight chuckle. "You guys can tickle each other's pickles on someone else's time. We've got plays to run. Let's go."

"Pickle Pumper," August murmurs, shaking his head with quiet laughter before he skates off to the other side of the rink.

Fantastic.

There's no way that won't become a nickname.

Bodhi Roche the Pickle Pumper.

Oh well. That's the least of my worries now. It's time to show off my skills once again to prove to these guys that I'm just as much of a player as they are. I've been busting my ass during our preseason to show these guys what I'm made of and that I can live up to my hot-shot reputation. I can be a monster on the ice, but every time I go for something flashy or try something they're not used to doing, they roll their eyes or give me a tough time about it. They don't seem too interested in Bodhi Roche the superstar hockey player.

Maybe the joke's on them because that's who they hired.

I've spent years refining my strengths and eliminating most of my weaknesses. I'm bringing notoriety to the Anaheim Stars. They're lucky to have me.

When I was in Boston, if we won it was because Bodi Roche scored or assisted in more goals than anyone else. If we lost it was because Bodhi Roche had a bad night. Why they put so much pressure on me as the new guy when there were older, more experienced players on the team I'll never know. But when you come onto a team as a college superstar, and the franchise expects a lot from you, you do what you're told. When I started in Boston I was told to skate fast and score goals and that's what I did.

I won.

Because I'm a winner.

These Anaheim guys though, they don't seem to give a shit about that.

They have no interest in my stats as a player.

And none of them seem to give two shits that I'm out here on the ice with them trying everything I can think of to show them what I can do. I'm showing off all my skills during this morning's practice, but it's almost like I'm not even here.

Maybe they're all jealous of my pickle pants.

"Hit the break, Roche! Hit the break!" Coach Hicks shouts as I speed down the ice. "Be the double threat. Give yourself the opens."

"Ugh, I don't need to be a double threat when I can fucking sink the puck right now."

Harrison Meers swings up behind me and caps my shoulder with his gloved hand. "We don't give a damn how fast you can skate, kid."

"Well, you should because I'm faster than a lot of you."

Oliver chuckles from a few feet away. "Mmkay."

"Fast is nice," Barrett says from the net, irritated. "But it doesn't get the job done when you end up missing the pass or worse, you miss nine out of the ten shots you take."

Fuck.

He's not wrong, I suppose.

I have missed almost every shot I've taken today.

I'm blaming the damn pickle pants.

"We don't need a superstar out here, Bodhi!" Hicks shouts when he sees I'm talking to Harrison and Barrett. "The guys need a reliable teammate. Someone who can shoot when he knows he can and pass when it's best for the team."

And here lies the difference between the Boston Brews and the Anaheim Stars. Boston didn't stress much about being a team. They wanted to breed star players and that's what I was for them. I'm not going to lie, it's a little aggravating that these guys don't seem to appreciate my competence on the ice. I worked my ass off in Boston in hopes that when my contract was up, I could finally find a team that would accept me for who I am and what I can bring to the franchise.

Anaheim was one of my top five dream teams, so when my agent called and told me I received an offer from the Stars, I was stoked. They've had a winning record and haven't traded a player in the past four seasons. That has to mean something in terms of how this team functions on and off the ice and over the past few weeks I've seen it firsthand. These guys aren't just a team.

They're a family.

Walking into a team that is as tightly bonded as these guys are though, that's a hard door to step through. They've been welcoming, yes, but I can tell I'm not really part of their family just yet. I'm like their annoying little brother that they're forced to play with. They've set their bar high and I know it's my job to do all I can to reach it.

"Run it again," Hicks commands.

"Nice job out there, Pickle Pants," Griffin says to me when we enter the locker room after practice.

I toss my glove on the bench in front of me not sure if Ollenberg is being sincere or sarcastic. "Could've fooled me."

Griffin cocks his head, pursing his lips. "Aww is someone a little butthurt that he didn't get to be the super star out there?"

I stand a little taller and puff my chest. "I'm damn good on the ice. You know it and I know it."

He nods, his expression growing more serious. "Yes. It's true. You have stellar form, Kid but here's the difference between us and you," he says, gesturing between me and the rest of the team. "*We* are a team. *We* have always been a team. *We* will always be a team. We run like a well-oiled machine. It's a give and take. There isn't one of us on this team who is better than the other. We all have different strengths and weaknesses and we know how to use them to our advantage in a game setting."

"It's true," Ledger says as he walks by. He gestures to Griffin. "This guy is the king of assist. He'll set you up for the killer shot almost every time and we know we can trust him to always be there."

"Right." Griffin nods and gestures to Ledger. "And this guy can skate rings around me. He's fast as fuck so if I can get him a pass he can take the puck down the ice in seconds. Like I said, well-oiled machine. And you can either learn how the machine works and become a part of it, or you're left standing on the outside looking in wondering where the power button is. You've got a lot of talent, Roche. A lot. But if you want to feel like a member of the team, you've got to act like a member of the team. Got it?"

I huff out my frustrations in a tight breath. "Yeah. I got it."

He pats my back and gives me a smile. "Good. Now clean yourself up Pickle Pants, it's time for lunch."

I hop in the shower, mulling over what Griffin and Ledger had to say after practice, and remember what my father once said to me after a particularly frustrating high school hockey practice.

"It's not right," I whine, grabbing a can of cola from the fridge. "I work my ass off for him but it's like Coach doesn't even know I exist. He knows I can skate better than any one of them. They all know it. They all call me lightning for a reason."

"Speed is nothing if you can't sink a puck, Bodhi."

"But I can sink the puck! If they would just pass it to me, but they never do!"

Dad lays his hands on my shoulder and gives me a patient smile. "Let me give you a piece of advice, son. You are a fantastic athlete. You're strong. You're hardworking. You're smart and you are kind. But perhaps you're not always coachable."

I tip my head. "What is that supposed to mean?"

"As you go forward in all you do, surround yourself with people who will challenge you to be a better version of yourself," he says. "Listen to what others have to say before making rash decisions. And never be afraid to look at yourself in the mirror to try to see what someone else sees. And if they're not seeing what you want them to see, ask yourself why. Perception is reality, son. Even when you don't mean it to be."

"But maybe they're just perceiving me all wrong."

He nods. "That is absolutely true. And that's what I mean when I say perception is reality. If someone perceives you to be a non-team player, then to them, that's what you are. If someone perceives you to not be a kind person, then to them, you are unkind. See what I'm saying?"

I take in his words and repeat them to myself. "Yeah, Dad. I hear you."

"Great things are going to happen for you, son. One day you will be a star."

A star.

I smile to myself and wonder if Dad knew back then that I would one day be an Anaheim Star.

After I'm showered and dressed, I grab my cellphone and tap the screen for any missed messages. My brows furrow at the lone text waiting for me.

UNKNOWN

Hey Dad. I left spaghetti in the fridge for you. Garlic bread is wrapped in foil. Good luck tonight.

"Dad?" I chuckle. "Afraid not, asshat. No dad here." Giving my thumbs a quick workout, I text back a reply.

ME

Uh, last I checked I'm 24 and very sure I haven't fathered any children just yet. I'm sorry to say you've texted the wrong number.

Shoving my phone into my back pocket, I make my way to the conference room where the team is having lunch before continuing with the rest of the day's game-day routines. When I sit down, my phone buzzes in my pocket so I pull it out to check assuming it's an apology from whoever just mis-texted me.

UNKNOWN

Dangit! Who's going to eat all this spaghetti then?

I huff out a laugh at the witty response appreciating their sense of humor and text them back.

ME

Well that all depends. Are we talking alfredo sauce or marinara?

UNKNOWN

If I had made alfredo, wouldn't I have told my Dad there was alfredo in the fridge? 😅

ME

Touché. I'm sorry I'm kind of busy tonight or I'd definitely be interested. I love Italian food. Perhaps some other time. 😔

UNKNOWN

Perhaps...

Staring at the reply, I can't help but smile and shake my head. After a rough practice it's nice to be reminded there's life outside of hockey.

"What are you grinning about over there?" August asks. He's seated next to Ella Blackstone, his wife and mascot for our team.

"Oh, nothin' important. Just a random text."

Ella's brows wag. "From a giiiirl?"

"Nah." I shake my head and then shrug. "Well, maybe. Whoever it was they were texting the wrong number. Called me Dad and told me there was spaghetti in the fridge."

"Hey, you got a girl to call you daddy." Griffin winks. "Isn't that one of those kinky things you kids are into these days?"

"Kids?" I scoff, amused. "You know I'm not that much younger than you right?"

Griffin waves off my comment. "Semantics."

"So, is there someone special in your life, Bodhi?" Ella asks curiously as she takes a bite of her chicken. "A girlfriend? A wife?"

August's eyes grow mischievous. "A secret lover?"

Ella elbows him in his side. "Give him a break. Not everything about Bodhi has to be scandalous, you know. He's a perfectly normal guy."

If she only knew.

When it comes to relationships I'm probably the most scandalous one here, but I don't mean scandalous in an I'm-fucking-a-forbidden-woman kind of way. Just the opposite really.

I'm not fucking at all.

In fact, I've never fucked anyone in my life.

I'm a twenty-four-year-old professional hockey player.

And I'm a virgin.

CHAPTER TWO
CORRIGAN

"Can you tell me your name, Sweetheart?" I ask, doing a quick assessment for any external injuries that need my attention other than the laceration above her right eye.

Her little voice responds to me. "My name is Mandy."

"Hi Mandy." I smile at her reassuringly. "My name is Corrigan but everyone calls me Corri because it's easier to remember." I lift her left arm remembering that her mom said she thinks she may have injured her right one. "Does this arm feel okay?"

She nods with glassy eyes. "Yeah, but my other arm hurts."

"I know, Sweetheart. We're going to take good care of you, okay?"

I can tell she's trying not to cry. "Mhmm."

"I'm just going to wrap this cuff around your good arm right here so I can take your blood pressure, okay? It's going to give your arm a hug."

"Mhmm."

"And this is little thing is going to help me measure your pulse." I hold up the fingertip pulse oximeter to show her. "It's just going to go right over your finger, like this. Doesn't hurt a bit," I tell her as I press it open and close it over her finger. "Good girl. You okay so far?"

"Mhmm."

Working as quickly as I can, I wrap the blood pressure cuff around her arm and push the button on the receiver for it to inflate. "Can you tell me what happened?"

"I fell off the ladder at recess."

"Oh no. That must've been very scary."

"Mhmm."

"Well, you are being so super brave right now."

I take note of her normal blood pressure and pulse and then gather the supplies needed to treat her laceration. "We're going to get this nasty cut cleaned up and make sure we don't need stitches and then we're going to get an x-ray on your arm so we can see what we're dealing with." I make sure to keep my focus on her even though I'm also keeping her parents aware of my plans. "How old are you Mandy?"

"I'm nine."

"And what grade are you in?"

"Fourth."

"Oooh fourth grade. I loved the fourth grade when I was your age," I tell her. "We got to do so many fun things in fourth grade. What's been your favorite thing so far this year?"

She thinks about it with a furrowed brow but then winces when her right eyebrow moves. "Um, we got to do a living wax museum."

I gasp excitedly as I dab her laceration with a gauze pad. "Oh, that sounds like fun. Is that one of those things where you get to pretend to be someone famous or historical? Like you're really them in a museum?"

"Uh huh." She nods. "And I was Queen Elizabeth."

I lift my brows. "Oh, then I should curtsey in front of you since you're such a royal young lady."

My curtsey makes Mandy smile for the first time since she was wheeled in here.

"Did you know I used to live in London?"

Her little eyes grow. "You did."

"Yep. I lived there for two years. That's where I was living right before I moved back here." I don't bother telling her that I only moved back because my boyfriend cheated on me with an Attending at the hospital where I worked and my job and enthusiasm for what I do started to fade. I've always loved being a nurse though and knew if I stayed in London any longer, I'd end up a nasty old hag feeding the birds in the park instead of living my best life.

But back to my patient.

"And you probably know from your project that London is where the Queen lived."

"Did you ever see her?"

I nod. "I did see her once, yes. She was outside her huge palace and had flowers in her hands and she was saying hello to all the people who were standing around wanting to get a glimpse of her."

"Did she say anything to you?"

"Nah." I shake my head. "Sadly, I couldn't get close enough to her."

In my very best attempt at a British accent, I tell her, "Well, your highness, the cut above your eye seems to have stopped bleeding for now so I think we can patch it up with no need for stitches." I finish cleaning the small wound and place a band aid over it. "And if you're ready, we'll wheel you down the hall so we can get a good look at that arm."

Mandy nods one more time. "Okay."

I give her a friendly smile and then scrunch my nose and whisper, "Sorry my accent isn't very good."

With her parents following behind, I wheel Mandy to the

radiology department for her x-ray and wish her and her family well before heading back to the emergency room. After working a nearly double shift it is well past time for me to go home.

I need sleep.

And food.

And then more sleep.

"Hey Corri, you heading home?"

My keys in hand, I turn to find my very best friend in the whole wide world, Layken Hobbs leaning on the counter of the nurse's station. "Yeah what are you doing down here?" Layken is the Development Director for the hospital's Foundation and her office is on the fourth floor. I rarely get to see her during workdays.

"I knew your shift was about done and wanted to be here to walk out with you."

"You're leaving now?"

"Yep. Should've left an hour ago but I had enough to do to keep busy so I waited for you."

"You're the best." I smile, albeit sleepily. "I feel like I'm sleepwalking already. Thank God my last patient was a simple one."

"We still on for tomorrow?"

"The book signing, right? Hell yes, I'm so there." I point at her. "And next year, you're going to be there as a signing author and I'm going to be your book bitch."

She laughs and rolls her eyes. "Doubtful."

I shake my head, disagreeing with her. "Nope. It's time to put that shit out into the universe, Layken. Positive affirmations. You've got this. I believe in you."

Layken took the job as the Development Director about a year after I started with Pacific Children's when I told her about the position. She's great at it and has made the hospital a lot of money over the years thanks to her outgoing personality and willingness to roll up her sleeves and get to work. But her real passion lies with writing. She's a hopeless romantic and started writing her first romance novel about seven months ago. One day we're going to see that book in all the bookstores throughout California, I just know it.

"Well, I'm not quitting my day job just yet."

"Good! I don't see you often enough as it is. I need my bestie close by always!"

"Cause living in the same apartment building as you isn't enough." She snickers and links her arm with mine as we walk to the parking garage together. "I'm really glad you're back."

Does it feel good to be back home?

I suppose it doesn't feel bad.

At least Layken and I never lost touch and were able to pick up our bond right where we left off.

And I'm far away from Leo Abbot and his tiny pin prick of a penis.

"Good to be back. G'night."

Once I'm home I kick off my shoes and toss my keys onto the table right inside my door. I stop at the fridge and pull it open hoping to find a five-star meal waiting for me. Maybe an entire cooked turkey that I can tear the leg off of and dig into on my way to the shower. Or even a bowl of homemade ramen I can slurp while the water washes away the grossness of the E.R. Alas, my refrigerator is empty except for a half gallon of milk, a few slices of cheese, some butter, grape jelly, a jar of mayonnaise, and a few expired packages of half-eaten lunch meat.

I need to do some serious grocery shopping.

"Tomorrow," I murmur, closing the door to the fridge. "I'll do it tomorrow."

That's what I always say.

Pulling my phone from my pocket, I send a quick order to my favorite take-out place for Chinese dumplings and sweet and sour chicken and then hop in the shower to clean the last eighteen hours from my body. When my phone dings twenty minutes later, I expect it to be Door Dash letting me know my dinner is approaching, but instead, I get an unsolicited picture of a bowl of pasta and a message that reads,

UNKNOWN
Told you I loved Italian. World's best lasagna.

My stomach growls but my eyes grow when I spy the to-go container in the picture. I know exactly where this picture was taken and now I'm so jealous.

ME
OMG is that MARIO's?

Those three little dots appear that tells me whoever I'm texting is writing back.

UNKNOWN
Wait...you know Mario's?

ME
Heck yes! It's my favorite Italian place! My dad and I go there often. He's a sucker for their fettuccine alfredo. Does that mean you actually live in Anaheim?

UNKNOWN
Ah. I'm usually a chicken parm kind of guy but tonight the lasagna was calling to me. And yeah, I'm in Anaheim. Why?

I gasp when I read the last text. "It's a guy."

I don't know why I'm surprised by that given I had no reason to think I was talking to a girl the other night. It actually surprises me that he thought to write me at all. I had already deleted the random text from my phone without another thought.

He must be lonely.

I chuckle to myself, though I shouldn't be laughing at all. A man eating his favorite Italian food by himself isn't that much different from what I'm about to do.

Plus, he never said he was alone.

Ew, I hope he's not on a date because that would be hella weird.

MR. STRANGER

> Oh, I just reread your text. So, you're telling me you sent a text to me the other day instead of your dad and managed to find someone who also lives in Anaheim and not on the other side of the country? That's impressive.

ME

> I'm also a chicken parm kind of girl but when you want good food, fast, Chinese is the way to go. And...yeah...I guess I did. Though to be fair, there's only a one-digit difference between your number and the correct number so maybe it shouldn't surprise me that your number is also an Anaheim number.

My doorbell rings, alerting me to my dinner delivery. I thank the woman standing outside with my food in her hands and give her an extra tip for delivering it while it's still hot. Once inside, I grab a fork, a spoon, and my chopsticks along with a few extra napkins and then set up my to-go containers on my coffee table. My chopsticks in hand, I open the container of dumplings and snap a quick picture.

I toss my phone on the floor beside me and flick on the television to the latest episode of *Say Yes To The Dress*. Why I have some sort of obsession with this show, I'll never know. Maybe it's that gut feeling that I'll never be one of those brides, especially now that

I'm basically starting all over again in the relationship department. Twenty-six and single in California doesn't seem possible, but here I am eating Chinese take-out on my living room floor all by myself.

My phone dings next to me and I glance down at it as I stuff a dumpling into my mouth.

MR. STRANGER

Except I got my phone when I was living on the east coast. So, you're a girl, huh?

ME

Last time I checked. And oh...so I guess I must just have magical powers then. Fancy that.

Swallowing my mouthful of dumpling I look down at my phone again, cringing at what I really want to say to this guy.

"You know what? Fuck it. I don't know him and he doesn't know me so..." My thumbs make quick work of my thoughts before I hit send.

ME

Also, I know this is none of my business but please tell me you're not sitting at Mario's on a date right now completely ignoring some nice naïve girl while texting me your food porn.

MR. STRANGER

Food porn! That's good. And I could be saying the same thing to you. What if some hopeful guy is sitting across the table from you assuming he's getting laid tonight and you're paying more attention to my food porn instead of setting yourself up for an epic night of...you know...adult porn.

ME

Who said I was an adult?

MR. STRANGER

Oh fuck! I mean shit! No. Hell! I'm sorry, kid. Please delete these texts and pretend I didn't say a word. Won't bother you again. My apologies. It was just an innocent text, I swear.

ME

LOL. Relax perv. You're not messing with an underage brain. I promise, I'm an adult.

MR. STRANGER

That's exactly what I would expect a kid to say. "I promise I'm an adult." What are you going to do next, pinky swear?

ME

Hey, don't knock the pinky swear. That's like a blood promise to some. 😊

MR. STRANGER

How can I be sure you're an adult? You going to send me a pic?

ME

Yeah. Let me hop into ChatGPT and see what AI can come up with. 🙄 You want blonde? Brunette? Big boobs and kissy lips or old woman in daisy dukes?

MR. STRANGER

LOL. Alright good point.

ME

For the record. I'm not on a date. I'm sitting on my living room floor watching T.V. and eating alone.

ME

Also, I don't know why I'm telling you this other than to make it clear I'm not a shallow human who ignores people around her. Not that it matters what some total stranger thinks of me, but still.

MR. STRANGER

I get it. And just so you know, I'm also not on a date. Just moved to town not too long ago and don't have a ton of time for making friends. Work keeps me pretty busy.

ME

Same. I just got off an 18 hr shift. I'd ask what you do but I feel like that's too personal considering you're a complete stranger.

MR. STRANGER

Alright then. Make up my job. What do I do?

ME

LOL You sure you want me to go there?

MR. STRANGER

😊 Do your best.

ME

Well, I could go the dirty jobs route and make you out to be someone who has his hands in shit all day, but the thought of hanging out with someone who might not wash his hands properly is a little off-putting. So maybe I should go with something more fun like you're a world-renowned food critic and professional ice cream tester.

MR. STRANGER

You know me so well. LOL. So, we're hanging out now, are we?

ME

shrugs I mean...you're still writing me, aren't you?

MR. STRANGER

I guess you have a point.

ME

So, are you going to make up a job for me?

MR. STRANGER

No need. You're a nurse.

"What the fuck?" I drop my phone like it's just seared my hand and stare at it for several long seconds.

How does he know I'm a nurse?

Does he know who I am?

Is he stalking me?

No, he can't be. I wrote to him first. Not the other way around.

Another text comes through, making me jump when it dings.

MR. STRANGER

If you're panicking because I got it right, you can relax. You said you worked 18 hours and made a big deal about having clean hands. I used my context clues to make an educated guess.

I scroll back up through our messages to find that he's right. I did say both of those things.

I roll my eyes. "Way to keep yourself private Corrigan."

ME

Alright, you got me. I am in the medical profession. But for all you know, I might be a brain surgeon.

MR. STRANGER

You're right. My apologies. I shouldn't have assumed. So, does this mean we're kind of friends now? Since you know what I do and I know what you do? 😊

ME

LOL. Sure. I guess so. Secret friends who have never met.

MR. STRANGER

Like virtual pen pals.

ME

Or a virtual diary. 😅

MR. STRANGER

Oh! Scandalous! Alright then diary, tell me something about yourself.

ME

Like what?

MR. STRANGER

I don't know. Something wild? Something nobody else knows? Something you need to get off your chest? Anything. I'm just over here stuffing my face with lasagna bored out of my mind.

ME

Alright. 😊 Dear Diary, I lived in London for two years and just got back to the States last month after my stupid pencil dick of a boyfriend cheated on me with someone who outranked me.

MR. STRANGER

Ouch. That must've hurt a lot.

ME

The pencil dick? Nah. It wasn't very sharp and quite frankly was kind of the size of those mini pencils you get when golfing. Did it hurt mentally though? Yes and no. I could feel something was off so when I found out I wasn't shocked. But when it feels like an entire hospital is looking at you weird because someone you were close to is now suddenly fucking your boss...I knew nothing good would happen for me if I stayed there.

MR. STRANGER

So, you work in a hospital. Maybe you really are a brain surgeon.

ME

Dear Diary, pretend I didn't just tell a strange random man what I do for a living and where I work.

MR. STRANGER

Ha-ha! I promise not to come looking for you. *Googles how many hospitals there are in Anaheim...*

ME

I didn't say anything about WORKING in Anaheim... But okay, okay. Your turn. Tell me something about you.

MR. STRANGER

Alright. Here goes. Dear Diary, I'm a physically fit, relatively attractive (if I do say so myself) man.

ME

Nothing bad about that.

MR. STRANGER

And I'm a virgin.

CHAPTER THREE
BODHI

"Shit. Why did I tell her that?" I shake my head, chastising myself for being so forward. I'll be lucky if she doesn't respond with a huge laughing emoji. Or worse, maybe she won't respond at all. Not that I should care in the slightest. I realize I'm sitting alone in my darkened apartment eating a dinner I didn't make and talking to a stranger who accidentally texted me a few days ago.

Her opinion doesn't matter.

She has no idea who I am.

So, it's not like my name is going to be splashed all over the tabloids in the morning.

Rolling my eyes at my overshare I toss my phone down and lean back in my chair to take a long sip of the cola I grabbed from the fridge. I poke around my plate with my fork so irritated with myself, I'm now not at all interested in this ridiculous dinner.

Maybe I should just go back to the arena and practice.

Or to the gym downstairs for a workout.

Or maybe I should just go the fuck to sleep.

Either way, I no longer want any more of this lasagna, but

as I stand up to pitch it in the garbage my phone dings. Expecting to see nothing but a bunch of laughing emojis litter my screen, I smile at the message waiting for me.

DIARY GIRL

That's not a bad thing but I'm guessing it bothers you.

ME

If you knew what I did for a living, you would probably be shocked.

DIARY GIRL

Is this where you tell me you work in the porn industry but yet somehow you're still a virgin? Is this like one of those always the bridesmaid, never the bride kind of things? Like always the fluffer never fluffed?

ME

LOL no. I promise it's not. I am not a fluffer. Also no, I do not work in the porn industry.

DIARY GIRL

Hmm. Alright. *thinks* Is it because you have a third and fourth nipple or something and women just aren't into that kind of kink?

ME

Is there a third and fourth nipple kink that I'm unaware of? *Hey Siri...*

DIARY GIRL

🤔 💭 Hell if I know, but I've certainly seen some things in my day.

ME

See? That right there. You're definitely a nurse.

DIARY GIRL

ignores last statement Are you a Eunuch?

ME

Nah. All genitals are attached and in fine working order (sorry if that's crass).

DIARY GIRL

Okay so your chastity is a personal choice.

ME

Yeah I guess you could say that.

DIARY GIRL

Again, not a bad thing at all. Saving yourself for marriage?

ME

Hell no. I want my future wife to know I can satisfy her before she agrees to spend the rest of her life with me.

DIARY GIRL

Okay, I suppose that's fair. So, you just haven't found the right partner yet.

ME

I guess...

There's a bit of an awkward lull in our conversation and I'm not sure what to say. I'd love to tell my Diary girl that I'm more than interested in sex. It's not like I don't think about it and jack off to the newest porn video or simply soap up my dick in the shower because it feels good. I like the idea of sex. I want to experience it. I want to know what it feels like to slide inside a woman. I've just spent so much goddamn time focusing on my career, I haven't allowed myself to give in to the physical temptations.

Sure, there are numerous women hanging out at hotels when we pull in after a game. And yeah, they're wet, willing, and waiting for me to say the word but I never do. Every time I consider it, I hear my father's voice in my head.

"Great things are going to happen for you, son. One day you will be a star."

My father gave me so much.

He gave his life up for me.

Okay maybe not really, but that's how I've always seen it.

He spent days, weeks, months, and even years traveling all over with me so I could get the very best hockey training he could buy.

He spent his money on me instead of cancer treatments.

He knew what he was doing, but by the time I found out it was too late.

I was going to lose my strongest supporter. My number one fan.

Dad died four years ago.

He never saw me move into the major leagues.

He never saw me become an Anaheim Star.

So how could I even begin to consider defiling all he's worked for by whoring myself out to a few puck bunnies when we're on the road?

I owe him everything I have.

I owe him my very best.

I'm too busy climbing the ladder of success to become a father or be tied down to anything. My hockey career is growing in the right direction and could skyrocket with the Stars if I continue to push myself to be the best I can be.

But then again...

I watch some of the other players like Hawken Malone or Milo Landric in Chicago.

They're married and Milo's even a dad. And they're both huge successes. Hell, I think everyone on their team is married and some have more than one kid. Even on our own team, Oliver has his fiancée and August and Ella are married.

Those guys are making a name for themselves *and* getting laid.

Best of both worlds.

If they make it work, why can't I?

Wiping my hand down my face, I stare at my phone for a second, noting the blank screen void of any other incoming texts, and take it as a sign that I should just shower and get to bed. Ice time comes early tomorrow. I tap out one last text to Diary Girl and then leave my phone on my nightstand to charge while I jump in the shower.

ME

Well, I guess I should grab a shower and head to bed. I have to work pretty early. Good night Diary girl. That's what I call you now, by the way.

DIARY GIRL

Sleep tight, Mr. Stranger. That's what I call you. 😊

"HEY ROCHE!" Coach Hicks calls out to me from down the hall as I'm about to enter the gym for my workout.

"Yeah?"

"Stop upstairs and see Marlee Remington when you have a few minutes. She wants to go over your upcoming charity visits."

"Alright."

"I hear you're planning to spend some time visiting the kids at Pacific Children's Hospital." He claps me on the shoulder when he finally reaches me.

I nod. "Yes, Sir. I'm actually planning to help them with their annual Children's Art Auction."

"Well done," he says with an approving nod. "That's a very admirable thing to do."

I give him an easy shrug. "I enjoyed working with the children's hospital back in Boston so when I came out here, I asked Marlee to set me up with the same kind of thing here."

"I like it," Coach Hicks says with a smile. "Alright, well be sure to touch base with her sometime today." He points at me as he starts to walk backwards toward his office. "Don't forget."

"Got it, Sir. I promise I won't forget."

"Oooh," Griffin teases when I step into the gym. "Roche just got a stern talking to from Coach. You already gettin' yourself in trouble Bodhi?"

"In your dreams, Ollenberg. He just wanted to make sure I stop in and see Marlee this afternoon."

"What?" Ledger spins around on his workout bench. "Wh-wh-why? Why do you have to see Marlee?"

"So, he can ask her out," August tells Ledger with a smirk. Ledger doesn't seem to find it funny though.

"Why would I ask out Marlee Remington?"

Bear gestures to Ledger. "Because this asshat here has been crushing on her forever and won't do anything about it."

"Shut up," Ledger admonishes. "I don't have a crush on her."

"Oh, then you're good if I ask her out?" I ask him. "Because she looks damn good today in that pink skirt she's wearing."

Ledger's eyes narrow and for a moment he looks like he might just pounce off the bench and pummel me. I hold my hands up and chuckle at him.

"Only kidding, man. You can relax. I'm not asking anyone out any time soon." I lower my hands. "But also, I hate to be the bearer of bad news, but when I walked into the front office yesterday it sounded like she was gushing over a text from someone…if that means anything…" I shrug and pass Ledger an empathetic wince.

He does look rather disappointed to hear that news.

"Sorry, Ledger."

"It's fine," he says with a shrug. "She's an adult and free to see whomever she wants."

"Or you could just buck up and ask her out," Griffin tells him.

Ledger shakes his head. "If it's meant to be, it'll be. Just leave it alone, alright?"

Wow. I didn't take Ledger for one of those leave-it-to-fate types. I kind of assumed he was one of those guys who sleeps around and enjoys the single-guy life.

Maybe I have a lot to learn.

"How do you guys do it anyway?" I ask after I hop onto the nearest treadmill.

Oliver glances at me from the treadmill next to mine in a full run. "Do what?"

"How do you make time for full-blown relationships? Or marriage and all the stuff that comes with that?"

August smiles widely and shrugs. "You just do."

"Yeah, but don't you worry that your relationship responsibilities will take away from your career? Make you less of a player?"

Even with a face dripping with sweat, Oliver raises a brow as he slows his run. "Do I look like less of a player to you, Roche?"

Sensing his irritation I quickly shake my head. "No. No. And I'm not saying either of you are. I'm just…ugh. I'm clearly not articulating my thoughts very well."

"Have you never been in a relationship before, Roche?"

Griffin asks. At that moment, I can feel the guys staring at me, but I proudly shake my head.

"No. I don't do relationships. No time. Too much effort."

"Pity," August chuckles.

"Why's that?"

He wipes his face with his towel and then turns toward me. "Because having someone special in your life to just...be your person is one of the best feelings in the world."

"Says the guy who married his childhood best friend," Harrison adds. "She's been your person since you guys could walk and talk. She would've been your person even had you not married her."

"Not true." August shakes his head. "If she would've married someone else, she would've been that guy's person. She would've been in love with someone else. Lucky for me, that's not how it worked out and yeah, she'll always be my person now. I'm a fuckin' lucky guy. Same for Oliver and Scarlett, right, Magallen? And you two dated during the season."

"Yep. And semi-long distance for a while until she moved to Anaheim to live with me." Oliver looks at me and says, "Scarlett was originally from L.A. but we met when her fiancé didn't show up for their wedding and she wanted someone to celebrate part of her honeymoon with her. A Halloween party in New Orleans."

"That's cool. How did you make it work with her during the season?"

"We just did. We did because we wanted to be together. When she could, she'd come here to visit. On days off, I'd try to go there or we'd meet halfway. But I never missed a practice or a workout if that's what you're worried about."

Harrison smirks. "One could say you even had a little extra cardio."

"Oh, there's nothing little about it." Oliver laughs before

making eye contact with me again. "But August is right. There's something to be said for having another human standing beside you through life. It's a good feeling to know you're not alone in the world, and I can't lie. The sex is out of this world."

"Same, bro." August and Oliver bump fists.

"You mean you aren't bothered by having sex with the same person every day for the rest of your life?" I tease, but both guys shake their heads with a scowl.

"Not at all bothered," Oliver says. "In fact, I find it relieving. I've got the girl now. I don't need to work at figuring out what some other woman wants or doesn't want. What she likes or doesn't like. I know how to pleasure my woman and I can rock her world any time she needs it, wants it, hints at it, you name it. I have zero interest in ever being with someone different ever again. One and done, man. One. And. Done."

Harrison steps toward me and claps my shoulder. "I think what they're saying, Pickle Pants, is that if you want what they got, you have to be even better than you are. You have to be able to afford the time and effort it takes to build a relationship with someone. The moment your game suffers, your relationship will suffer too because you'll resent her for taking you away from hockey—your career. All the things you've worked for."

"Bingo," Oliver says with the point of a finger.

"Is that what happened to you?" I ask Harrison innocently.

He bobs his head. "I was with someone years ago. At the beginning of my career. But she broke it off. She didn't want to be the reason I didn't try to get where I am today. She knew I had my heart set on professional hockey. She knew it was within reach for me, but her job wasn't one that she could randomly pick up and move away, you know?"

"Did you love her?" August asks.

"Of course I did. At the time, I would've done anything for her. And I still think about her every once in a while."

"Where is she now?"

He shrugs. "No clue. I have no doubt she's married with kids and living a fantastic life. And good for her. She deserves that happiness just like anyone else does."

"You know what, Pickle Pants?" Griffin snaps his towel to my ass. "We just happen to know someone who enjoys playing the match-making game. I'm sure she'd be happy to help you find the woman of your dreams." Griffin glances at August who throws his head back in laughter.

"Oh fuck! Trust me dude." August stands to move to the battle ropes. "You do not want to get her started."

"Who?"

"Ella." He rolls his eyes, still chuckling. "She'll never leave you alone about it, I swear to God. Do yourself a favor and just go get laid a few times. Maybe one of those partners will stick."

Go get laid a few times.

Yeah.

Okay.

If only it was that easy.

CHAPTER FOUR

CORRIGAN

"**W**hich one are you getting today?" Dad asks as we peruse the menu.

"I think I'm going for the Big Papa." I point to the item described as a hotdog topped with two slices of bacon, jalapeno scallion cream cheese, a shredded cheese blend, fresh jalapenos, and finished with a dusting of crushed potato chips.

He nods. "Impressive."

I smile and ask which one he's choosing.

"I've got to go for my favorite."

"Ah. The mac and cheese dog?"

"Mhmm." He pats his stomach. "It's the mixture of the mac and cheese, bacon, and fried onions for me. I think it's becoming my regular."

"Alright, I'll let it pass this one time," I say, pointing to him. "But next time you have to choose something new. That's the whole point."

Before I moved to London for a couple years to study and experience life as a nurse across the pond, Dad and I would meet for lunch once a week at Harold's Hotdog Diner. The retro décor gives off a fun and nostalgic vibe and the food is fantastic. There is no other place I've ever known to have as many different hotdog topping combinations as Harold's. When we would come here before, the rule was we could never order the same hotdog twice so that we could experience as many combinations as possible.

Some of the times the combos were so amazing I forgot I was actually eating a hotdog. Other times?

Well...best not to remember those times.

Let's just say some toppings really don't need to be put on a hotdog.

Snapping a quick picture of my lunch, I send it to Mr. Stranger since we seem to have bonded a bit over food.

ME

My lunch for the day. Ever had a hotdog like this? #foodporn

"It's really great to have you back here, Sweetheart," Dad says with an appreciative smile as he takes a messy bite. He chuckles and grabs his napkin to wipe his face. "I missed these lunch dates."

"Same." I nod to my dad with a mouth full of food. "They definitely don't make them like this in London."

"So, have you gotten yourself all settled in? Anything you need? You know I'm more than willing to—"

"Dad," I say for the twelve-hundredth time since I got home a few weeks ago. "I don't need your money. I promise I'm good. I handled life an ocean away all on my own. I can certainly handle it here in California."

Although the boxes in storage that I have yet to pick up and unpack tell a bit of a different story.

"I'm just saying, Corri. I make more money than one person

could ever need. I could've made sure you were set up with a state-of-the-art house if you would've just let me."

"And that's precisely why I didn't, Dad. Come on, we've been through this before. You can't just be the guy in my life who spoils his daughter so rotten she forgets to learn how to do things for herself. You know, one day you won't be around anymore and then what will I do if you've always done everything for me?"

He shrugs and passes me a smirk. "Marry a rich man and hope that he's half as good to you as I was?"

"Dad." I chuckle this time.

"I know, Sweetheart. I know. I'm sorry. With your mother not around and you in another country, it got a little lonely around here. I just want to feel like I'm doing something good."

I cock my head. "Dad, what are you even talking about? You do loads of good! You give so much money to so many organizations in need. You might think that's just a normal day for you but think about the millions of people who could never give back the way you do."

"I guess that's true but it's just money."

"It's not always money. You've played Santa for the kids at Pacific Children's for years. That's not money. It's time. It's effort. It's compassion. You know I'm right. Not every man gets to be the head coach of a professional hockey team. If you don't think that's special in and of itself, or that you didn't work your ass off to get that position, you need to walk yourself into my hospital and have your head examined."

"Don't you work at the Children's Hospital?" He grins, referring to the fact I spend most of my days with children.

"Yeah, but they'd take a peek at your brain if I asked them to. Then I can tell all the kids what a whacko you are. Speaking of the kids, even when I left you never stopped being Santa for them."

Dad shakes his head. "And deny them a little bit of Christmas magic when they're lying in a hospital bed? I would never."

"See?" I pat his hand across the table. "You do good things, Dad. And I have so much respect for what you do. You've taught me well. Now you have to let me spread my wings a bit, okay?"

He nods, quietly watching me with a glint in his eye. "Alright. I promise I'll try. But you have to promise you'll come to me if you ever need help. With anything."

"You know I will, Dad." I smile at him and squeeze his hand. "Now tell me how the team is looking. I know it's early but hockey is hockey. How are Barrett's knees holding up?"

Dad laughs as he wipes his mouth with his napkin again. "That grumpy bear wouldn't tell me if his knee literally came unattached from his body. He'd just strap on his guard and put himself back out there on the ice. But I've got to tell you about the Pickle Pants."

A goofy grin spreads across my face. "Pickle Pants?"

"Ollenberg's latest prank on the new kid."

"Bodhi Roche?"

"Yeah. You know how Ollenberg likes to wear his stupid pajama pants?"

I grin. "Yeah."

"He told Roche that they all wear pajama pants to the last practice before the season opener and even got him a special pair for the occasion. They had pickles all over them."

I gasp, sitting back in my chair and covering my mouth. "Oh no! Let me guess. He was the only one in pajama pants?"

"You guessed it. And now the team calls him Pickle Pants." Dad laughs. "Definitely knocked the kid down a peg or two. He came onto the team with this righteous, pompous, star-child mentality, you know?"

I shrug. "Meh. He's young. I imagine getting to be an Anaheim Star can get to just about anyone's head. He'll learn."

"Yeah. The guys will set him straight. The kid's a great player. He's got tons of potential. I can see it."

"Well, there's nobody better than you to help bring it out of him."

"Thanks, Sweetheart." He gathers up his garbage and places it on the tray we were sharing. "I should probably get going. I've got an interview with Sports Network before we board the plane for tomorrow's away game."

I roll my eyes playfully. "As if you need to prepare."

"The moment I don't is the moment someone will get me to say something stupid and then I'll really be in trouble."

"Well thanks for lunch. Same time next week?"

"Absolutely." We stand from the booth and Dad leans over to place a kiss on my temple. "I look forward to it."

AFTER A GRUELING WORKWEEK, I finally have a day off. An entire day to myself to do God knows what. Lying in my bed, I weigh all the things I need to do against things I would rather do. I could be scrubbing the bathroom or organizing my closet, but I would rather shop...or do nothing at all. There are still several boxes in my storage unit to pick up and unpack. I need to work on making this place look more like a home than a low-key dorm room, but when I come home from work over-stimulated and exhausted the last thing I want to do is put my home together. Dad would offer to hire someone to do all the work for me, but I want to do these things on my own.

It's time to create my own happiness.

Build my life the way I want to live it.

I suppose that means a day of shopping is in order because I need more shit. And then I could grab some boxes and bring them back here to unpack.

But maybe I need a shopping buddy.

We could make a day of it!

Grabbing my phone from my bedside, I tell Siri to call Layken and wait for her to pick up.

"What up, Bitchachos?"

"Hey! Want to hang out and shop with me? Maybe have lunch or dinner somewhere?" I ask. "I'll probably watch Dad's game tonight if you feel like doing that too."

"Oooh! A whole day with Corrigan Hicks? Who would I be to say no? And you know me! I live to shop. Can we go to that new ramen place?"

"Hopeless Ramen-Tic?"

"Yeah! It's all everyone has been talking about for weeks and they're finally open. There might be a wait, but I hear it's worth it."

"Alright. That's cool with me. I can stop downstairs and get you on my way out."

"No need. I'm already out so how about if I swing by and pick you up? Be there in ten?"

"I'm literally just getting out of bed," I tell her with a laugh.

"Well, it's eleven o'clock bitch! You've slept almost half the day away. Get yourself up and throw on some clothes. I'll be there soon."

"Alright, alright. I'll drop the kids off at the pool and brush my teeth and be ready when you get here."

Layken blurts out a laugh. "You know you can just tell me you're going to poop, right?"

I shrug as I roll myself out of bed. "You know me. I'm fancier than that. Plus, I ate lunch at Harold's yesterday so..."

"You're fancier than that," she laughs. "But say no more. Harold's is always excellent, but it'll get ya in the end. Pun intended. I'll see you soon. Don't push too hard or else I'll be forced to make a show of it when we walk down the medical aisle at Target."

I giggle again. "I'll try my best to stay in control at all times. See you soon."

I carry my phone with me into my bathroom because let's be honest, who doesn't poop while scrolling through their phone anymore? As I'm scrolling, a text dings in from Mr. Stranger that makes me laugh.

MR. STRANGER

> Sorry, this is late. I was traveling yesterday. Harold's huh? A few coworkers took me there not too long ago. Excellent dogs but...

ME

> But what?

MR. STRANGER

> Never mind. Forgot who I was talking to.

ME

> What's that supposed to mean? And what do you care? You're literally talking to a stranger! 😄

MR. STRANGER

> Yeah but you're a girl and I'm a guy and we don't usually talk that way around girls.

ME

> Oh, so it was going to be gross?

MR. STRANGER

> Obviously.

ME

Did you forget I'm a nurse? I assure you I've seen it all. Come on. Hit me.

MR. STRANGER

Okay, okay. I was going to say their dogs are great but they make you poop.

I throw my head back in laughter noting only to myself where I am sitting right now. "Oh man, if you only knew."

ME

Yeah that's true. They do. 😋

MR. STRANGER

What one did you get?

ME

The Big Papa.

MR. STRANGER

😋 The Big Papa, huh? My girl likes 'em spicy!

I don't know why I smile at my phone. I don't know this guy at all. I don't even know his name but seeing him call me his girl gives me the warm-fuzzies. Realistically it's the first time I've had anyone call me their girl. Leo was always so prim and proper when it came to us being together. He wasn't much for public displays of affection and refused to treat me like his girl-friend during the workday. I respected that idea for the most part, as he was an Attending and I was one of the team's nurses, but still. He never made me feel the way I just felt with a complete stranger calling me his girl.

You're such a wanker, Leo.

ME

Your girl huh?

MR. STRANGER

Sorry. Didn't mean to offend.

ME

Oh, you didn't. I was just teasing.

MR. STRANGER

Well, if I'm being honest, you're kind of my only friend outside of work. I don't usually give myself much time for a social life.

ME

Right. I can see how professional ice cream testing could do that to a person.

MR. STRANGER

Ooh! She's witty too ladies and gentlemen. 😊
So what are we eating for dinner tonight?

ME

Actually, I'm heading out with a friend today. Thinking about trying that new Ramen place in town. You can come if you want. We could actually meet in person. Side note: my friend would die to know I've been texting a complete stranger. 😊

MR. STRANGER

Damn. I would love to, but I'm out of town for work today. Lots of ice cream parlors to hit before the week's end. 😊 Maybe a rain check?

ME

LOL! Of course. I'm not going anywhere. Safe travels. Have some cookies and cream for me!

MR. STRANGER

Will do. Can I ask you a question before you leave for the night though?

ME

Sure!

MR. STRANGER

I suppose you could lie and I would never know, but do you have a name and am I allowed to know it?

ME

My name is Corri.

MR. STRANGER

Corri. That's a beautiful name.

ME

Thank you. 😊 And what's your name?

I watch the three dots appear on my screen and then disappear...and then reappear again before my Stranger man finally replies.

MR. STRANGER

Alan.

ME

Nice to finally sort of meet you, Alan.

MR. STRANGER

The pleasure is all mine Corri. Hope you have a great night. Slurp some Ramen for me.

ME

Haha! Will do!

"Wait, WHAT?" Layken's jaw drops mid-sip. She saves the noodle hanging out of her mouth and I watch as she sips it down. "You've seriously been texting some guy you don't even know?"

I sift my spoon through my ramen bowl, because I'm lame and don't know how to use chopsticks correctly, after a long afternoon of shopping. I love shopping with my best friend, but sometimes I forget she's one of those people who likes to walk down every single aisle of the store to make sure she doesn't miss a good bargain. Also, I promised a stop at the local bookstore on our way to dinner and of course that took longer than expected with her. A warm bowl of ramen to end our day out is hitting the spot perfectly.

"Like I said, it was an accident at first. I hit the wrong number on my phone when I was texting my dad."

Her brows pinch. "You know that's what they make contacts for in your phone, right? So, you don't even have to type in a number?"

"Yeah but you know I'm not that organized and since I knew his number I figured it was just as fast to type it in than search through my contacts. I don't know. I'm weird that way."

"Yeah. You are, but I guess that's beside the point. You're texting a stranger. Like still..."

I nod. "Yeah. Do you think that's bad?"

"I mean..." She shrugs. "It's weird. He could potentially be some sort of oddball perv or what if he's a sex trafficker?"

I cock my head. "He is not a sex trafficker."

"How do you know?"

"Because I..."

She's right.

I suppose I really don't know.

"Okay so it's always possible, but I just don't get that vibe. He's never asked me to meet. He's never asked where I work. There's no way for him to locate me unless he works for my cell phone company. He's never asked my name. I mean, until today. It's just been harmless chat about food."

"Wait, so did you give him your name?"

"Yeah. I told him my name was Corri."

"Well, that was smart of you at least."

I shrug. "I mean, I'm no dummy."

"And did you get his name too?"

I slurp a spoonful of my ramen, savoring the chicken flavor. "Yes. His name is Alan."

Layken scrunches her face. "Alan? What the hell kind of name is Alan?"

"What's wrong with Alan?"

"It's...I don't know. Old."

"Okay, so he has an old name. Maybe it's a family name."

"Are you planning to meet him? Like for real?"

"I invited him here."

Her eyes bulge. "WHAT?" She looks around for a lone man but I chuckle and pat her arm.

"Relax spaz. He's away for work. I just thought meeting in a public place would be easy and we could've bolted if we wanted to had it gone badly."

"You mean if he was ugly as hell?"

I grin over my noodles. "Yeah. That too. So, how's the book writing going?"

She swallows another bite and shrugs. "It's slow going for now. Work is a lot, so I write when I can. And my best friend keeps tearing me away to do stupid shit like shop and suck ramen down our pie holes and watch hot guys play hockey."

"God, she sounds like a real bitch."

She rolls her eyes. "Don't even get me started."

"Well, I'm sure it's going to be a masterpiece and I can't wait to read a few chapters when you have them done."

"I promise you'll be the first to know."

"Do you have an exciting main character?"

"Yeah I think so. He's going to be this guy who—"

DING!

My phone dings with a text, lighting up the screen. I nearly choke on my ramen when I see what the message says.

MR. STRANGER

I think I need sex lessons. Is that a thing?

CHAPTER FIVE

BODHI

Tonight's game was a disaster.

I don't know what came over the team but every single one of us had a hot mess moment at some point during the game, which led to the Grizzlies ending the game with a 4-2 victory. Bear has been seething since we got off the ice because somehow he let Minnesota into his net four times, which is very unlike him. He hit the ice bath pretty quickly after the game.

Hopefully he's alright.

Once we got back to our hotel most of us stopped in the bar where they gave us a roped-off area to enjoy a late dinner and a few drinks. Oliver headed upstairs about forty minutes ago to call Scarlett and August and Ella went up together as well with their hands all over each other. Ledger said something about the two of them still living in their honeymoon phase. Either way they're lucky to have each other. Especially when we're on the road.

The rest of us are three beers in and have been discussing Griffin's collection of pajama pants and how even though he sometimes looks like a complete bum, he's never at a loss for women.

Ledger sips his beer, trying not to snort it through his nose. "Like, do they come up to you and tell you how fucking hot you look in your pants? Do they whisper, 'Nice pants, Ollenberg' in their husky sexy voice or something? Is that how you reel them in?"

Griffin laughs. "Dude, I can't help it if I'm just a sexy ass motherfucker who exudes all the things the ladies want. Plus, I've got a cock they all like to suck on." He shrugs helplessly. "What can I say?"

Harrison belches and then laughs. "You're so full of shit, Griffin."

"You think so?"

"Know so."

He leans forward in his chair, his arms stretched on the table. "I'd be willing to bet you a thousand bucks my dick will be in the mouth of a beautiful woman, if not two beautiful ladies, by the end of this night."

"No go, man." Harrison shakes his head. "How am I supposed to know if that really happens? You think I'm going to watch or something?"

Griffin sits back with a smirk on his face. "Guess you'll have to take my word for it. Or maybe I'll take a pic for good measure."

"Speaking of hot ladies," Ledger says, standing from his chair. "That one over there looks thirsty. I think I need to buy her a drink."

I whistle as he walks away and Griffin reminds him to wear a rubber. Then he turns back to me.

"What about you, Roche?"

"What about me?" I ask, licking my lips after a sip of beer. The tension in my body during today's game is finally floating away thanks to the alcohol.

"How come you're not prowling for someone to take to bed?"

"Why do I need to do that?"

"Because everybody does that." He laughs. "And your reputation precedes you."

I cock a brow. "It does?"

He nods. "Yeah. You think we didn't hear all about you before you joined the Stars?" He huffs a laugh and his eyes narrow. "We heard all about your playful ways."

"Don't know what you heard, but most of it was probably bullshit."

"Is that so?"

"Mhmm," I say, lifting my glass to my mouth again.

"I heard people call you the Puck Bunny Prince."

I nearly spit out my beer, some of it trickling down my chin. "I'm sorry, what?"

"Yeah. Rumor has it you're damn good at picking up the ladies."

"Not true, man." I shake my head. "Not even a little bit. Don't know where you heard that but you've been led astray."

"Really?"

"Yep."

"So why would I have read that somewhere?"

I laugh. "I have no idea."

"So, you haven't had hundreds of sexual partners over the last couple of years."

"Fuck, no. Where did you read this?"

"So not even like, I don't know...fifty puck bunnies?"

"Dude, not even one."

Griffin freezes, his drink halfway to his mouth.

"Huh? You mean you have a steady girlfriend?"

"Nope. Never had a girlfriend."

Harrison laughs next to me, having picked up on our

conversation. "Come on Pickle Pants. Don't tell us you're a virgin."

"Okay." I laugh nervously but shrug like it's no big deal. "I won't tell you."

"Wait." Griffin's eyes grow unusually large. Like, scarily large. I don't know how they're not just falling out of the sockets. But then he shouts, "Wait, wait, wait. Are you seriously saying you're a virgin?"

"Shhh!"

Jesus, fuck! Does he have to be so damn loud?

"Jesus! Can you say that any louder?"

"Yes. Yes. I can."

"Well, I'd appreciate it if you keep your voice down, alright?"

"Dude, is it true?" he asks, quieter this time. "You're a fucking virgin?"

I bob my head, weighing whether or not to be honest. "Yes. I'm a virgin. Why? Are you planning a sacrifice of some kind?"

"What? No, dumbass." He laughs. "But how the fuck are you a virgin?"

Harrison leans on the table and brings his fist to his chin, suddenly interested.

Griffin lowers his voice and murmurs, "Is it a limp dick issue? I mean it's nothing to be ashamed of. Lots of guys have that problem." He shrugs one shoulder. "Granted, they're usually in their seventies but still."

"No Griffin. I do not have a limp dick issue. But thank you very much for your concern." Ugh I really didn't want to have to go through this but if I don't give them the whole truth, I might never live this down. "I did it for my dad."

"Your dad asked you to remain a virgin?" Griffin scrunches his face. "Dude, that's—"

Harrison nods as if he gets it. "Did you have a strict don't-touch-the-remote policy growing up in your house?"

Cocking my head, I glance at Harrison and wonder what the fuck kind of childhood he must have had to even ask a question like that. "I feel like there's a lot to unpack in that question, Meers. But no, he didn't ask me to be a virgin," I say, shaking my head. "My father made it possible for me to have this life. He bent over backwards to give me the ability to play hockey and so I never wanted to disappoint him."

"Oookaaay..." Griffin says, clearly unimpressed.

"And then he died from cancer four years ago. Cancer that I didn't know he had until it was too late because instead of spending his goddamn money on cancer treatments he was traveling around the country watching me play college hockey. After all he did for me, how could I ever look myself in the mirror if I were to accidentally knock up some chick I fucked for the fun of it?"

Harrison sits back in his chair. "Wow. That's..."

"Deep." Griffin nods. "That's deep."

Harrison's expression softens. "I'm sorry you had to go through that."

"Ditto," Griffin says. "That must've been hard."

"It was. I just...didn't want to be a disappointment to my father after all this time, you know? I mean, when I was young I was just hyper focused on being the best so I didn't allow myself to give a moment of my time to girls."

"Wait, so you didn't even like..." Griffin pumps his curled fist up and down to which I roll my eyes.

"Of course I did. All the time when I was younger. I've just never..."

"Put the ham in the ham wallet?" Griffin suggests.

"Slap the beaver?" Harrison adds.

"Slam the hen?"

"Shoot the sherbert?"

"Take Willy Wonka to Wonderland?"

Harrison points at Griffin and smiles at him. "Ooh that's a good one, Bro."

The two of them fist-bump as I sit watching them with a deadpan expression.

"Yeah. I've never done any of those things. So, no way in hell am I walking up to some hot puck bunny who's looking for a good time when I'm really not at all confident that I can give it to her. I mean what if I suck balls and she tells every goddamn person she sees that I'm terrible in bed?"

Griffin lifts his finger. "Okay first of all, dude, you don't suck the balls. She does."

I roll my eyes again and let out a frustrated sigh. "You know what I mean."

He nods. "Yeah, I hear you. So, it sounds like you need to find a friend."

"A friend?"

"Yeah like, a friend with benefits. Someone you trust who you can practice with."

"Why a friend?"

Griffin cringes. "Because dude, what else are you going to do? Hire a hooker? Do you think that won't end up on the front page of every tabloid known to man? Besides, that's gross."

"How is it any less gross than the puck bunnies hanging around here?"

"Well for starters they're usually a lot cleaner and you don't have to pay them. They just want bragging rights," Harrison explains.

Griffin nods and then leans in and whispers, "Yeah, and if they're really good, they can become regulars whenever you're in their town so you're not whoring it up with hundreds of different partners. Not that that's a particularly bad thing."

"But also," Harrison says, swirling the drink in his glass, "sex comes pretty naturally really. You just need to make sure you're aware of the sounds your partner makes. If you touch her and she moans or something, that usually means she likes it. Most of the time, you'll know if she's not into something and then you can change things up."

I wipe my hand down my face. "But how am I supposed to know what to change up and how to change it if I've never done it before in the first place?"

Harrison glances at Griffin who smiles and nods before they both look at me and say, "Porn."

"What?"

"Dude, just watch some porn." Griffin shrugs. "Not like the wild and crazy stuff but just some general sex. You'll get the idea of what girls like and how to do things. But if you're really that worried about it, I'd seriously go find yourself a friend."

I slouch in my chair and drain the last of my drink. "Where the hell am I supposed to find not only a female friend, but one who wouldn't mind letting me fuck her a few times to see how good at it I may or may not be? I can't just put that out there on social media."

Harrison gives me a sympathetic half smile as he shakes his head. "Definitely can't do that, no. You seriously don't know anyone?"

I'm quiet for a moment as I consider the one and only female I know in California who, as luck would have it, happens to reside in Anaheim. My pause is just enough time for Griffin to raise a suspicious brow. "So, you do know someone?"

I tap my finger on my glass nervously. "There's...there's this one girl."

"Well, there you go!" Griffin says, sitting back in his seat and raising his arms in victory. "That's your in!"

"Wait, wait, I don't even really know her though."

"What do you mean?" Harrison asks.

"I mean she texted me a while back but she was texting someone else. I was the wrong number but I was just messing around and texted her back."

Harrison's brows pinch. "Weird. Why would you do that?"

"I don't know. I was bored? It was just this innocent conversation about spaghetti. It was stupid but then she texted me a day or two later with a picture of her dinner just as a funny add-on to our conversation and we've kind of been texting here and there ever since."

"But you've never met her?"

I shake my head. "Nope. All I know about her is that she's single and she knows I'm a virgin."

Griffin's eyes bulge again. "You TOLD her?"

"Yeah, why not? She has no idea who I am."

"You didn't give her your name?"

"Hell no. I'm a virgin, Griffin. Not an idiot."

Harrison asks quietly, "So, do you think she would go for the idea?"

I rub the back of my neck. "Ugh, I have no idea. And how would I ever bring that up?"

"Is she a virgin too? Because if she is, you guys could both work together."

I pause, trying to recall if she ever mentioned her sexual experience to me. "You know what? I don't think I know the answer to that."

"Well, maybe you need to find out. That might not be a terrible place to start."

"Yeah." I nod slowly. "I suppose maybe you're right."

"Okay well, good luck with that," Griffin says, eyeing a group of ladies giving him googly eyes. "I've got to go."

"Where are you going?" I ask as he lays a couple twenties on the bar and taps them with his hand.

He gestures to the ladies with the lift of his brows and murmurs, "At least three of those ladies over there are going to offer to suck my dick tonight." He smiles. "Who would I be to say no to that?"

"Me," I murmur as he walks away. "You would be me."

"Aw come on, Pickle Pants." Harrison caps my shoulder. "Don't be so hard on yourself."

"Why aren't you over there picking up a woman for the night? Don't let me keep you from them."

He lifts his shoulder. "Nah. I'm not feeling it tonight. And this isn't my scene."

"No?"

"Nah." He shakes his head. "I'm a relationship guy. Not a one-night stand kind of man."

"That's...admirable."

"Patience comes with age, Roche." He lifts his glass and clinks it with mine and then tosses money onto the bar making sure the bartender sees it. "When the right woman shows up in my life, I'll know it. And you will too. I promise."

"Thanks, Harrison."

"No problem. Have a good night, Bodhi."

"Yeah. You too."

Not wanting to sit by myself, I pay for my tab, leaving a generous tip, and then make my way back to my hotel room. Lying on the bed I try to come up with the right thing to say to Corri in order to find out if she's a virgin or not, but nothing good comes to mind.

Me: Hey, are you a virgin too?

Nope. Delete.

Me: Want to be virgin buddies?

No. That's stupid. Delete.

Me: I'll show you mine if you show me yours.

I chuckle, shaking my head. "Definitely not."

Delete.

ME

> I think I need sex lessons. Is that a thing?

Send.

"Shit! I hit send!" I bolt up on the bed frozen in place with my phone in my hand. "I fucking hit SEND! Oh fuck. I wasn't thinking. How do I erase it? She can't see this." I stare at my phone in my hand and shout at it, "UNSEND! No, wait, DELETE!"

Nothing happens so I tap the screen and say it again. "DELETE! UNSEND! UNSEND! UNFUCKING—"

Three dots appear...

"Oooh, fuck."

Standing from the bed I pace back and forth unable to tear my eyes away from the screen. I bite my lip and rub one very clammy hand down my pant leg.

God, it's hot in here all of a sudden.

Do those windows open?

Shit. They don't open.

Fuck. What am I going to do now?

She's going to tell me to fuck off. I just know it.

I shouldn't even care, but for some reason I do.

I swear to God I'm breaking out into a nervous sweat anticipating what she might say.

Corri: Uh. You're a loser bye.

Corri: Sex lessons are not a thing. Are you that stupid?

Corri: You want to pay someone to teach you how to have sex?

Corri: Just watch porn dumbass.

Finally, the three dots disappear and her message comes through.

CORRI

Sure. But I don't work for free. Might fuck for food though.

CHAPTER SIX

CORRIGAN

"Oh my God!"

"What? What's going on? Was it the guy? The mystery man?" Layken asks, perplexed with my shocked expression.

As I'm staring at my phone with my jaw hanging open, all I can do is nod.

"Well, what's he saying? Wait, don't tell me." She palms her forehead. "Did he send you a dick pic?"

"No but...he asked if sex lessons are a thing."

She spits her water all over herself and blurts, "He... what?"

"That's what he said," I tell her, gesturing to my phone. "It says, 'I think I need sex lessons. Is that a thing?'"

"Oh, my God!" She laughs. "Do you think he's being serious?"

"How the hell should I know?" I blurt. "I barely know the guy! What the hell am I supposed to say?"

"What do you want to say?"

"I don't know! What do you say to someone who has been texting you for days but all you know about him is his name, his taste in food, his sexual experience, or lack thereof, and that he thinks he needs sex lessons?"

Layken laughs out loud. "Fuck, this is too good. Gimme that phone." She doesn't give me the chance to deny her before she snatches my phone from my hands and reads several of our last texts.

"Aww, Corri. This guy sounds...relatively nice."

"Right? He doesn't come off as a weirdo or a perv or anything like that."

"Agreed." She glances between my phone and me and then finally smirks. "What if he's like a beast in the sheets but he doesn't know it?"

I scrunch my face. "What if he's some homeless man with a dad bod and a plumber's crack?"

"Hey, don't knock the dad bods of the world. Those bodies hold some of the world's biggest hearts."

I raise my hands in front of me. "You're right. I shouldn't have generalized."

"Plus, he says in his text that he's physically fit."

"Yeah but you can't believe everything. Until I see him for real I—"

"Yes! Great idea!" The smile that crosses her face as her thumbs speed across my phone screen is alarming.

"Whaaaaat are you doing?"

"Sending him a reply."

"But what are you saying?"

"I think it's time for you to meet this mystery man."

"WHAT? Are you CRAZY?"

She hands my phone, proud of herself as she smiles at me. "Corri, in case you have forgotten, I write spicy romance books when I'm not at my day job so yes, I'm just crazy enough to want you to meet this guy because who the hell knows?" She shrugs. "He could be the love of your life!"

"Oh please, that's cr—"

"Crazy?" Layken's eyes grow huge, as does her grin. "That's right. It is crazy! But even you can't say it's impossible because you don't know. This guy might be hung like a fucking horse and besides, you told me enough times about pencil dick London Leo, and honestly honey, that bridge fell down. So, I think we both know you deserve a good dicking right about now."

"But—"

"And maybe this guy is just the guy! He clearly wouldn't be someone who thinks his shit doesn't stink if he's a virgin, but with enough mentoring you could literally mold this guy into the lover you've always dreamed of. And then maybe you'll fall in love and live happily ever after and have all his little mystery babies and then I can write a bestselling novel all about it!" Her hand to her chest, she sighs against the back of our booth with a dreamy smile on her face.

"You're not honestly suggesting I sleep with this guy?"

Her cheeks turn pink and she giggles as she gestures to my phone with her eyes. "I mean, I may have already offered it up."

"WHAT?" My jaw hangs open as I drop my head and look down at my phone screen.

ALAN

I think I need sex lessons. Is that even a thing?

ME

Sure. But I don't work for free. Might fuck for food though.

"OH MY GOD, LAYKEN!" I whisper shout as she bursts out laughing. "I can't believe you told him that!"

"Come on!" She waves her hand. "Live a little. You never know if—"

"Shit! He's writing back!" Like a deer in headlights, I stare at my best friend, my hand starting to sweat as I hold my phone. I cannot believe this is even happening. That we're encouraging this conversation. "He's totally going to tell me to fuck off. That was way too strong of a—"

ALAN

•• Oh. I didn't mean...Uuuh, I mean...wait... are you...are you seriously offering?

Without speaking, I swallow the knot in my throat and turn the phone toward Layken so she can see what he said.

She claps her hands excitedly. "Eeeeeeek! This is perfect!"

"What. Do. I. Do. Now?"

With a helpless sigh she peels my phone out of my hand once again and texts Alan, the mystery virgin.

ME

Sure. I have a nice pair of chesticles. I could definitely teach you a few things. What do you want to learn specifically?

ALAN

All of it. Also, I just spit out my drink at the word chesticles. That's a new one for me.

ME

All of it, as in, you've never done anything with a woman? Like, ever?

ALAN

I told you I was a virgin, didn't I?

ME

Yeah but that can mean a lot of things.

ALAN

Okay so full transparency: I had to work hard to get where I am today. My father paid for a lot of opportunities for me and I didn't want to let him down by accidentally knocking up a woman I wasn't in love with. So, I just never got involved. Lame, I know, but that's my truth.

ME

Not lame, Alan. There's nothing wrong with being a responsible man. It's wise and honorable. So why the sudden change of heart?

ALAN

I could probably better explain in person but long story short, I'm seeing a lot of my coworkers finally settling down and realizing they have the best of both worlds. They have love and they have career. And they're happy men. So, I kind of want that too.

ME

Okay. That's understandable. Are you saying you're unhappy?

ALAN

Not unhappy. Just...I don't know. Lonely? And I don't want to date some girl and fall for her and be bad in bed. I want to be able to pleasure her and worship her and show her what she gets when she's with me. Ugh but I don't have a fucking clue how to do this. For all I know, I suck at it. How do you find out if you're bad in bed if you don't have anyone to tell you you're bad in bed?

ALAN

PS. You can laugh if you want. I know how bad this all sounds.

ME

Actually, I think it's endearing. In my experiences, men don't seem to care about pleasuring their partners as much as they care about getting off inside a warm vagina. Or down a throat.

ALAN

I don't want to be that kind of guy. That guy sounds like an asshole.

Layken lays my phone on the table and looks at me. "Listen, this guy sounds like he's too good to be true so if you don't teach him to fuck like a beast, I will. But also," she adds practically bouncing in her seat, "I really need you to do this because I just get a good vibe from him and plus, c'est la vie, Corri."

"What is that supposed to mean?" I ask, amused.

"It means you're living your life." She allows me to scroll through the things she was saying to Alan while she explains, "You moved abroad to learn and work and you fell in love and that guy ended up being a douche. So here you are back in the States. You accidentally text some guy, who rather than just ignore you or tell you 'wrong number' and never speak to you again, has been texting you multiple times a day for several days. He comes across as a ten so far, except he has zero bedroom experience. And now you have the opportunity to literally teach him all the ways you like to be pleasured."

"Yeah but he's not in it for me. He says he wants to learn so he's ready when he meets his—"

"Yeah, yeah, yeah." She waves me off. "I know what he said. But who's to say you aren't the love of his life?"

I chuckle at her slightly pushy albeit hopeful attitude. "You really are the hopeless romantic, aren't you?"

She puts both hands on the table and raises her brows, her eyes filled with glee. "Does that mean yes?"

Taking a deep breath, I glance down at my phone again to see another message from Alan.

ALAN

Look, I didn't mean to say all this. I'm really sorry. You deserve a man who knows what he's doing and treats you like gold. I totally understand if you want to think I'm a fucking douche and never speak to me again.

Steeling myself for what I'm about to do, I pick up my phone and move my thumbs over the letters forming my next text:

ME

We start tomorrow.

CHAPTER SEVEN

CORRIGAN

"I can't believe I'm doing this."

I take one more look at myself in my bedroom mirror, making sure I look hot enough in my green floral mini wrap dress for Alan to possibly think I'm attractive, yet classy enough to not look like a whore. My hair is down, styled in tight curls as it's the only thing my hair knows how to do, and I've applied minimal makeup. Enough to feel pretty but not overdone.

"You know what? Fuck it. I'm ending this night with an orgasm one way or another. Layken is right. C'est la fucking vie."

Approving of my look for the night, I remind myself not to bend over too far in public, fluff my hair, grab my purse and keys, and head out.

When Alan texted me this morning that he was back in town and looking forward to our date, he suggested we meet at Topside Peaks, a rooftop bar not far from where I live, though he doesn't know that. I liked the idea of Topside in particular because it's relatively dark with only soft lighting so it feels a little more private, and also, it's never extremely busy as it tends to be on the pricier side. The fact Alan recommended this place at all impressed me. He must make decent money in whatever job he does to be able to afford this place. When my Uber drops me off, I make my way to the elevator while double checking his last text to remind myself how to best identify him.

ME

I'll be in a green floral mini wrap dress and heels. Light brown very curly hair.

ALAN

I'm sure you'll look stunning. I'll be wearing black pants and a light black sweater.

ME

Perfect, you'll blend in well with the shadows. 😏

ALAN

I promise I'll find you.

The elevator doors open and I step out to the rooftop bar overlooking the city. It's a modern take on a tropical oasis above the fray of the streets below. There are beautifully adorned open cabanas lining the center of the rooftop while firepit lounges line the back wall. Up front it's standing room only with a wide-brimmed bar edging the banister where patrons can mingle while taking in the views of the city's nightlife. It really is a magical view. As I look left and right, I notice the space is just dark enough to feel a sense of privacy yet not enough to make me feel any less on edge.

I'm literally about to whore myself out...for free.

Nothing a stiff drink can't help fix, right?

A man standing behind a podium smiles at me when I approach him. He's in black dress pants, with a white dress shirt, and black tie. His blond hair styled meticulously.

"Welcome to Topside Peaks. Can I interest you in one of our cabanas or fireside lounges this evening?"

I return his warm smile with one of my own. "Uh, hi. Actually, I'm meeting someone here. The reservation is under the name Alan."

The man checks his iPad and then nods. "Of course. It looks like you two will be at our cabana in the far back corner. If you'll follow me, I'll take you there."

"Thank you."

He leads me across the rooftop to the last cabana near the corner of the bar. It's the best of both worlds as there is a comfy loveseat for two along with a small table and chairs plus access to the ledge where I can stand and see the city streets below.

"Can I get you a drink ma'am?"

"Yes please." I turn back from admiring the view. "A vodka cranberry."

He taps a few things on his iPad and nods with a smile. "Coming right up. Make yourself comfortable."

"Thank you very much."

When the host disappears back across the rooftop I nervously glance around for any sign of Mystery Alan, but there's only a small handful of people here. One party of six is laughing together several cabanas away, a party of four is seated around one of the fireside lounges, three individual couples are standing near the ledge, and then there's me. Adjusting my dress from the warm coastal breeze, I take a deep breath and remind myself that confidence is key. I feel like one of those girls Layken reads about in her romance books. The ones who make a deal with the rich billionaire having no clue what they're getting themselves into.

Oh my God what if this is like that?

What if Alan is some billionaire business mogul?

What if he wants to Alpha me?

No, that's insane. I would be the alpha in this scenario.

What if he intends to lavish me with gifts in exchange for sex lessons?

Sex lessons?

There has to be a better name.

Sex mentor?

Titillating Tutor?

Intimacy coach?

Yeah, intimacy coach sounds classy.

He has to be rich if he suggested this place, right?

Fancy dates in exchange for some intimacy coaching.

I mean, there could be worse things.

Okay. You've got this Corri.

I'm sure he's very nice.

And hopefully mildly attractive.

Oh God, what if he's horribly unattractive?

I mean he said he thought he was attractive but that could mean anything.

He never mentioned the way he smells.

Maybe that's why he's still a virgin.

Maybe he's a super attractive guy with horrible body odor.

What if the smell makes me gag and I vomit right in front of him?

What if his scent is all I can think about all night?

Oh! Or worse! What if he's old?

What if he's my dad's age?

Oh shit, what if he knows my dad?

"Shit. Maybe I shouldn't do this." Glancing down at my phone I tap out a quick text to Layken while I wait for my date who is now three minutes late.

ME

> Layken what if this guy is old and wrinkly? Or smells really bad? And what if he knows my dad? I don't think I should go through with—

"Corri?"

"Huh?" Startled, I nearly drop my phone when I turn toward the male voice. I catch it against my stomach, but then I step back and almost trip over my own foot in the process. "Whoa!" Raising my arms, I reach for whatever I can so I don't fall backwards. His arm wraps around my waist just in time to save me from imminent peril and certain embarrassment.

"Sorry about that. Didn't meant to startle you," he says. "You okay?"

"Oh! Uh, yeah. Uh hi." Slipping my phone into my purse hanging at my side, I check my hair with my hands and then fidget with my dress making sure it's situated perfectly and then finally look up and meet the eyes of my—

Oooh noooo.

Is this...

What...

Is this a prank?

He can't be serious, right?

Was this all a set up?

What's going on here?

I don't understand.

Does he really think...

He has to know I...

"Hi. I'm Alan," he says kindly as he hands me a glass. "Your vodka cranberry."

His whiskey brown eyes stare back at me as my drink is shuffled from his hand to mine. My fingers brush against his as I take my glass and I notice the warmth of his skin. His facial features are gorgeously sharp, with dark brows and black hair that's short around the sides but hangs messily near his left eye. He's clean shaven with an angular jaw and a smile that could literally melt my panties right off.

He looks every bit the spitting image of his pictures online and on T.V. so I don't understand why he's here unless...wait...

Does he know who I am?

He's new to the team so maybe he has no idea.

And if that's the case then...

Oh, my God.

His name is definitely not Alan.

This is Bodhi Roche! The newest player for the Anaheim Stars!

The team my dad coaches!

Shit! Fuck! Shit! Hell!

Oh, my God.

Bodhi Roche asked me for sex lessons!

Oh, my God! Oh, my God! Oh, my GOD!

Why does he call himself Alan?

Is he trying not to be Bodhi?

Isn't his middle name Alan?

Bodhi Alan Roche...do I remember that correctly?

Ugh! Who cares? It's definitely him and he's not using his first name.

What the hell do I do?

Do I run away?

Ugh if I do that, I'll never be able to be around him again.

It will always be hella uncomfortable.

I don't want that.

He isn't going to want that.

Okay I have to stay cool.

Don't react Corrigan.

He clearly doesn't know who I am.

I suppose I haven't used my entire name either sooo fair is fair.

And so far I haven't given him any indication I know who he is.

If he thinks I know who he is, he'll bolt.

Fuck, how am I going to keep this from Dad?

Corri, he's trusting you.

This is like doctor-patient confidentiality.

Easy peasy.

Okay. Yeah.

I can do this.

"H-H-hi...Alan."

Alan.

Alan.

Not Bodhi.

Call him Alan.

I try my best to steady my voice as I offer him my hand to shake. "It's a pleasure to meet you."

"The pleasure's all mine." His strong hand connects with mine, his fingers squeezing as his eyes rake over my body and then float back up to meet mine. "You look...beautiful tonight. That's a...wow...a stunning dress."

Stunning dress?

Stunning...dress?

Bodhi Roche just told me I'm wearing a stunning dress!

I mean Alan! Alan told me I'm wearing a stunning dress.

"Thank you very much. You look amazing as well." He really does have fantastic fashion sense but what else would I expect from a professional hockey player? At least it's not Griffin with his goofy pajama pants.

I cannot believe I'm here right now.

How is this even happening?

Quickly, I scan the rooftop for signs that anyone else here recognized him—or me for that matter—but just like before, everyone else up here is focused on their own conversations. We have the area completely to ourselves.

"Have you ever been here before?" Bodhi—I mean Alan—asks me.

"A couple times but it was years ago. It's gorgeous up here. I had forgotten just how far you can see."

"Right? It's the best on a clear night like this too."

"So, you've been here before then?"

"Only once with...uh...a client. It's a nice place to wine and dine."

I take a long sip of my vodka cranberry and then boldly ask, "Is that what you're doing with me? Wining and dining?"

"Well..." He shrugs. "You did ask me to take you to dinner first."

Actually, Layken's words were 'Might fuck for food though'...but I digress.

His innocent honesty breaks the ice and I let out a laugh, my anxiety dissipating little by little. "Except this isn't dinner. It's just drinks."

"You're right." He nods in agreement. "But I find that preventing dehydration is key."

With a smirk, I retort, "Right. Definitely wouldn't want the dreaded Big-D. Best to curb the dehydration with a whiskey sour and a vodka cranberry, am I right?"

He passes off an innocent shrug. "We do what we can, but I can get you a water if you prefer."

"Nope." I lift my glass to clink with his. "You've just met me and I'll be doing things with you by the end of this night that I've never done before on a first date. The alcohol is making me brave."

Looking equally nervous, he nods. "Understood. Do you want to sit?" he asks, gesturing to the loveseat under the cabana.

"Yeah. Sure."

As we take our seats I run through a few possible scenarios of how this night could go.

Is Bodhi really a virgin?

His reputation makes it seem like he's a player, but what if he's not and that's just how the media, or an old marketing team, likes to spin his personality because in reality he's just the opposite? Wouldn't be the first time I've seen it done with professional athletes.

There's only one way to figure this out.

I've got to ask the right questions.

"So, Alan, what is it you do for a living?"

"Uh." His brows pinch slightly. "I'm in team building and physical fitness."

Hmm. So, he doesn't want me to know he's a hockey player.
Why?

"That sounds exciting and busy."

"Very busy." He nods. "It's a lot of travel and a lot of time management. My company keeps a busy schedule but the job makes me happy."

"And you know what they say," I tell him. "If you love what you do, you don't work a day in your life."

"That's true." He smiles. "And what about you? Is nursing something you've always wanted to do?"

Moving the conversation away from him. I see what he's doing.
So, he really doesn't want me to know who he is.
Which means he also has no idea who I am.
God, this could get awkward very fast.
Or...I could play it out because obviously this is happening for a reason.
And who better to understand his need for privacy than his coach's daughter?
But damn if he ever finds out who I am...
Actually...what is there to lose?

If he finds out who I am, he's not going to run to my dad and tell on himself.

That would be professional suicide if I know my dad.

And I'm certainly not going to tell Dad.

I have to earn his trust.

I have to make him feel safe.

That's the only way this will work.

"Yeah I love nursing. I've wanted to be a nurse since my mom got sick twelve years ago."

"Oh. I'm sorry to hear that." His features soften and he touches my knee. The contact alone sends a spark up my spine. "Did she pass away?"

I nod. "Yeah. Bone cancer eleven years ago. It was hard because I was still a teenager. Not that it would be any easier now but..." I shrug. "Anyway. She's not suffering anymore."

He's quiet for a brief moment before he swallows and says, "My dad passed from cancer four years ago."

My mouth falls open as I gasp lightly. "Oh, Alan I'm so sorry. I had no idea."

How many years did Dad say Bodhi had played in Boston?

Two? Three? Four?

Damn! That means...

His father was going through this at the start of his hockey career.

"I guess that means we have something in common now, huh?"

"Yeah. Welcome to the dead parent club," I tell him. "I wish I could say we're happy to have you, but...you know...it sucks. I'm not going to lie."

He huffs a soft laugh and nudges me with his elbow. "Is it terrible to say it's nice to know I'm not alone?"

"Nah. I think that's pretty normal. How old are you, Alan?"

"Twenty-four. Almost twenty-five. You?"

"Twenty-seven."

He wags his brow playfully. "An older woman, huh?"

Cringing, I ask, "Does that bother you?"

"Not at all. Does it bother you?"

I shake my head and take another sip of my drink. Moistening my lips with the tip of my tongue, I allow my gaze to trail down his body taking note of the way his broad chest fills out his sweater, the thinness of the material expertly revealing his rounded biceps. His sleeves pushed back bring my attention to the sinews of his veiny forearms and the size of his hands that I know grasp and maneuver a stick on the ice with a prowess most players would envy. In looks, he's the kind of man any woman would drool over. And up until today, I would have thought that was the case for Bodhi Roche, hockey superstar.

"Can I ask you a personal question?"

The corner of his mouth draws up. "If you can't ask me a personal question, I have no business being here."

"If you don't mind my saying so, you're insanely attractive."

The side of his mouth turns up. "Don't hate me because I'm beautiful."

"I just mean you seem to have the whole package."

His brow quirks. "I wasn't aware we were talking about my package."

"Well, we weren't but maybe we are now, because in the looks department you're a ten and so far in our conversations, you haven't come across as some kind of sex-crazed douche whose only point in life is to carve another notch in his bedpost. So, unless your package is abnormally small..."

Staring into my soul, albeit with a look of amusement, he murmurs, "I assure you it's not. But I imagine you'll see that for yourself soon enough and then maybe you can tell me."

Cocking my head and taking in his answer, I finally ask,

"Then forgive me saying this, but I don't get it. Is your dad really the reason you're still a virgin?"

"He is," he murmurs, nodding slowly. "He gave me everything. Paid for my schooling...all my uh...activities growing up."

Hockey...I know he means hockey.

"I knew he was giving up so much of his time and money for me so I never wanted to let him down." He bows his head and quietly adds, "But I didn't know he was spending his money on me instead of cancer treatments. By the time I found out, it was too late."

"I'm so sorry, Alan. It sounds like he loved you very much."

"He did. And I loved him. My parents were my world growing up."

"Is your mom still around?"

"Yeah. I see her a few times a year. She still lives at home, back where I grew up."

"Which is where?"

"Pittsburgh."

"Wow. You're far from home."

"That's the job," he says, tossing back his drink and motioning for the waiter to bring another.

"So now that your dad has passed away, you're ready to lose your virginity? Just like that?"

He smiles. "Well, when you put it that way, it sounds a bit ungrateful. But in reality, my dad's death is finally making me notice life around me that I guess I took for granted until now. I see my colleagues all falling in love and living these happy lives and their careers aren't suffering. If anything, they're blossoming because they're happy. I want that too. I want that happy life but..." He smooths his hand down his face. "I'm like the lamest fucking virgin you will probably ever meet."

"Why do you say it like that?"

"Because when I say I haven't done anything with a woman

I mean it. I haven't even kissed a woman. I mean, I kissed a girl in high school but that was nearly ten years ago now. I stayed away as much as I possibly could during my college years so I wouldn't make any stupid mistakes."

"And now you're okay with mistakes?"

He bobs his head and chuckles. "I'm okay knowing if for some reason a mistake is made, I'm responsible enough to be able to handle it."

"Meaning you can pay for a child's upbringing if it comes to that."

He winces slightly. "Again, that makes me sound like the pompous ass that I assure you I'm not, but yeah. If something happened, at least I know I could provide for a child and its mother." With his hand on the back of his neck, he adds, "And I'm not saying I would be some dead-beat dad. I wouldn't. I want kids one day. I want to be the father for my kids that my father was for me. I just feel like I have a lot to learn if I'm going to make a woman happy. Life isn't like it was back in high school, you know?"

"Totally get it. So have you um..." I bite the corner of my bottom lip. "Have you thought about how you want any of this to go? You and me, I mean?"

He shakes his head and winces. "Not really. I mean, I've obviously thought about sex loads of times before but right here, right now? I guess I really wasn't sure what or how to plan for tonight." He dips his chin to his chest, avoiding my eyes.

Okay.

So, this is up to me.

I've got to make him comfortable.

I can do this.

"Alright well I say from here on out we put our nervousness aside and pretend this is one of the best dates we've had in a long time."

"Okay. I can do that. It wouldn't even be too hard," he says, smiling. "You're stunning, and you haven't run out on me yet."

"That's right." I nod. "I'm right here looking like a million bucks. So, kiss me."

His head shoots up and his eyes meet mine. "What?"

"You heard me." I place my glass on the table in front of us and take his glass and do the same before I turn my body toward him and lay my hands on his knees. "Let's rip off the band aid. I want you to kiss me."

"Right here?" His brows lift. "Right now?"

"Mhmm. I promise I won't bite. Let's see what you've got?"

"What if I suck at it?"

"You won't." I grin. "But if you do, I'll tell you and we'll go from there. Okay?"

He nods and pushes his hands down his thighs. "Yeah. Okay."

"Okay."

I close my eyes in anticipation and hear him blow out a nervous breath. He slips his hand into my hair and cups my cheek. "Here I go."

His thumb strokes my skin and I wonder what he might be thinking right before he presses his warm soft lips against mine. I expect to not feel a thing, after all, this is simply a test kiss so I can decide on a lesson plan. But when his lips touch mine he pauses for the briefest moment before he angles my head and goes for it and hooooly shit.

This is a kiss.

My heartbeat pounds in my ear and my stomach bottoms out as our mouths move together. He's smooth, gentle and slow, like he's savoring every second of our connection. Like he's truly tasting me. And for just a second, I find myself wishing we could have this first kiss over and over again, because dang, he's pretty damn good at this.

His tongue slides gently against my mouth and I open my lips for him. The slightest feel of his tongue against mine sends a jolt of lust through my body, warming me from the inside out, and oh my God, I'm kissing Bodhi Roche! I press my hand lightly against his hardened chest, his muscular physique under the tips of my fingers. I want to slide my hand down his taut body but I keep myself in control even though my heart is racing inside my chest.

Can he feel that?

Is his pulse racing too?

The last man I kissed was Leo but even on his best day, it was nothing like this. Alan slowly pulls his lips from mine and as he does, a sigh escapes my mouth, though on the inside it feels like my breath has been sucked out of my lungs. I take a moment to open my eyes only to find him watching me.

He cringes slightly and in a whisper of a voice showing his vulnerability asks, "How was that?"

I tilt my head and give him a reassuring smile. Bringing a finger to my lips, I revel in the lingering tingling sensation reminding me of the moment we just shared.

"It was...wow."

CHAPTER EIGHT
BODHI

Wow is right.

She didn't give me time to think about what kissing her might feel like, but hell, what I wouldn't do to kiss her again. I know I'm not supposed to feel anything and I'm not saying I'm gushing over this girl, but also, I'm a fucking lucky bastard. Corri is drop dead gorgeous. Her light-brown hair is full of curl, but she has part of it pulled up behind her. The rest hangs in ringlets passed her shoulders, a few tendrils blowing in the evening breeze. Her bright blue eyes are as mesmerizing as her friendly smile. She has a narrowed facial structure with high cheekbones, a dainty nose, and lips that taste like marshmallows.

The green floral dress she's wearing wraps perfectly around her small waist but flaunts her curvy hips. The tie of her dress hangs loosely along her left side. And those heels...fuck. Maybe I have a shoe fetish because those heels make her legs look killer.

"Okay, so I don't think you have to worry about kissing." I watch as she trails her finger from her lips down to the top of her chest. "I uh..." She clears her throat. "I don't have any critique for you because that was...good. Very good."

Thank fuck.

The last thing I wanted to do was give her a bad impression.

But also, she's very easy to kiss.

And I really want to do it again.

"I like marshmallows."

Her lips turn up in a smile. "What?"

"Shit," I whisper, shaking my head like an idiot. "Sorry. It's just that uh, your lips tasted like marshmallows."

"Marshmallows huh?" She touches them with her finger again and I find myself wishing I could be touching them again. *With my tongue.* "That's definitely one I haven't heard before."

"You're a good kisser, by the way," I say. Hell, I have no idea if what I'm saying is cool or totally ridiculous. "You made it very easy, I mean."

Her smile widens so I'm going to take that as a good sign. "Good. That's what this arrangement is supposed to be all about, right? Making things easy for you so you can feel confident?"

Heat spreads across my cheeks, my ears, and my neck. "Yeah. I guess so."

Sensing my embarrassment, Corri places a tender hand on my knee. "There's nothing to be embarrassed about, Alan. I promise I'll be a safe space for you." She sits back and leans against the loveseat cushion. "There's no judgement and no preconceived notions. I can usually read another human being pretty well and you give off a friendly vibe."

"You think?"

"Mhmm." She nods but then gives me a quizzical look. "Should I be worried? Because I'm not."

"No." I shake my head. "Not at all. I know you don't know me, but I promise, at my core, I'm a good guy. I'm just..."

Lame as fuck.

"Inexperienced but curious?" she offers.

I nod. "Yeah. That sounds better than what I was saying in my head."

Though I should also add liar to my list.

Now that I've met Corri and she seems like a decent woman, I feel guilty that I'm lying to her about who I am.

Okay, maybe not really lying as much as omitting.

Lying by omission. That's a thing, right?

Because that's what I'm doing. But there was no way I could tell her who I am and then turn around and tell her I'm a virgin. And I certainly couldn't tell her who I am and then take her up on her offer for intimacy help.

Talk about professional suicide.

She could tell anyone and it would kill me.

I'd be the embarrassment of the team for sure. Coach would bench me immediately and I've only just gotten started. I have so far to go with the Anaheim Stars.

But at least when Corri turned around and saw me she didn't gasp and say, *"Oh My God, you're Bodhi Roche, the rich pro hockey player!"*

I'll count myself very lucky that she doesn't recognize me.

I wonder if I should have her sign an NDA.

But how would I do that without revealing who I am?

And if I tell her, she could refuse to sign and walk away and then tell the world.

I guess I'm in this now for better or worse.

Maybe it's not so bad.

She seems pretty easy going.

And she didn't talk sports at all when I told her what I do.

I have to keep myself from chuckling when I glance at her because she probably doesn't know shit about hockey. She probably works all day as a nurse and then spends her evenings shopping online or hanging out with friends. Nothing about her screams sports fan.

Thank God.

"So, now that we've gotten the kissing part out of the way," she begins, "maybe we should talk about what else you want to, you know, try. Or learn. Or practice. Or whatever."

"You mean like, a list?"

"Yeah." She smiles. "Let's make a list. That will keep us on track."

She pulls her phone from her purse and opens an app. "So, what comes to mind when you think about your experience or rather, what you want to experience?"

"Umm, well." I glance around quickly to make sure nobody could be listening to our conversation. Even still, I lower my voice to a soft murmur. "I want to feel comfortable pleasuring the woman I'm with so I guess I need to learn how to touch her?"

Corri nods. "Yes. For sure. There's a fine line between flirty touching and touching that means a whole lot more. In fact, if it's okay with you, maybe we should start out with something easy like touching. I can show you what most women like in terms of, you know, genital touching..."

Fuck, she just said genital touching.

"Finger stimulation..."

Fucking finger stimulation.

"And how to bring her to orgasm."

Orgasm.

She said orgasm.

And I'm sitting here nodding like we're discussing hockey stats in a press conference.

How is this even happening right now?

"Yeah." I nod, trying fucking hard not to move my head too eagerly. "Yeah, that sounds good."

She grazes her thumbs across her phone murmuring words

like touching, fingers, and orgasm. "Okay. What else? What about oral?"

Jesus Christ.

"Yeah. Definitely oral."

Her gaze flits to mine. "Has anyone ever..." I watch as her eyes fall to my crotch and, swear to God, I feel my dick twitch in my pants knowing that one, she's looking there and two, she's asking me if anyone has ever sucked my cock.

"Uh no." I shake my head. "Nobody."

"Is that something you'd like to experience?"

My mouth just went fucking dry because how the hell do I say to this beautiful woman that I'd be a fool to stop her if she wanted to suck my dick. I try to conjure up any remaining saliva in my mouth but there is literally nothing there. To my extreme delight our waiter delivers my second drink and I swallow almost all of it in one fell swoop before I answer, "Iiiii think I would probably like that very much."

"Great." She smiles, holding back a laugh, I think, as her head dips back to her phone and her lips form the word *blowjob*.

"So other than plain old fashion sexual intercourse, we could try things like toy play, or maybe work on a little dirty talk."

"Do women like dirty talk?"

I see the mischievous grin form across her lips before she brings her head up to look at me. "Alan, there is nothing hotter than a man who can take charge in the bedroom and praise his partner for a job well done. I may just be speaking for myself, but nothing turns me on faster than a dirty talking sexual partner who tells me all the ways he wants to pleasure me."

"Was your ex a dirty talker?"

She surprisingly laughs out loud. "Good God, no. There wasn't a dirty bone in his scrawny British body."

"Then how would you know if you enjoy dirty talkers?"

"Oh. I read books."

My brows peak. "Dirty books?"

"Is there really any other kind?" She smiles. "My best friend writes steamy romance books so she got me into the genre. I'd be lying if I said some of those reads don't turn me on more than I've ever been turned on before."

"That's setting the bar high for all the future men in your life."

"Maybe." She shrugs. "But if the guys in this world aren't reading romance books as sex how-to manuals for their women, what are they even doing?"

"Romance books. Kinkier the better. Noted." I match her smile and then watch her as she notes the words *toys* and *dirty talk* into her phone.

I am flabber-fucking-gasted that we're sitting here discussing the sexual relationship we're about to enter into as if we're discussing what to pack for my next away game. Yet, Corri is making this the easiest experience I could have ever asked for.

"One more question."

"Alright. Shoot."

"Have you ever seen a naked woman, Alan?"

"Are you asking me how much porn I've watched?"

She laughs quietly. "Uh, not necessarily. You said before that you've never been with a woman. I was just trying to gauge what that really means for you. Not that sex has to equal nudity, because it doesn't if we're talking just the physical act of penetration."

"Right. Penetration." Good God I don't know why I just said penetration. "Umm." I swallow the knot forming in my throat. "I've seen naked women before on television and I've been to clubs with my colleagues a few times so I've seen plenty of topless women, but I've never uh...you know, been in bed with a naked woman."

"You've never touched a boob?"

My eyes inadvertently fall to Corri's chest.

She's right.

She has nice chesticles.

"Nope." I shake my head. "Definitely never done that."

She nods. "Gotcha."

She's quiet for a moment, the space between us filling with awkwardness the more each second passes by.

Fuck, this is so weird.

Why is this weird?

Because you're literally using a woman for sex, asshole. That's why.

"Look, I'm really sorry. This is like the craziest thing I think I've ever done." I shake my head. "I'm sorry if I'm making you uncomfortable."

She gives me a sympathetic smile and covers my hand with hers. When she touches me something in my chest tightens. "It's fine, Alan. I completely understand. If I'm being honest, this is probably the craziest thing I've ever done as well. And if you feel too uncomfortable and you don't want to—"

"I do," I interject, trying to nod confidently but not appear over-eager. "I do. I want this. I...I need this." I sigh. "Look, I know it's lame, but I don't want to be a virgin anymore. I want to know what the fuck I'm doing when I'm with a woman. I want to know how to make her feel good. I want to be able to pleasure her in every way possible. But to do that I need to experience what it feels like to be inside a woman. I want to know what a woman tastes like. I want to know how my body is going to react so I can be prepared. It's one thing to experience those feelings as a teenager but as an adult I..."

"You want to be prepared. You want to be in the know."

"Yeah."

Corri swallows the last of her drink and sets her glass on the table in front of us. "Well, drink up Alan. And then perhaps we should go somewhere a little more private. I actually don't live too far from here. It's just a couple blocks. We could walk, if that's alright with you?"

I toss back the rest of my whiskey. "Perfect."

I stand and offer her my hand, which she takes. Her skin is warm and soft and she doesn't try to disconnect from me so I don't let go of her either. I lead us to the elevators and when the doors close in front of us, she turns and lifts up on her toes and kisses me again. Not as long this time, but enough that I've gotten another taste of that sweet marshmallow. She wobbles against me and I place my hand on her waist to steady her. She squeezes my other hand with hers and then her mouth opens and her tongue swipes against mine. I can feel her tits pressed up against my chest and it's all I can do not to reach up my hand and touch them. Fuck me, why didn't anyone ever tell me that kissing a sexy woman could feel so good?

I feel like I'm walking on air right now.

I feel like I could skate drills faster than lightning if I wanted to.

Also, with her lips on mine and her tits brushing against me, the sensations taking over my body are making my dick hard.

"You know if you keep this up I'm going to be walking home with a teenage boner, right?"

She smiles and chastely kisses me once more. "I'm about to get naked with you, Alan. Kissing you is giving me something to think about so I'm not nervous and so I don't make you nervous."

Holy shit.

She's going to get naked.

That idea isn't doing a thing for my boner.

But fuck if it's not making my heart race.

Okay. We're doing this.

It's happening.

Fuck. I'm nervous.

"I'm not nervous," I tell her, trying to hide my smile. "I'm… cautiously excited."

"Good." The elevator dings and the doors pull open. "Let's go."

.

CHAPTER NINE
BODHI

Corri's apartment isn't much once we get inside. It's a beautiful space, and it's actually in a building I know to be relatively upscale. I only know this because it's one of the buildings I looked at before Coach Hicks suggested I move to the complex where most of the team lives. Her place is very sparsely decorated but there are several moving boxes scattered around the entryway. I guess when she says she just moved back to the States, she meant it. The only thing I know about her apartment is that the kitchen area flows into her living room, and I only know that because I can't keep my eyes off her. I watch her hips sway in her dress as she crosses the floor and I ogle when she bends over slightly to find the switch to the lamp.

She's fucking mesmerizing.

Once she's done she weaves through the boxes back to me.

"I'm uh…" She clears her throat. "I'm not exactly sure of the best way to start this. I didn't exactly write a lesson plan."

"Me either," I admit anxiously. Tonight wasn't something I could prepare for. It's not like I could open a textbook and study all the ways I could potentially pleasure a woman. Though I understand the internet is full of wild ideas, I didn't want to give myself any preconceived notions on what someone like Corri might like. Or rather what she might think are the important parts for me to learn.

Staring at each other in the middle of her kitchen, I notice how she tends to bite her bottom lip.

She's nervous.

Just like me.

I have to put her at ease.

I have to do something.

Anything.

With a fluttery feeling in my stomach, I finally offer, "What if I uh…maybe I kiss you again?"

She nods and shakes her hands out nervously. "Yeah good idea. We've already proven we're good at that so we'll let that lead us."

"Good idea."

"Yeah. Agreed."

Smiling at her beautiful if not slightly flustered face, I whisper, "Here I go."

"Okay." She closes her eyes waiting for me and rather than second guess myself, I lean in, wrapping an arm around her, pulling her against me, and press my lips to hers. She immediately relaxes in my hold and kisses me like it's something we've been doing together since the dawn of time. The curve of her mouth, the way her lips separate, the way a tiny little moan comes from her as our mouths move together.

Damn.

Corri is fire and kissing her might just be my new favorite thing.

She fists my sweater as I hold her face in my hands, angling her head for better access, and dip my tongue into her mouth. She meets me stroke upon fucking stroke and Christ, this girl's mouth is like a little piece of Heaven. If she can kiss like this I can only imagine what her mouth can do when it's wrapped around my cock one day.

Jesus. My cock just stiffened in my pants.

"I think it's time for your first official lesson," she boldly murmurs between kisses.

"I'm all yours, Corri. Show me. Teach me. Tell me what to do."

Her lips parted slightly, breathing against my mouth, she takes my hand and slowly moves it to her breast.

Holy shit, my hands are on her breast.

"Touch me, Alan."

I fold my hand over her rounded breast, palming it and rubbing my thumb over the silky fabric of her dress, feeling the taught peak of her nipple. She hisses in a breath and I immediately let go.

"Sorry! Sorry. I'm sorry," I tell her with my hands up in front of me. "I didn't mean to hu—"

"No, no, no," she says, shaking her head and grabbing my hand again with a soft giggle. "That was a good sound." She brings my palm to her breast again. "It felt good and I liked it."

"Oh. Good. Amazing. I mean you feel amazing. In my hand."

"Good. Keep going. I have two breasts and you have two hands."

I nod and whisper, "Right."

Bringing my other hand up, I hold both of her beautiful breasts in my hands. I don't know what makes me brave enough to do it, but when I make eye contact with her she smiles at me. "Good boy, Alan. It's okay to squeeze. I'm not going to break."

Fuuuck. Me.

She called me a good boy and now all I want to do is make her feel like fucking magic so she'll say it again. I back her up against the wall as I fondle her breasts, slipping my thumbs over her nipples simultaneously and smiling when her head falls back against the wall and she moans. "Yeah...God that feels good. You're a quick study."

"I aim to please, Corri."

I fucking aim to please.

"My dress," she gasps. "Untie my dress."

The tied fabric isn't a far reach for me. When I wrap my hand around it she steadies me and says, "Slowly. You don't want to just yank clothes off and come across like a horny toad. Well..." She considers her words. "Okay sometimes you do but for the sake of this lesson, take your time. Savor your partner. Make her feel like she's the only one you desire and that peeling her clothes off and admiring her body is one of your greatest pleasures. I promise it will make her feel special. You can consider it delayed gratification."

I nod as I lazily pull the tie to her dress. I keep my eyes on Corri's, noting the quickened pace of her breathing and the way her chest rises and falls with each breath she takes.

My touch is affecting her.

And that is affecting me.

At the last pull of the tied fabric, her dress falls open and I allow my eyes to drop.

My God.

She's perfect.

She's wearing a pair of dark red lace panties and a matching bra that pushes her breasts up like two of the softest round melons I've ever seen.

Hmm.

A green dress and red lace undergarments...

She's like the perfect Christmas gift.

And suddenly I feel like a kid in a candy store. I just want to touch it all. Refusing to take my eyes away from her gorgeous tits, I drag my fingers across her shoulders and slowly pull her dress down her arms until it falls in a pile on the floor. Finally, I lift my eyes locking with hers and lick my lips before I say, "You're fucking gorgeous and I am one very fucking lucky man."

The smile that beams back at me makes something in my chest swell as she grabs my face and kisses me again. Her hands make quick work of my sweater, which makes me chuckle given the explicit instruction she gave me to go slow, but I don't give a shit. Her hands gliding up my pecks and across my bare chest is hands down one of the best feelings in the whole goddamn world.

Her touch alone makes me want to come just standing here in front of her. I've never had a woman touch me the way Corri is touching me and it feels so fucking good.

"Bedroom," I nearly growl, picking her up and walking her out of the kitchen.

She smiles and giggles. "End of the hall." She wraps her arms around my neck and her legs around my waist as I carry her down the darkened hallway and into her bedroom. When I sit down on the edge of her bed, she's straddling me, and I can feel the heat of her lace covered pussy. She leans back slightly and switches on the bedside lamp. When she does her beautiful body is illuminated in a soft glow.

She gives me a teasing smirk and murmurs, "Now let's see if you can take off a bra."

"Challenge accepted."

Reaching around to her back I fiddle with the clasp to her lacey bra. I try pulling them apart like magnets but that doesn't work so I try maneuvering things another way. I twist and turn, all the while Corri is chuckling because I'm on the bra struggle bus.

"What the hell is this magic?" I grunt, trying but failing to separate this damn thing. "You know what? Fuck it. I can afford to buy you twenty more just like it." In one tight yank, I rip the fabric apart. Corri's mouth falls open but she smiles.

"Well, that's one way to get the job done."

"I mean it. I'll buy you a new one. And ten more to go with it. But right now, I really want to see your body." I drag the straps of her bra down her arms and wait patiently as she slips her arms out of it and then she flings it to the floor, her bare chest now on display for my viewing pleasure.

"Fucking Christ," I murmur as I bring a hand up the side of her torso and over the top her breast.

"Alan," she sighs when I touch her and my dick twitches underneath her.

"You're beautiful."

"Am I?"

"You know you are."

"You want to know something else?" she asks as she nibbles my earlobe.

"What?"

Whispering into my ear she tells me, "I'm even prettier when I'm coming."

Her sexy confidence turns me the fuck on. "Is that so?"

"Mhmm."

"Well, this I need to see, so tell me how to make it happen."

"I could ride your cock just like this. I can feel how hard you are."

She does feel incredible sitting on me like this.

"Is that what you want?" I ask her, knowing I would absolutely do any fucking thing to help her get off because if there's one thing I need to do before this night is over, it's watch Corri orgasm in front of me.

"I want to come by the touch of your hand, Alan," she says to me. She stares into my baby blues and whispers, "And my legs are already spread for you, so what are you going to do about it?"

What am I going to do about it?

"Well, if I have anything to say about it, I'm going to glide my fingers through your slick pussy and you're going to tell me what feels good."

"Good boy." She smiles. "I like the way you think."

"I just need to do one thing first."

Her brows furrow slightly. "What's that?"

I bring a hand to her breast again and lower my mouth over her nipple. "This," I say just before I suck her nipple into my mouth and circle my tongue around it.

"Oh, my God!" She groans and bucks against my stiff cock.

Fuck that's too good.

If she keeps that up, I'm going to lose control.

"Yes, Alan. That feels amazing."

With a slide of my other hand, I sneak a few fingers between the lacey fabric of her panties and her warm wet center. "Fuuuck, Corri." I coat two fingers in her arousal, reveling in the welcomed softness of her body. "You're so wet."

"You made me that way," she breathes. "That's how turned on I am for you. Now put two of those fingers inside me and then curl it up like this." She makes a come-here motion with two of her fingers. I do just as she instructs, finding her opening and sliding two fingers inside her pussy.

Holy fuck this is...

Mother fucker she's warm.

And wet.

And tight against my fingers.

"Oooh God, yeah," she moans as her head falls back. "Nice and gentle." Her lips separate as she gasps once, twice, three times and then bucks against my fingers. "Now move your fingers in that same position but as if they're riding a bicycle."

I move my fingers inside her slowly and she moans a little louder. "Yes, Oh my God, yes. Just like that. Now press your thumb against my clit until I come."

Press on the clit...

Okay...

With my...

Where exactly is the...

Hmm.

If I were a clit where would I be?

Is it down here near my other fingers?

Yeah...inside her, I think.

Has to be.

Wait no. That can't be right.

Why would she tell me to use my thumb if I already have fingers inside her?

Isn't it at the top somewhere?

Here clitty clitty...

Oh fuck. Don't be stupid Bodhi.

She's naked and waiting.

I've got to give her the clitty clitty bang bang or I'll never be able to look her in the eyes again.

Fuck, I should've looked at a diagram before tonight.

Why can't I find this thing?

Why is it such a mystery?

Thank God the guys aren't here to see this.

"Here," she says softly, her hand grasping mine. She places my thumb on top of a small mound just under her pubic bone. The moment my skin makes contact she gasps. "See? Just like that. You're doing great. The trick is to not stop touching her clit no matter how much you're turning her on. The clit is where the nerve endings are. You find her clit and she'll be putty in your hands, Alan."

"Like this?" I ask, coating my thumb in her arousal and then rubbing it over her clit in small circles.

She gasps a breath and nods. "Exactly like that. Fuck! Please, whatever you do, don't stop."

For extra bonus points, I lean down and pull her nipple into my mouth again and she cries out, bucking against my hand.

"Yes! Fuck! Yes! Please, Alan!"

"God, You're beautiful like this."

She moves across my cock as she rides my fingers and it's all I can do to keep breathing as my cock presses firmly against the seam of my pants.

Fuck, I'm not going to last like this.

It's too good.

She's fucking riding me.

And I've sucked on her pretty pink nipples and her tits are bouncing in my face and holy shit this is too—

"AUNNNNGH! FUCK!"

Corri wraps her arms around my neck, holding on for dear life, as she rides me until she's screaming, "YES! YES YES! Oooooooh fuuuuuck. Yesssss." She has a death grip around my neck when she orgasms. I wrap my arms around her and smooth my hands up and down her back while her body settles and she comes back from her high. The feeling of her breasts against my bare chest is surprisingly intimate.

And I really fucking like it.

"That was..." She pants. "That was unbelievably amazing."

"It absolutely was."

"Are you sure you've never done this before?"

I chuckle against her body, tightening my hold on her. "As I just fucking lost control and came in my pants, I'm going to answer that with a resounding yes."

Guess I can't win them all.

But then again...pretty sure I was a fucking winner tonight.

CHAPTER TEN
CORRIGAN

ME

OMGEEEEE!!!!!!

LAYKEN

Well, well, well, I haven't received a late-night text like this from you in ages. You're usually asleep by now.

ME

I know. And tomorrow morning is going to come very early but this can't wait and I kind of want to see your face when I tell you.

LAYKEN

Are you going to tell me you got laid?

ME

Not quite.

LAYKEN

Not quite...okay so you didn't get laid but you did have a happy ending kind of night?

ME

LIKE YOU WILL NEVER BELIEVE. NOT IN A GAZILLION YEARS.

LAYKEN

😵 Oh fuck, please tell me that Mystery Man ended up being some A-list celebrity like Chris Hemsworth or Chris Evans or...oh my God, Chris Pratt!

ME

Uhh...aren't they all married?

LAYKEN

Don't know don't care. I just like to look at them but judging from your response I'm going to guess it wasn't one of them.

ME

Correct.

LAYKEN

Am I going to have to come up there?

ME

shakes head yes vigorously

LAYKEN

Okay but I'm not putting on a bra. And there better be cookies.

ME

I shall provide all the necessities. Just get your pretty little titties up there.

LAYKEN

Two minutes.

There was no way when I moved back to the States that my best friend was going to let me live anywhere other than the same building she lived in. And I can't say I hate it. We're mature enough to give each other privacy when it's needed but intrusive enough to barge into each other's homes half naked and poop in each other's bathrooms. Living just a few floors away from my best friend brings back all the college dorm vibes, only we're actual professional adults who have to pay bills and clean our own toilets.

Grabbing my robe off the hook in the bathroom, I wrap it around my body and tie it closed at my waist and then grab two glasses of milk and a package of chocolate chip cookies from the pantry. Just as I unlock my door, Layken turns the knob and waltzes inside. She takes one look at my barely dressed self and whistles.

"Wow...she didn't even put her clothes back on before texting me. Impressive!"

I yank on her hand and pull her into the living room, my body still thrumming from the way Bodhi Roche brought me to orgasm less than an hour ago.

"Okay before you tell me anything, I want to try to guess who this guy was."

"Alright." I nod, failing miserably to hide my smile.

"Okay, twenty questions."

"Go," I tell her.

"Do I know him?"

"Uh...no?"

"No...question mark?"

"I mean you don't...*KNOW* him."

"Do you *know* him?"

I smirk. "I do now."

She rolls her eyes, amused. "Okay smartass. So, he's someone we don't know personally but we know *of* him?"

"Yes."

"Is he famous?"

"Yes."

"Is he a movie star?"

"No."

"T.V. star?"

"No."

"So not an actor at all?"

"Nope."

"A model?"

"Could be."

"So, he's hot?"

My cheeks pinken and my eyes bulge as I nod. "Hot is an understatement."

Layken mirrors my expression. "Wow! Really?"

"Really!"

"Okay so he's not an actor. He's hot enough to be a model. Does he sing?"

I shrug. "Not what he's known for."

"You're really bad at twenty-questions, you know that?"

"Sorry! I can't stick to just yes or no answers!"

"It's okay. So, if he's not an actor and not a singer and most likely not a model then he has to be..." She rubs her chin between her thumb and forefinger. "An athlete?"

My smile says it all and she gasps. "OH MY GOD you lucky bitch! Is it baseball?"

I shake my head.

"Football?"

Shake again.

"Soccer?"

"Not soccer."

Her brows furrow. "Golf?"

"Nope."

"Tennis?"

"Huh uh."

"What else...oh shit." Her eyes bulge even more and her smile drops. "Is it hockey?"

"Bingo."

"Oooh fuck! Dear baby Jesus tell me it's not a player on the STARS?"

When I don't answer her she knows the answer is yes.

"Holy fucking shit, Corrigan! Wait..." She raises her hand to her chest. "Please don't tell me it's Griffin Ollenberg because as much as I know I'll never have a chance with that man, his penchant for pajama pants and the donations he makes to the kids at the hospital melts me every time. He's the cutest and if you tell me you got to fuck the one person who makes watching hockey worth it for me, we might have to never be friends again."

Laying my hand on her forearm I reassure her, "I promise you I will always, always, always consider hoes before bros and will never fuck Griffin Ollenberg. You have my word. I know how long you've admired his cuteness."

"Okay so if it's not Griffin and it's not Oliver Magallan or August Blackstone," she starts, eyeing me as she puts the pieces together. "And you don't know him very well..." She stares at me shocked. "And he didn't know who you were...?"

"Nope." I shake my head. "No idea."

She gasps and then whispers, "Oh my God Corrigan, did you just fuck Bodhi Roche?"

Letting all my pent-up excitement out, I fall back against my couch with my arms out and a huge very satisfied smile plastered on my face. "Layk, with his tongue at my tits, I rode that man like the bull he is meant to be and I enjoyed every fucking minute of it."

"Oooh...my...God. Tell me every fucking thing! First, what the hell did you do when he showed up? Did you tell him you knew who he was?"

"Hell no!" I laugh. "I mean on the inside I was battling over whether or not I should say something and then graciously bow out, but then I realized he had no idea who I was which made me think to myself that here's this new guy in town, new to the team, who I thought was this badass know-it-all..."

"Well, that's the way the media has hyped him up," Layken says with a bob of her head.

"Right, but he's totally not that guy! I mean maybe he is on the ice. Obviously he is on the ice, but off the ice...phew." I fan my face. "He's just this hot as sin super virgin who refused to give in to temptation because he didn't want to let his father down. Now he just wants to be able to please a woman so when the time comes, he knows what he's doing."

Layken considers my explanation and then adds, "Well, think about it Corri. If he's never had sex a day in his life, he can't just pick up some random woman and take her to bed not knowing what to do or how to do it. He could end up all over the front page of every tabloid if he were to be bad at it."

"Exactly. And I considered all that. I really did consider being honest with him, but the more he spoke, the more vulnerable he was, and the more vulnerable he was, the more I realized he was trusting me...this random female stranger, with his biggest secret. How could I say no then? Also, he is so far from bad at anything. He's the model student if I do say so myself."

She smirks. "I mean it helps that he's hot. No question."

"One hundred percent. I lucked out there for sure."

She tosses a cookie into her mouth and with a mouthful asks, "So how did you guys even get started with...you know?"

I shrug. "I basically told him to kiss me. Straight up."

She laughs. "You did what?"

"It was the only thing I could think to do. We were both a bit nervous and going through idle conversation and I needed to smash the ice, not just break it if the night was going to go anywhere, so I told him to consider the two of us on a fantastic date and to just kiss me. And so, he did."

"Aaaand?"

"Aaaand I still can't wipe the smile off my face because that man can kiss."

"Not too sloppy?"

"Nope. Perfect amount of lip and tongue action. Not too hard. Not too soft. Lips were warm. It was...wow. That was the only word I could find for it. Wow."

"Eeeeek!" Layken claps her hands excitedly. "I am so fucking happy for you. So, you brought him back here, obviously."

"Mhmm."

"And then?"

"And then I made him take my clothes off. Taught him how to do it nice and slow and then he saw me in my bra and underwear and kind of took over from there. He kind of went with his instincts, which I thought was excellent. I talked him through using his fingers...oh, my God his fingers...and the rest is—"

"Orgasmic."

"Yeah." I laugh. "Orgasmic."

Shaking her head in astonishment, her bewildered smile falters and she asks, "So what about your dad?"

"What about him?"

"What happens when he finds out? He could make Bodhi's life a living hell."

"He's not ever going to find out."

"Girl, these things always have a way of getting out."

"Well, it won't be me who says a word and I can't see Bodhi saying anything because that would be admitting that not only was he a virgin but that he sought out sex lessons with his coach's daughter."

"I guess you have a good point there." She snickers. "What about feelings? Do you see yourself catching feelings for him?"

He *was* kind.

And courteous.

And friendly.

And one hundred percent present with me.

But I seriously doubt I'm his type.

I shake my head confidently. "Nah. I don't think so. He's very focused on his sport. But will I enjoy the fucking as long as I absolutely can because who wouldn't want to ride that man until the sun comes up? Absolutely."

"Speaking of riding...just how big is the bull?"

I bite down on my bottom lip trying not to laugh. "Well, that's the part I can't exactly answer."

Layken frowns. "Okay now you've lost me. If you rode him, how do you not know how big he is?"

"Well, I never got the chance to get his pants off because we were just supposed to be focusing on fingers and touching. I mean, it felt pretty large when I was straddling his lap but other than that, I don't know for sure." I shrug and bite my lip to keep from smiling. "Plus, he kind of came in his pants as I was doing my thing so I never got to actually see for myself."

We lock eyes with each other and within five seconds we're bursting into a fit of giggles.

"Oh, my God," Layken says with a snort. "You sure do know how to have a good time and I am officially a jealous bitch. But I love you just the same."

CHAPTER ELEVEN
BODHI

"Your vanity is showing , Roche!" Coach Hicks shouts from the bench. "Play through it, not to it!"

"Shit. He's right. He's right," I say to myself as Barrett sends the puck back up the ice for me to try again. I flicked the puck too hard and watched it slide to the net rather than following through and charging in for the rebound. This time though, when I have possession of the puck I take it down the ice and pass it to Ledger and then I hustle toward our goal to support his forthcoming shot. He dribbles the puck between his stick and then bounds around the net where he flicks the puck and sneaks it in for the score.

"Yeah! That'a boy, Roche." Finally, Coach Hicks smiles and claps his hands. "Way to support your teammate. That's how we get the job done gentlemen!"

Fuck yeah!

That actually felt damn good!

"Nice job, Pickle Pants!" Harrison says before we set up another play. "You might just learn how to be a team player yet."

Griffin taps me with his shoulder as he skates by and then

turns and skates backwards. "Yeah Roche. You're a different player this morning. What gives?"

I give him an easy shrug. "Can't a kid just learn from his teammates and get better?"

"Sure, he can. But when you're on the ice your M.O. is to leave everyone else in the dust."

"Well maybe I've decided I like dust."

"You know, now that you mention it," Ledger adds, listening to our conversation, "Pickle Pants did waltz into the locker room this morning with a little extra pep in his step."

I roll my eyes but grin nonetheless because he's not wrong. I practically floated into the locker room this morning.

I do have a little extra pep in my step.

A little jizz in my jeans...

Not that I should be at all proud of creaming my pants last night but I can't stop smiling about it.

It's not like I have a smoking hot woman wearing nothing but a pair of lace panties dry humping me every night.

Also, sidenote: She was anything but dry.

Watching Corri come undone under my touch, my tongue, my fingers...fuck me. There was no way I was going to be able to keep myself in control. I've never come at the hands...er...dry humping of a woman before so that was a first for me.

And by God, I hope it's not the last.

But I'm not going to admit that to these assholes.

"I didn't waltz to anything. I don't even know how to waltz."

"So, what's got you so happy then Bodhi?" Griffin asks, his knowing smirk telling me he has a couple good guesses.

"Dude, why are you grinning like that?" August asks Griffin.

"I don't know. Maybe you should ask Bodhi"

August turns his head and glances my way. "What's going on? What did I miss?"

"Nothing. You didn't miss a thing."

"Not true." Griffin shakes his head. "Pickle Pants is keeping something from us. I can see it all over his face."

"What's wrong with my face?"

"Alright, next play. Let's go!" Coach shouts from the bench at just the right time.

Phew! Saved by Coach.

When we enter the locker room after practice though, Griffin still hasn't let it go. "Did you win the lottery?"

"Nope," I say, tossing my stick to the equipment manager.

"Get a new sponsored deal from your agent?"

"Nah."

"He probably had a hot date. Leave the guy alone," Barrett chides, finally chiming in to the conversation. Leaning down to untie my skates, I don't say a word and Griffin is quick to notice.

"Yeah! There it is!" he says with a snap of his finger. "You saw the girl."

Oliver's head snaps up. "What girl?"

"There's a girl?" August asks.

Oliver wags his brows. "Well, who is she?"

"Wait, I was right? Bodhi's got a girl?" Barrett scoffs. "Like for real?"

Why does that seem so hard to believe?

"Well, will you look at that," Harrison says with a shit-eating grin. "Pickle Pants has found himself a pickle tickler."

August laughs. "A pickle tickler. That's amazing!"

"I didn't say anything about a girl," I tell them.

Griffin caps my shoulder. "Yeah but you didn't say you weren't with a girl either. And since I happen to know things, I'm now invested and need to see this through."

"You know things?" Oliver questions. "What's that supposed to mean?"

Ledger smirks. "He means Bodhi's a little less experienced between the sheets than the rest of us."

Fuck. Me.

If looks could kill, Griffin would be a lump of cold hard shit on the floor right now.

Barrett turns, shirtless at his locker. "How do you know this, Ledger?"

He shrugs. "Griffin told me the other night after our last away game."

"Thanks Griffin," I mumble.

Asshat.

"You're welcome little buddy." Griffin pats my back. "I told you it's nothing to be ashamed of." He stops and thinks for a moment and then asks me, "I did tell you that, right?"

"Not that I reca—"

"No matter," he says with a wave of his hand. "So, you're a virgin. Big whoop. Lots of guys are virgins, right gentlemen?"

Crickets sound through the locker room.

Oh...that's right. How silly of me.

There aren't any crickets in the locker room because we're not out in the middle of the goddamn woods so that would be ridiculous.

It's eerily quiet in here as my gaze shoots around the room at each of the guys. Some are scratching their heads; the others are trying to do anything but look at me.

"Uh huh. Sounds like it, Griff. Thanks."

"But hey!" Griffin raises his arms up in victory. "You were with a girl last night, no?"

"Wait, back up a second." August has his hand raised. "Roche, are you really a virgin?"

I guess the cat's out of the fucking bag now. No use denying it. None of them are going to let this go so I may as well come clean.

"Yeah."

He shakes his head completely befuddled. "What...wh... how? Like seriously how?"

"Easy Blackstone. I keep my penis in my pants and out of any kind of hole."

"That includes glory holes right?" Griffin winks and then leans in and loudly whispers, "You know I had to ask."

"Bodhi Roche is a goddamn virgin," August states as if him saying it over and over again will help him believe it. "But you've like, done stuff with girls, right? Like, you've made out with them and shit."

I shake my head. "Nope."

Barrett's jaw practically unhinges from his face. "Nothing?"

"Nothing."

"At all?"

"Nothing at all," I say matter-of-factly. "Look long story short, my dad spent all his money on me growing up instead of on the cancer treatments he needed so how could I have ever disappointed him by making a colossal mistake and knocking up a girl and ruining my career? It was just easier to keep my nose to the grindstone and be the best fucking hockey player I could be."

The expressions around the room change and they all begin to respond with agreeing nods and shrugs of understanding.

Oliver pulls off his shirt and grabs his towel. "So why the change now? Is your dad still alive?"

I shake my head. "Nope."

"I'm sorry to hear that, man."

"So yeah, it was at first me not wanting to disappoint my dad. But now, I've started to notice all the hockey greats settling down and I just think that now a relationship or a family might be something I would like. You and Scarlett seems happy." I turn and gesture to August. "And you and Ella are good. You guys are great players and you have happy lives. I'm going to want that too one day but I don't want to be the laughingstock of the hockey league by being bad in bed with the possible love of my life. Especially when the media has categorized me as a walking ladies-man. So, yes. I was with a girl last night."

Whistles and cheers come from the guys as they each congratulate me. "Well, way to go, Roche!" August exclaims. "Did you stick your dick in her?"

"Yeah," Ledger smiles. "Did you take her to Pound Town?"

"Whoa, wait." Olver raises his hand. "Bodhi, forgive me for asking but I have to because you're young aaaand a virgin therefore making you a little bit stupid, but please for the love of God tell me you didn't hire a prostitute last night."

With a roll of my eyes, I shake my head. "I did not hire a prostitute last night."

He brings a hand to his chest and lets out a sigh of relief. "Good. Don't do it. Ever. You don't want that shit all over the tabloids. They will take that news and run crazy with it."

"I would never do that. And for the record, no, I did not stick my dick in her."

"So does that mean you asked her?" Griffin asks, plopping down next to me as I pull off my skates.

August's brow furrows. "Wait, who is her? What girl are we talking about?"

"Okay, okay." Harrison stands. "Storytime. Roche met some girl who texted the wrong number and accidentally reached him. He texted back and now they've been talking and I'm guessing he either asked her for some sex lessons or she offered or maybe they just went out to Chuck E Cheese for all I know."

The guys chuckle around me.

Har har. Very funny.

"But Griffin and I encouraged him to find a friend to...you know..."

"Practice on?" August asks.

Harrison nods. "Yeah."

"And?" Oliver prods.

I shrug my shoulder. "And she said yes."

Griffin folds his arms in front of his chest and cocks his head. "Aaaand?"

"And we met last night for the first time."

Griffin's brow raises this time and I know he's waiting for more.

"And she's drop dead gorgeous and I don't know how I got so fucking lucky."

"Did she recognize you?" Harrison wonders.

"Not even a little bit. She asked what I did for a living and I told her I worked in team building and athletics. She could clearly see I'm physically fit so she didn't question me any further."

Griffin clears his throat, still staring at me and waiting. "AAAAAAND?"

"And I kissed her."

Oliver smirks. "Did you use tongue?"

"Hell yeah, I used tongue."

"Did she like it?"

"I believe her words were, 'wow'."

Griffin wipes his hand down his face. "For the love of fucking Christ, did you make her come, Roche? Did she teach you how to do that?"

A smile spreads across my face and I finally give Ollenberg a nod. "She taught me how to undress her. Nice and slow and then she asked me to touch her and once I had my hands on her breasts and saw her nearly naked in front me, my instincts sort of took over and she let me go. I fingered her while she dry-humped me and I got to watch her fall apart right in front of me."

Griffin nods his approval with a satisfied smile on his face. "Alright. Way to go, Champ! Next time let's get a little oral action up in there and then you're well on your way to Pussy Palace."

Harrison caps my shoulder before heading to the shower. "Proud of you Roche. You hit a milestone. Onward and upward from here."

"Thanks Harrison."

"Yeah man," August claps his hands, "we're happy for you."

Griffin wags his brows. "And you know we're all here to give you pointers along the way if you want them. Really even if you don't want them. You know we're going to tell you all kinds of shit."

"Are you going to tell me there's a special pair of virgin PJ pants out there?"

Griffin's eyes grow huge and he gasps. "No but that would be amazing!" He snaps his fingers. "I need to think about this. Maybe something like chastity pants..." I watch amused as he walks away from me completely distracted by my idea and chuckle at how easily his brain switches from one topic to another.

As the rest of the guys disperse, I grab my towel and head to the showers feeling that little pep in my step the guys were talking about earlier. Because it's true. I woke up feeling better this morning than I've felt in a long time. I laid in bed before falling asleep last night replaying every moment with Corri over and over again as many times as I could so I wouldn't forget a thing.

I thought about what she looked like the first time I spotted her in that sexy green dress that showed every curve of her body.

I thought about the way she looked at me when I said her name. No judgement. No awkwardness. Just...Corri.

I smiled like an idiot thinking about the kiss we shared and the taste of her lips.

Marshmallows.

How soft her tongue was against mine.

How hungry for more she left me when our lips finally separated.

Her smile when she brought her fingers to her lips and said the word, "Wow."

Her gentle guidance in having me remove her dress and then what she looked like standing in front of me in that sexy as fuck lacey bra and panties. I've never wanted to rip material from a woman's body as much as I wanted to last night. Which reminds me, I need to find out where she got that bra and order her more as promised.

All in all, last night was one of the best nights of my life and I'm eager to do it again. After jerking off to thoughts of Corri, I slept peacefully through the night. Now, as the warm water hits my body, I work my way through this shower contemplating when I'm going to see her again.

Will she text me?

Should I text her?

What's the protocol when you're taking sex lessons from someone?

Is this a weekly thing, like taking trombone lessons?

Trombone...

Bone...

Boner...

Boner lessons...

Hehe.

Hell, I'm such an immature fuck.

Wait...

If she's giving me lessons, we never talked about payment.

Shouldn't I be paying her?

Shit.

We never discussed it.

I can't see her again and make her think she's doing all this for free.

I quickly rinse the soap from my body and then grab my towel and wrap it around my waist before moving to my locker to grab my phone.

ME

Hey Diary Girl. I'm sorry for the straightforward text but it just dawned on me that we never discussed payment for your...you know. The lessons. Please name your price. I'll pay whatever you want.

CORRI

Uh...hi. Good morning. I'm good thanks for asking. And if you pay me even a dime that would make me a whore. And I'm not a whore sooo I don't want your money.

"Shit! I didn't mean for that to sound..." I stare at my phone, realizing I'm talking to it like Corri can hear me rather than texting her back.

ME

Fuck, Corri I'm sorry. I didn't mean to make it sound like that. Please know that's not how I feel. I just feel bad that you're doing this for me, and I'm not really giving you anything in return. I'm happy to take you out. Dinner? Drinks? A beach day? Whatever would make you happy.

CORRI

Orgasms make me happy, Alan. 😊 And you'll be giving me multiple orgasms as you complete your...lessons. Consider that payment enough.

ME

Then I guess it's a win-win for both of us.

CORRI

Hence why I agreed to this arrangement. 😊

ME

Well, now that we're talking I'm really glad last night happened. And if it's okay that I say so, I haven't been able to stop thinking about it.

CORRI

What was your favorite part?

ME

Uh, well, there was that part where we shared an amazing kiss. But then also your dress falling to the ground and you placing my hand on your breast. It's a stunning breast by the way. Very...plump. Luscious. Soft in my hand. Pliable...Are they all like that?

CORRI

😊 I'm glad you liked them. I told you I have a nice pair of chesticles. And sadly, no. They're not all like that. Boobies come in all shapes and sizes.

ME

Well, I really like yours.

CORRI

Of course you do. They're all you know.

ME

But I think my very favorite moment was watching you come apart with my fingers curling inside you. Touching you like that was like nothing I've ever experienced and I enjoyed every minute of it.

CORRI

Me too, Alan. And I'm excited to get to play
with you again soon.

Play with me again soon.

Like a play date?

Is that what we're calling what we do?

Whatever she wants to call it is fine with me.

I'm all in.

And I'll be thinking about it every minute of the day and
night until the moment we meet again.

CHAPTER TWELVE
CORRIGAN

"Can you not see my child is in fucking pain? Do they even train you people in here or do they just pull in all the homeless bums off the street and ask you to pretend you're nurses?"

You people.

Fuck you lady.

If she seriously says that one more time.

"Ma'am. I understand that Makenna isn't feeling better yet, but she is maxed out on Tylenol and Motrin and I am not cleared to give her more. Taking too much, especially mixed with her antibiotics, can and will cause her way more harm than good, I assure you. All we can do now is make her comfortable and wait for these meds to do their jobs. I promise you she will start to feel much better in a matter of hours."

"Hours? Hours?" The woman flails her arms in front of me. "My child shouldn't have to fucking suffer because you're too stupid to do your job. I want to talk to the nurse in charge. Get me her name!"

Fuck you twice.

"Her name is Corrigan Hicks, ma'am and she is me," I tell

her with a confident lift of my chin. "I am the one in charge so if you'd like to tell me again how stupid I am or how badly I do my job, I'd be more than happy to listen to what you have to say but I will not, under any circumstances, be giving your daughter meds that her little body cannot handle."

With her finger in my face and her brows drawn together she seethes, "Then you can be prepared to hear from my lawyer because I will fucking sue you for murder since you refuse to give my kid the Tylenol she desperately needs."

I can't even remember the last time we lost a patient because of an ear infection.

Gun shot wounds, yeah.

Sepsis after a blown appendix? Sadly yes.

Car crash with no seatbelt? Way too many.

Cancer? Every single fucking day and it never gets easier.

Drowned in their own swimming pool? We see a lot of those too.

But dying from an ear infection?

Nope.

Can't remember even one.

A quick glance at little Makenna lying in her bed, her eyes bulging at her mother's words of anger, has me swallowing back the bile in my throat.

"I look forward to chatting with your lawyer, ma'am, because one thing I am very proud of in this hospital is how accurate our charting is. That means every tiny step we take with each of our patients is documented. Every I is dotted and every T is crossed so when the time comes, I'll be happy to share Makenna's charts with the appropriate people. Also," I mention, gesturing to the ceiling where we're standing, "you've been on camera for this entire conversation. Is there anything else you would like to say?"

Translation: Fuck you, you fucking fuck of a mother.

When she curls her lower lip over her teeth and bites down, for once choosing not to respond to me, I continue. "That's what I thought. Perhaps if you spent the time and energy you have for spewing anger and hatred at me to, instead, comfort your little girl, she wouldn't look so scared right now. She'll be feeling much better in a couple of hours. If she were to close her eyes and simply take a nap, she'd feel better when she wakes up. I am going to walk away now as I have a few other patients who need me. The doctor will be here to see you momentarily."

Quietly, and with as much calmness as I can muster, I turn and head the opposite direction from sweet little Makenna's bitch of a mother. As soon as I turn the corner Layken is standing at the nurse's station silently applauding me. I love that she's worked her schedule out to be relatively on par with mine. She's almost always standing here when my shift is about to end. She's like my happy face at the end of a shit day.

"Woof! That woman was a piece of work."

"Tell me about it," I say with an exaggerated roll of my eyes. "What a way to end a shift, huh?"

Layken smiles at me. "Yeah but now, you can fix your face and slap your smile on because..." She waits for me to finish her sentence.

"It's hot hockey hunk night!"

"That's right!" She claps her hands excitedly. "Just two girls settling in to feast our eyes on a bunch of hot men as they battle it out on the ice for a few hours."

"Do you even know the rules of the game?" I ask her, chuckling.

She shakes her head. "Hell no. Why do I need to worry about rules? Just bring on the hot men and a couple glasses of beer."

She curls her arm to her hip and I lace my arm through hers. "Sounds like Heaven to me. Let's get out of here."

"Did you tell Bodhi...oops!" She covers her mouth and then grins. "I mean Alan that you were coming to the game."

I shake my head. "How could I tell him when he doesn't know that I know who he is?"

She shrugs. "Well, you could've just mentioned that you were going to a hockey game tonight with your best friend. Maybe he would've told you the truth then."

"Doubt it. It's too soon. At some point I'll have to tell him because I can't stay away from my dad every time I'm in the arena. I mean, we meet for lunch once a week. Bodhi is bound to see me around here at some point."

I grab a tray of nachos and my beer, thanking the concession stand associate, and then follow Layken to our seats. I told my dad we were coming to tonight's game and he offered to put us right behind the bench so I can really feel the action. I politely declined because I didn't want to risk Bodhi spotting me in the crowd. Not knowing for sure how seeing me would affect his game, I asked Layken if she would mind if we sat farther back. We're still close enough to get a good show and I made sure to dress like every other Stars fan. I chose a comfy pair of jeans and a team hoodie and even grabbed my Stars hat. Looking around at the fans seated within close proximity to us, I think I blend in pretty darn well.

"Oooh here they come!" Layken points to the team as they move onto the ice for their warmup and I can't help but sit up straighter and watch anxiously for him to appear.

"Where's number thirty-seven? Do you see thirty-seven?"

Layken glances at me and laughs. "Girl, you already know his number?"

"What?" I shrug innocently. "I Googled him as soon as I had the chance. Of course, I know his number."

"You're not smitten at all." She turns back to watch the players for a minute and then gestures with the tip of her chin. "There he is. On the left."

My eyes rake through each player as they circle around the net and then split into sides, some shooting a puck and others rebounding. And that's when I spot him.

Not that he looks any different from any of the other guys on the ice when they're all in uniform but to me he's very different from anyone else out there. His strong arms carried me down my hallway to my bedroom. His sculpted chest and broad shoulders have pressed against my bare chest. He explored my body with those large soft hands.

I can still feel his touch when I think about it.

I can still see the sense of wonder and pure lust in his eyes.

"What position does he play?" Layken asks, pulling me from my thoughts.

"Uh, he's a sub for the left. I think sometimes he's a left wing and sometimes he's left defense."

"Wow, he plays two positions?"

"It's not uncommon, really. Players move around a good bit even during game play. I'll have to ask my dad the next time we have lunch what his plans are for Bodhi since he's not necessarily a starting player."

"Do you think one of the guys is considering retirement or something and that's why they brought him on board?"

"I don't know. I suppose it's not out of the realm of possibility. I wasn't following the team much while I was in London. You would probably know more than me at this point."

Layken shakes her head. "Nah. I'm a fan but I'm not the super-know-every-detail kind of fan. All I know is that the guys have always been great to work with whenever we've had charity events for the hospital. And thanks to your dad, they almost always come around to visit the kids. Especially around the holidays."

"Dad loves being Santa for those kids. I imagine he'll do it until he physically can't anymore."

"Hmm." Layken smirks bringing a finger to her chin. "Maybe I could write the next great holiday romance where Santa shows up to see the children in the small-town hospital and ends up falling for one of the single moms who sits with her son day in and day out. She spends so much time taking care of her ailing son but nobody is there to take care of her... until Santa shows up and then BAM. Christmas miracles everywhere and happily ever afters for everyone."

"Wow. How do you do that?" I ask her, amazed.

"Do what?"

"Just come up with storyline ideas like that on the fly?"

She smiles. "You mean like the story about the girl who accidentally texts the virgin pro hockey player and he writes her back and then somehow she's offering him lessons on how to be great in bed so he's ready when he meets the love of his life except he think he's already met the love of his life and it's her?"

Nearly spitting out my drink, I cover my mouth with my hand and roll my eyes. "Oh please. That's pretty far-fetched, don't you think?"

Without response, she merely shrugs with a mischievous grin and then gives her attention to the pregame ceremony. After the national anthems are sung and the teams get into their starting positions, she leans over to me as I'm watching the players and murmurs, "Far-fetched maybe, but not out of the realm of possibility. Just saying."

I shake my head silently, not wanting to give her any more fodder for her wildly creative mind. Though now that she's planted that seed in my brain, would a hot hockey player falling in love with his coach's daughter be so bad?

Not for me.

Pretty sure Dad would not say the same.

For the first couple minutes of the game Bodhi is on the bench but the minute Ledger Dayne comes off his first shift, Bodhi hits the ice and sprints to his position to get into the action. Magallen has possession of the puck and forces it to August Blackstone in the corner. August is checked by one of the Pittsburgh players and the puck is taken over by them.

"Dammit! Come on Stars!" I shout along with Layken and the other fans surrounding us. We watch as Pittsburgh moves the puck down the ice to our goalie, Barrett Cunningham, but that man is on point tonight. He stops the puck from entering his net three times before the Stars take a solid possession again. Griffin being the closest to Barrett, he swings the puck back around the net to the corner and shoots it at Bodhi.

YES! Let's GO Bodhi!

I want to scream and shout for him simply because I feel some small connection to a player on the ice, but I stop myself out of fear that he might actually hear me screaming for him. I know that sounds ridiculous but what if they can actually hear certain fans? What if he were to look up at just the right time and see me? Something tells me that would be the end of our playdates and after the orgasm he gave me a few nights ago, not getting to experience that again would make me very sad.

There. I said it.

I liked falling apart to Bodhi Roche's touch.

And I'm antsy to do it again.

Knowing Bodhi's reputation for being the killer player on his last team, I expect him to take the puck all the way down the ice and score the team's first goal.

But he doesn't.

Instead, he passes to August who is presently in a position to make the better shot and then advances toward the net to assist him if needed. August fights against a few strong Pittsburgh defensemen and takes the shot but misses as the puck banks off the net. It slides towards Bodhi just in time for him to hook it with his stick, reposition, and shoot for the net and this time it slides right in!

The crowd jumps to their feet. Layken and I do the same. I raise my arms above my head and scream for our home team, so incredibly happy for Bodhi. His shift comes to an end as he races back to the bench where he's met with a high-fives from his teammates. I smile when my dad gives him a proud slap on the back.

"Aww look. Daddy likes your boyfriend," Layken teases.

"Oh my God! He is not my boyfriend."

"Okay...playmate. Does that sound better?" She wags her brows. "I mean don't tell me you haven't been sitting here wishing his face was between your legs right now. Look at that man." She gestures to the where Bodhi is seated on the bench, his helmet off and a Gatorade bottle being lifted to his mouth. Sweat pours down his face but his smile when he looks at the player next to him, and the fire in his eyes...phew. Layken is right. That man is sexy as hell.

"I wasn't necessarily thinking it until now."

"Well, you better tell him it's time for his next lesson as soon as he's available. And that it's going to be of the oral variety."

CHAPTER THIRTEEN
BODHI

We won our game four to one and I am flying high. Scoring the first point of the game was a highlight for me. It set the tone for the rest of the game, which was amazing if I do say so myself.

Which I don't because the entire team rocked it tonight.

The moment I scored that goal I pictured Corri sitting in the stands cheering me on like I've seen Scarlett do for Oliver. For Ledger too since they're family. I pictured Corri jumping up and down, a bright smile on her face and that look in her eye that says *we'll celebrate when you get home.* And the more I thought about her being there supporting me, the more I realized I really want that. I want someone in my life who cares about me and supports my endeavors. And I want to be that person for someone else. I want to dote on a woman and bring a smile to her face. I want to be the one she turns to when she's having a bad day. I want someone I can wrap my arms around and snuggle with when I'm at home. I want that intimate connection with a woman. Someone who can look into my eyes and feel loved. Someone who can trust me one hundred percent.

Someone I can call mine.

"Hey Bodhi!" Ella smiles and waves as she walks down the hall. I'm out of my uniform and about to head to the gym for a quick leg stretch. "Great game! And congrats on that first goal. You were amazing out there!"

Her compliment brings a sincere smile to my face. "Thanks Ella. These guys make me better and I love that I can be a help to the team."

August follows me out of the locker room headed for the gym too but claps my shoulder when he hears my response to Ella. "Spoken like someone who's learning what we're all about around here. Proud of you, Roche."

"I want to be a team player and I also want to be the best."

"You'll never be the best as long as I'm around, Pickle Pants," Griffin teases, messing up my already wild hair. "But you're alright, Kid. You stretching?" he asks, hitching his thumb toward the gym doors.

"Yep. I'm coming. See ya, Ella."

She gives her husband a quick kiss and waves. "See you in a bit guys."

Once inside the gym the three of us head to the exercise bikes to work our legs before heading out.

"You guys going to Jay's?" August asks, staring at us I in the mirror as we ride.

"Heck yeah," Griffin says. "I've got to find someone to fuck around with tonight or else it'll just be me and my fist and what's the fun in that?"

I hear that.

I'm ashamed to say I've gotten used it over the years.

Maybe I should text Corri and see if she wants to get together.

And say what? Hey, you don't know that I'm a pro hockey player but I am and I won my game tonight and scored a goal and now I have all this adrenaline and really don't want to end up alone at home with my dick in my fist so how about we get together for a playdate?

Get real, Bodhi.

Corri's not a plaything and she's not mine to play with whenever I want.

She's a teacher. A tutor. A mentor.

She's doing me a huge favor.

I won't take advantage of that no matter how much I've thought about her body since the moment I left her apartment.

"Bodhi? What about you?"

"Yeah, I guess so. I don't have any other plans."

"No hot sex girl tonight?" Griffin wags his brows.

"Nope."

"How did you not have her on standby tonight? That's poor planning, Pickle Pants."

"First of all, she doesn't know I'm a hockey player. And I'm pretty sure it's not normal to just call someone like her late on a Saturday night and ask her if we can fuck around."

"I disagree." He shakes his head, the corner of his mouth turning up. "That is, in fact, the exact definition of a booty call."

"Well, she's not a call girl. She's a friend and if I have any chance of learning how to pleasure a woman, I want to stay on her good side."

August nods. "Her good side. Would that be the front of her or the back of her?"

Griffin laughs. "Yeah man. The tits or the ass?"

For a minute I consider not answering them but since they're both staring at me and waiting to hear what I'm going to say, I swallow my pride and tell them, "All of the above. Her body is...everything. Perfect tits *(that fit wonderfully in my hands)* and perfect ass *(that I can grab on to)*."

Fuck. I wish I could see her tonight.

I wish I could walk into my apartment and see her lying on my couch waiting for me.

Or in my bed.

Hell, I'm going to need a cold shower before I fall asleep tonight.

"Sounds like you found yourself a great partner. Maybe she'll end up being the perfect girl for you."

I shake my head. "Nah. I doubt it. I mean she's been cool about this arrangement we have going on and luckily there's enough chemistry between us to make it not feel forced, but I seriously doubt that I'm her type. I didn't get the impression from her that she's a sports fan at all."

"Not her type?" August laughs. "You mean a rich attractive young man who has the body you have and a willingness to give her anything she wants in the bedroom? Who the fuck doesn't like that type?"

Griffin leans over and gives August a fist-bump. "Amen brother!"

Finally, dressed in my suit and leaving the arena, I head out to the parking garage with my keys and cellphone in hand. Moving toward my parking spot, I hit the unlock button on my key fob as my cellphone chimes. When I turn it over, I see a text from Corri and stop dead in my tracks.

CORRI

I know it's late on a Saturday night, but I also know you're usually sitting at home alone crying over a bowl of pasta so...

ME

Who said anything about crying? What would I be crying over?

CORRI

Mario's forgot to give you your free bread?

ME

LOL that would be a tragedy. What else?

CORRI

They gave you veal parmigiana instead of chicken?

ME

Definitely worth a hearty cry. Anything else?

CORRI

They ran out of cheese?

ME

OMG where have you been all my life? You totally get me. I'm sobbing already.

CORRI

I knew it 😊

ME

Actually, I got out of work pretty late tonight and never ate dinner. I'm starving and Mario's sounds fucking delicious.

CORRI

Sooo if I ordered some, you would pick it up and bring it here? You provide dinner, I'll provide dessert? 😏

ME

By dessert you mean…

CORRI

Your second lesson.

ME

Order right now. I'll pick it up and be there in twenty.

"WHAT IF I can't get her off?" I can't believe I'm even asking this. My cheeks are turning red. I can feel them warm as I trail my fingers over Corri's naked body. The moment I got here, she met me at the door in nothing but her pink silk robe and I knew dinner was going to be a little later still.

"I hope you don't mind," she said to me as I set our take-out on the counter in her kitchen. "I thought maybe you might want dessert first."

I tugged on the tie of her robe as I pulled her in against my body, wrapping my arm around her. "I know this is just you being extremely generous and teaching me how to navigate a woman's body, but I'll need you to forgive me."

"For what?"

"I haven't been able to stop thinking about you since the other night."

The way she smiled at me...

I want to see that smile every damn day.

"You were pretty great the other night," she told me. "And I guess I'd be lying if I said I didn't want to see if maybe it was beginners luck or..."

I inched my mouth closer to hers as her eyes dropped to my lips and then with two fingers, pushed her robe over her shoulders, letting it fall to the ground. I feathered my fingers over her skin and cupped her beautiful breasts in my hands. Her eyes fell closed as she tipped her head back and she gasped when I smoothed my thumbs across her nipples. "Maybe you're just a spectacular teacher."

"I guess there's only one way to find out," she whispered against my lips.

It was then that I lifted her like I did the other night, wrapping her legs around my waist, and carried her to her bedroom where we made out for several long minutes before she stripped me of my clothes and asked if I was ready for an oral lesson.

Fuck yes, I'm ready for it.

"Trust me," Corri says reassuringly. "First of all, the way you worked your fingers the other night was...well, let's say it was magical."

"Magical?"

"Mhmm. So, you do not need to wonder if your ability to get a woman off is strong enough because the answer will always be yes. Yes it is. But oral sex has to be something you both want. You may find some women can't bear the thought of someone licking them there or smelling them there. It's just not their cup of tea, and that's okay. Every woman is different and every *body* is different."

"Do you think men are the same?"

"Do I think there are men who don't want their dick sucked?"

I nod. "Yeah."

A light chuckle comes from her mouth. "Honey if there's a man out there who doesn't want a warm tight mouth wrapped around his dick, I have yet to meet him."

"So why wouldn't a woman want the same treatment?"

She shrugs. "My guess would be either she had an asshole partner who made her feel insecure in the past, in which case you may just have to slow down and make her feel as comfortable as possible..."

"Or?"

"Ooor she's a fucking prude and may never change her views and if that's the case, RUN. You don't want that in your life."

"Well how will I know if she doesn't want it?"

"Oh, she'll let you know. Maybe you'll go to touch her and she'll stop your hand from exploring, or maybe you'll be kissing her body and working your way down..."

"Like this?" Corri lies naked on her bed once again, and I hover over her, my lips pressing against her collarbone before I move my mouth to the top of her chest, her left breast, her right breast, her stomach, and then her pelvis.

"Mhmm. If you get that far, I'm sure if she doesn't want it, she'll stop you."

"Are you going to stop me, Corri?"

"Do you want me to stop you?"

I shake my head meeting her gaze, noting her darkened pupils and the uptick in her breathing. Her nipples have hardened into tight peaks and her face is flushed.

"Not a chance," I tell her. Smoothing my hand down her leg I curl it around her calf, feeling every inch of her warm silky skin. She bends her knees, resting her feet on the mattress. Her chest rises and falls a little quicker the closer my fingers get to where I'm longing to be.

Is she wet?

As wet as the other night?

Because fuck that was sexy as hell.

"Teach me. What should I do next?"

"U-uh..." She clears her throat and I nearly grin at the effect I know my touch is having on her. "If you're taking things slow, I would uh...I would recommend kissing up her inner thigh, teasing her a little, you know? Making sure she's ready."

Doing as she instructs, I tenderly pull her legs apart and

then bend down to pepper slow kisses along her inner thigh, curling my tongue in small circles with each kiss. When I peek up at her, I notice she's watching me, her mouth hanging open, and her eyes heated. "Like this?"

"Mhmm." She nods. "And then when you're ready, and you feel like your partner is good and ready..."

"How will I know?" I ask, my voice sounding gruff. "Will she be wet?"

"Yes," she answers but her answer sounds more like a sigh as my fingers trail through her soaking pussy.

"Fuck," I whisper. "You're...Corri, you're glistening."

"You're very good at this."

Swallowing the lump in my throat, I stare are her beautiful pink center and lick my lips. "I really want to taste you right now," I murmur. "You look...fucking sweet."

She opens her legs further, allowing me to raise one of her feet and hook her leg over my shoulder. "Let's see how a man eats his dessert," she says.

Hell. Yes.

Leaning down, I separate her with my thumbs and then flatten my tongue against her and drag it through her sweet pussy.

"Oooh my God!" Corri moans, lifting her hips in response to my tongue. "That is..." she says, trying to breathe calmly. "That is...perfection."

"Yeah?"

"Yeah."

"You taste good Corri." I lick through her a second, third, and fourth time, flicking her clit with the tip of my tongue on each stroke. She rewards me with sensual moans and tight little gasps of breath that tell me she's loving this.

I'm loving it too.

Hearing her pleasure is a huge turn-on for me. Like she has

me under her spell, the more sounds I can pull from her the more I want to pleasure her. The more I want to hear her voice. Every sound that escapes her. Making her come is like a new reward for me. The sound of her orgasm better than the sound of the siren when I score a goal on the ice.

"Change the word good, Alan," she says. "Tell me again how I taste."

Swirling my tongue through her soft pussy, lapping at every available drop of her, I murmur against her body, "Fucking delicious."

I feel her hand slide through my hair, gripping the strands and practically guiding me through her sweet center. "God, yes, Alan! Just like that. Now dip your tongue-OOOOH God!"

Call me an overachiever, but dipping my tongue inside her, stroking inside like I'm pulling honey straight from the tree, causes her to lift her hips and fuck my face with wild abandon.

It also causes my cock to harden in my pants.

"Come on, Corri. Keep fucking my face," I tell her with my face buried in her heated pussy. God, I could die like this, suffocated by pussy, and die a ridiculously happy man. "I want to hear you when you come. I want to taste your release, baby," I mumble between flicks of my tongue on her clit as she moans louder, breathes faster. "I could eat you for hours."

And that's no lie.

The way her body responds to me makes me feel so alive.

Like I'm a fucking warrior.

Her grasp on my hair tightens as I continue my assault on her clit. Unwilling to show mercy now that I have her in this heightened state, I flick, flick, flick, flick, with my tongue until her pussy clenches and she's finally screaming. "OH MY GOD! I'M CO-I'M COM-FUUUUCK, I'M COMING!"

When she lets go of my hair, I pull back and press my lips a few times to her inner thigh before lowering her leg back to the mattress. "You know," I say as I work my way back up her body while she comes down from her climax, "I think I'm starting to become addicted to hearing you come. Your excitement seems to be going straight to my head."

She cups my extremely stiff cock with her hand. "I feel that."

"That's not what I meant." I chuckle, realizing that's probably exactly how it sounded. "I just meant—"

"I know what you meant." She pulls her gaze up to my eyes as she unzips my pants and pushes them down along with my brief. When she frees my cock, she palms it in her hand. My eyes roll back in my head and I hiss a breath through my teeth begging myself to stay in control and revel in the feel of someone touching me. "I find it so hard to believe that no woman has ever sucked this beautiful piece of your body into her mouth."

Fuuuuuck me.

She said my cock is beautiful.

I shake my head. "I want to tell you it's happened , hundreds of times, but that would be a lie."

She wraps her hand around my length and I swear to God I just grew another goddamn inch. She slides her thumb over the head spreading the precum around before pulling her thumb into her mouth.

"Mmmm."

Sexiest. Thing. Ever.

"So, you're saying I would be the first woman to have this beautiful cock in her mouth?"

"You would, yes."

The proud smile that crosses her face makes my chest tighten.

"Well since you've been such a great student, I can't think of a better reward."

"Corri, you don't have to—Oooh shiiiiiiit." I gasp loudly when she sits up and sucks my cock into her mouth, sinking over it completely until I feel the back of her throat against the tip. "Fuuuuuuuck, Corri."

Reaching down, I cup her face in my hand as she circles her tongue around my shaft and pulls off of me only to swallow me once again. "Jesus fucking Christ."

Don't come yet.

Don't come yet.

Please for the love of Jesus...

Do NOT come.

Her hand wrapped around the base of my shaft, she squeezes me as she sucks in my head a few inches at a time, her flattened tongue trailing along the underside of my cock and then twisting and curling as she sucks me in. I can't tear my eyes away from the sight of this woman with my cock IN. HER. MOUTH.

It's stunning.

It's sexy.

It's...fucking unbelievable.

She looks up at me and it's all I can do not to tell her I love her because fuck, I'm overwhelmed by sensations and feelings right now that I have never experienced before. If I'm not careful, I'll come violently down her throat way faster than I want to.

"Corri." Her name is a pleasured whisper. "It's so fucking good, Corri. Your mouth is...fuck, it's...it's incredible."

She pops off my cock, using her own saliva as a lube as she pumps up and down with her hand. With her other hand she pulls gently on my balls, rolling them between her fingers and oh. My. Fuck.

I think I'm dying.

Am I dying?

Am I dead?

I'm dead.

Gone.

Is this what Heaven feels like?

I tilt my head back, squeezing my eyes closed and letting the pleasure roll through my body and that's when the feeling changes. That's when she tilts her head under my parted knees and pulls one of my balls into her mouth rolling it around with her tongue.

"Mother fuck..."

She comes back to my cock, bobbing up and down as she fondles my balls with her hand. I bring my hand to her hair just as she did me and watch her mouth open wide as she takes me in as far as she can. I push a little bit more and she takes me in completely hitting the back of her throat with each and every goddamn thrust. "Corri...fuck...Corri!"

She doesn't say a word but she does moan loudly with my cock in her mouth, the sound sending fucking shivers through my entire body. I watch her suck me several more times, her head bobbing up and down as I guide her with my hand fisted around her hair. My God, this is..."Fuuuuuuuck, Corri, I can't hold on." A white-hot heat shoots through my body from my toes to my chest. My cock swells and my balls tighten and I come so hard I fear she'll choke on my cum. Thank God, she doesn't. She takes it like the goddamn queen that she is and then licks me clean for good measure.

Unable to remain upright, I lower my body to the bed beside her and then pull her into my arms, her head against my chest.

She fits there perfectly.

"Whatever the fuck you just did to me," I breathe, "I am absolutely certain there is nobody in this world who will ever do it any better."

With a proud grin on her face, she responds, "Well, if I

ruined you for any and all women who come after me...sorry not sorry."

If there are women meant to come after her one day...Hell...I'm not so sure I want them after what she's done for me.

"TELL ME SOMETHING ELSE ABOUT YOU."

She lifts her head from my chest, the lazy smile on her face giving me every impression that she's sated and content which makes me happy if not a little proud. Being with her in a way I've never been with any other woman makes me feel things I've never felt before. Like she's awakened a spirit for life in me that I've never had before.

Only now I want it with her.

I like being here with her.

Holding her after she comes.

I wish I didn't have to leave.

"Like what?" she finally asks.

Trailing my fingers lazily up and down the bare skin of her back, I tell her, "Anything. I just want to know more about you. I want to know what makes you such a beautiful human?"

"A beautiful human?"

"Yeah."

She ponders my words for a moment, her chin resting on my chest. "I'm not sure anyone has ever called me that before."

My brows pinch. "How is that possible?"

She huffs a soft laugh. "There's not really anything of super-star quality about me. I'm just...me."

"I don't believe that for a second. Tell me what you love most about nursing?"

She inhales a deep breath against me. "Well, I got started in nursing because of my mom. But once I got a taste for the emergency room, I kind of fell in love with it."

"Why the emergency room?"

"The thrill of the chase I guess? The adrenaline rush of knowing you don't have a ton of time to assess a situation or a patient before you have to know what to do or how to do it. Plus, it's different every day so my job is never monotonous. Sometimes it's a roller coaster and sometimes it's a Sunday drive along the coast. No two days are ever the same."

"What's your favorite cookie?"

Her smile widens at the change of subject. "Uh...are we talking everyday cookie or Christmas cookie?"

"Any cookie. What's your absolute favorite?"

"Bakeless oatmeal cookies, hands down."

I close my eyes and moan. "Mmm hell yeah those are pretty damn good."

"Right? A handful of those and a tall glass of milk? Perfection."

"Agreed. What's the perfect date for you?"

"Ooh, there are so many and I think it totally depends on the day or my mood, but really, the perfect date is one where I simply enjoy being with my partner. I want to laugh. I want to hold hands. I don't need someone to try to impress me or buy me a crap ton of gifts. The perfect date is one where I come home smiling unable to stop thinking about him." Her eyes flit to mine. "What about you?"

I think about my answer a moment. "I guess since I've never taken a woman out on a date before, my perfect date is one where I can make her smile no matter what we do together. A date where she feels like she's loved and cherished because I make her feel that way. I don't care if we're eating take-out food on the kitchen floor or we're dressed to the nines for a fancy dinner. The perfect date is the one I don't ever want to end."

"Yeah," she agrees softly with a sigh. "Same."

Kind of like this.

I know my time with Corri isn't really a date.

But holding her in my arms like this, my fingers trailing her back...

Her legs entwined with mine...

It's perfect.

And I wish it didn't have to end.

CHAPTER FOURTEEN

CORRIGAN

MONDAY

ME

> *Pic of fast food taco* That moment when you oversleep and barely make it to work on time, and then in your frazzled state, you drop the files you're carrying for two different patients which equals a solid forty five minutes of putting said charts back together and then checking and rechecking about ten times to make CERTAIN each patient has their correct information, you work through lunch because you feel bad for almost being late, you haven't had nearly enough to drink today.

ME

But when you finally get a restroom break you realize your period started so now you're tired, you're hangry, you've got cramps, and your best friend isn't even working in the building today so you can't cry to her about your day and then when you finally do get to leave you know your fridge is empty and you should order food but also you know your favorite restaurants are going to take too long because oh my God you need food like yesterday so you end your night on the living room couch munching on this soggy fast food taco that falls apart the moment you try to take a bite.

ALAN

Oh man. That sounds like a super shit day. I'm sorry you had it rough today. If I were in town, I'd bring you something better to eat.

ME

Is that an innuendo?

ALAN

LOL Uh, no. Sadly I did just mean I would've brought you Mario's...or Chinese. You did say it was your favorite. And I'd add all the chocolate for those cramps.

ME

Yeah. I just didn't want to go all the way across town because I'm cranky as fuck and should just put myself to sleep. Sorry for bothering you with my whiny text.

ALAN

Your texts never bother me. Hearing from you makes me smile. Plus, I'm out of town for work for a few days so it's nice to hear from someone a little closer to home.

ME

So, what are you eating then? Or have you not eaten yet? Or are you in Switzerland or something and therefore it's like middle of the night and I'm keeping you awake?

ALAN

LOL. Nope not in Switzerland. But I am in Ohio. I hear there's a little town about ninety minutes from here that calls themselves 'Little Switzerland'. Also, the town has the world's biggest cuckoo clock. 🐦

ME

Interesting. What is good to eat in Ohio?

ALAN

pic of steak, side salad, and baked potato Well I ate several hours ago but dinner was catered so I can't complain.

ME

Salivates over your dinner I hate you right now.

ALAN

Hey, don't hate on my food porn.

ME

I think I could get off to that food porn right about now. That's how good it looks.

ALAN

Now THAT I would pay to see. Maybe we should Facetime.

ME

Too bad for you. You don't get to watch since you ate that yummy food without me. *shrugs* Your loss.

ALAN

Fuck!

ME

Night Alan.

ALAN

Night Corri.

TUESDAY

ALAN

pic of runny scrambled eggs, burnt avocado toast, and two bruised bananas For the record, hotel room service isn't always the best. Hope your day is starting better than mine. At least the coffee is hot.

ME

As I'm currently standing along the side of the fucking road waiting for the police to show up, I think I have you beat yet again.

ALAN

Oh shit! Corri, are you alright? What the hell happened? What can I do?

ME

I'm fine. Just a fender bender of sorts. Stupid kid was texting and ran right into me at a red light. I'm sure I'll feel it later today but for now, I'm fine...except that I'm late for work AGAIN.

ALAN

Are you sure you're alright? Do you want me to call someone? I feel terrible I'm not there. I could have picked you up or...I don't know... something. Anything.

ME

You're sweet but it's okay. My car is drivable, so once the police get here to make a report I'll be on my way. My workday hasn't even started yet and already I can't wait for this day to be over.

ALAN

Hey. I know it's late. Just checking in to see how you're feeling.

ME

Head hurts. Neck is sore. Took a muscle relaxer and am heading to bed. Sorry, Alan.

ALAN

Never apologize for taking care of yourself. Go. Rest. Your body needs it.

WEDNESDAY

ALAN

Morning Corri. Hope you slept well and are feeling better. I was thinking about you a lot last night. Hope you're okay.

ALAN

Missed hearing from you today. Hope you're well.

THURSDAY

ME

OMG I am SO SORRY I never got back to you yesterday. Work was a madhouse. We were understaffed and of course ended up with a full emergency room all day. I swear to God Mercury must be in retrograde or it's a double full moon or something because we had all sorts of kids in yesterday for everything from a broken arm to a mother poisoning her kid with turpentine! My head just wasn't into talking to anybody by the time I got home. I stuffed a PB&J in my mouth and went to bed.

ALAN

Wow. What a week you're having, huh?

ME

Tell me about it. 😊 When does a girl get to catch a break?

ALAN

What would you do with that break?

ME

What do you mean?

ALAN

I mean if you had a day off to do whatever the hell you wanted, what would you do?

ME

Probably should unpack. I still have a living room full of boxes. I had to dive into a box in my bedroom just to find clean underwear because I'm that backed up on my own fucking laundry. My father would be so disappointed in my hot mess of a life.

ALAN

We'll come back and unpack your father and whatever hold he might have on your life later (because I get it) but you're not allowed to say you'll unpack on your day off. Tell me what you do for fun.

ME

You mean besides meet men by accidentally texting them and then offer to teach them everything I know about sex? 😏

ALAN

Whatever guy takes you up on that offer is an asshole. Tell him to fuck off.

ME

Are you kidding? That would be a terrible idea.

ALAN

Why is that? He's a total stranger who you don't even know and you're literally bringing him into your home and letting him do all sorts of ridiculously hot sensual things to your body.

ME

shrugs Maybe I'm a stupid naïve woman but 1. The guy is hot AF. 2. He seems relatively nice, and 3. He's a virgin, which means he hasn't been tainted by skanky-ass women. That makes him a hot commodity and I would be a fool to toss him aside.

ALAN

Well, whoever that guy is, he better consider himself a lucky bastard because it sounds like you might be the best thing to ever happen in his life in a very long time.

ME

blushes Well, I don't know if I would go that far. I'm not a perfect person. Maybe I'm just a horny slut who is taking full advantage of the poor guy.

ALAN

I seriously doubt that. But for the sake of argument, let's say that you are taking advantage. Is he at least...you know... comparable? To past playmates? I mean I'm only asking because obviously you wouldn't want to take advantage if the guy is less than stellar.

ME

You know, I can't lie...for a beginner, he's far superior to any other playmate I've ever had.

ALAN

Uh...wow. That's umm, quite the compliment. That guy really is a fucking lucky man.

ME

And I am equally lucky.

FRIDAY

I toss my keys onto the counter and kick the door closed behind me. The weight of this day, no, this whole week, has me wanting to curl up in a ball and sleep for days. I don't think I've experienced a week this bad since the day I found Leo bent over Gale Wittindom in the on-call room back in London.

Fuck you, Leo.

I move down the hall toward my bedroom and search through one of the open boxes for the comfiest pair of pajama pants I can find along with an oversized sweatshirt and toss it on my bed. I grab a clean towel but before I head to the bathroom for the longest hottest shower I can stand my phone dings in my pocket. I pull it out to see a text from Bodhi. Well, Alan to him, but only because he still doesn't know that I know who he is.

Maybe I should just tell him.

Having to remember to call him Alan instead of Bodhi is getting exhausting.

Ugh.

Nah.

I guess I don't really care right now.

I just don't feel like getting into it.

Not tonight.

I've had enough drama this week.

ALAN

Happy Friday! You made it through the week! What are you going to do to celebrate?

ME

Curl up in a ball on my couch and probably cry myself to sleep.

ALAN

Oh nooooo. I was wishing you a great day all day! What happened?

Well, one of the male nurses asked me out but I don't want to tell you that, so I guess I'll tell you the worst of my day.

ME

I lost a patient today.

Just typing the words out on my phone brings tears to my eyes.

ALAN

Oh shit, Corri. I'm so sorry. Do you want to talk about it?

ME

Maybe at some point but right now, I just want to stand in the hot water and cry. And then make myself eat something before I crawl into my bed and stay there for the next two days.

ALAN

Sounds like a fair plan. Is there anything I can do for you?

ME

No. This is all just part of the job I signed up for. Sometimes I win...and sometimes I lose.

ALAN

I understand that more than you know.

I chuckle to myself because I know what he's thinking, but losing a patient isn't the same as losing a hockey game. I won't tell him that though. I know he's only trying to be sympathetic.

ALAN

Enjoy your shower. Don't come out until you've used up the hot water for the entire building.

I try to smile at his last text and then toss my phone onto my bed, grab my clothes and towel, and head for the bathroom. The water is scalding as I step into it but I refuse to turn it down. The heat feels good on my skin. A reminder to my body that I'm still alive. That although I can't save every patient that comes through the doors, I statistically save more than I lose and I need to remember that.

Still, losing small humans is heartbreaking no matter how you look at it, so I allow myself as long as I need to cry for the little boy I lost today. To grieve the loss of a small innocent soul, to question why children are taken from this world way too soon. And when all that energy is gone, and those tears are shed, I finally allow myself the pity party I so desperately needed to have this week within the confines of my shower.

Because fuck this fucking shit week I just had.

It can all go to hell.

My shower turns into a nearly thirty-minute soak by the time I finally rinse my hair, wash my body, shave, and then switch off the water. I wrap my body in a fluffy towel and step out of the shower, cursing the air for not being the same temperature my shower was. I wrap a smaller towel around my wet hair and then slip into my comfy clothes, thankful to be without a bra for the rest of the weekend. Nothing says comfort like the oldest pair of sweatpants I wore while in college and a sweatshirt so well worn it's tattered in spots. Once I have them on my body, I wrap my arms around myself and inhale a deep breath. It's almost the same as a comfort hug.

Almost.

As I'm applying moisturizer on my face and neck, there's a knock on my door.

Layken.

She might not be a nurse, but she's the one person who understands what I need when I have a shit day like this one. She's already seen me cry once today. Hell, except for Monday I think she's seen me cry every day this week, so it doesn't surprise me at all that she's stopping by to check on me.

Padding down the hall, I grab the doorknob and pull my door open, completely taken aback when I see Bodhi Roche standing there with his hands full of bags.

"B-Alan..." I blink. "Wh-what are you doing here?"

He nods toward the stairs. "Someone was coming out as I was coming in so I didn't need buzzed in." He holds up a bag that is already making me want to drool. The savory scent alone makes me want to weep happy tears. "Thought you could use some comfort food and a friendly face."

"Alan," I shake my head, "I'm sorry. I just..."

How do I say this?

"I don't think I'm really up for lessons tonight."

He smiles kindly. "Good because I'm not here for that. I'm here for you."

"What?"

"You've had a fucking hard week," he explains. "And I thought maybe I could help make it even just a tiny bit better for you." He holds up the bag of Chinese takeout that he remembered I love. "So, I brought dinner because you need to eat..."

He lifts another bag. "And I brought way more snacks than either of us can handle, including cookies & cream ice cream because you said it's your favorite." Then he gestures to the third bag on his arm. "And in here is a comfy blanket, a bottle of vodka and some cranberry juice because I remembered what you ordered to drink that first night we met. And if your television is working, I have a streaming account so we can watch any and all sappy movies that give you all the feels."

I hold his stare as he lowers his arms and his smile fades. His voice becomes soft and tender as he says, "And if you don't want to watch television all wrapped up in a comfy blanket, then I'm still here. I'll sit with you in total silence if that's what you prefer. So, you're not alone." He swallows. "There's nothing worse than being in your own head after a shitty few days and I really just wanted to, you know, make sure you're okay."

The helpless expression on his face alone melts me into a gigantic puddle of overwhelming sadness. Not to mention the guilt that is building up inside me over possibly going out with another man when I have this...well, whatever this is with Bodhi.

Alan.

My eyes blur as my tears well, my chin quivers, and there's a heaviness in my chest just before I burst into tears, covering my face with my hands. "You're so sweet to me. God, I'm so sorry, Alan."

"Hey, hey, hey." His voice is even softer now. He steps inside and places the bags of food on the floor by our feet and then wraps his arms around me, his strong hand on the back of my head stroking my hair.

I'm not going to lie.

His touch is comforting.

"Shhhhh, it's okay, Corri."

"This has been the absolute shittiest week and I have nothing left to give." My voice cracks and my body trembles as I sob big fat tears into Bodhi's chest. "And I just can't seem to stop crying no matter how hard I try."

"Then don't," he murmurs against my ear as he holds me. "Cry it out. You never need to be ashamed of crying. Crying means you have feelings and having feelings means you're alive. You're human. You're a person Corri. And you don't have to hold the weight of the whole world on your shoulders." His hand smooths up and down my back as I continue to cry.

"Let me hold some of the burden for you. Even if it's just for one night."

I give in and wrap my arms around him, wishing I could somehow cover myself in his comfort. In his peace. In the calmness of him.

"I can't believe you're here," I sob. "You're so unbelievably thoughtful."

"I just wanted to make you smile. That's all."

My breath hitching against his chest, I try to nod. "I promise I'm smiling on the inside."

"I'll take that," he says with a soft chuckle. I feel his lips press against the top of my head. "Can I put some food on a plate for you? You haven't eaten much this week by the sound of it."

"Not yet," I answer meekly, grabbing onto his shirt. "I just... can you just hold me for a minute?"

He tightens his grasp around my body and it feels so good. Comforting and warm. I feel safe in his arms. Cherished even. Plus, he smells good. "There's nothing I would rather do."

This guy.

He's been here for me all week even when he couldn't be here in person.

He's checked up on me every day.

I don't know if it's selfish of me to be thinking these thoughts or not considering the arrangement we have together but, fuck. I've been a hot mess all week and he hasn't run from any of it. What has Sean, the nurse, done for me other than tease me at work or come on a little too strong because he has a penis and I have a vagina?

Why would I go out with him?

Why didn't I just say no the moment he asked?

Bodhi has been nothing but nice and compassionate and caring and a part of me wonders if I might be falling for him.

It's totally the wrong move though given the fact that my father won't approve, but I can't help it. How am I supposed to control the way I feel when he's here being all...Bodhi?

CHAPTER FIFTEEN

BODHI

"He was the sweetest little boy, but he was no match for the huge pick-up truck that rammed into his side of his family's car."

I watch as Corri takes a scoop of ice cream right out of the container, swallowing it down despite the tears still floating down her cheeks. My heart breaks for her. I know this is killing her but I knew she would need to talk about it.

"I can still see his sweet little face when the EMTs wheeled him in. He couldn't speak. His parents couldn't be with him because they were hurt too. He was all alone."

"I can't even imagine," I whisper, listening to her recount her workday.

"I was the only one he had." She shakes her head, crying a little more as she glances up at me with big round, glistening eyes. "I was all he had. And so, I held his hand and brushed his hair back and whispered to him that he was going to be okay, you know? I...I didn't want him to be scared. I didn't want him to feel alone so I held on to him while everyone worked around us."

She sniffles quietly and then grabs for a tissue to blow her nose. "I was holding his tiny little hand when he left this world, Alan," she cries. "I was literally holding him as he passed away." She crumbles against me on the couch and I wrap my arm around her, my hand smoothing up and down her back. "Why does God take the little ones? They never do anything wrong. They're kids! He was so little. So young."

"I wish I knew the answer," I tell her, knowing she doesn't need me to say anything at all. She just needs to feel her feelings.

"And since my shift was ending before his parents got out of surgery, I waited"—*sniffle*—"I waited for them to wake up in recovery so I could be there when the doctors broke the news to them that their son was gone." *Sniffle.* "I waited because I wanted them to know he wasn't in pain and that he wasn't alone and"—*sniffle*—"that the moment he left this world was peaceful for him." Her breath hitches with every sniffle. "It was the least I could do."

"And you did all those things because you are a beautiful, loving, compassionate soul, Corri. I can tell you care about people. You give your all to your job and the patients you care for, I can tell."

"I love my job," she whispers. "But I hate it at the same time."

"I have no doubt. It's okay to hate that part of your job. And it's okay to feel it with every fiber of your being."

God, what I wouldn't do to take away her pain.

Her grief.

Her sadness.

I hate this for her.

She sits up and wipes at her eyes with the back of her hand. "I'm so sorry you walked into me being an absolute mess tonight. I'm not usually like this, I swear."

My smile is faint but I study her face adoringly. The tears

streaming down her cheeks, her partially wet hair, her face without makeup that allows a few freckles to show across her nose.

God, she's pretty.

Even in this state.

She's raw and vulnerable and isn't trying to impress anyone.

"I think you're gorgeous just like this, Corri."

And I really mean that.

I don't understand how she's single.

She's a ten.

The total package.

Any man would be crazy not to go after her.

I don't get how some guy didn't snatch her up the moment she moved back to the States.

And I have no idea how I could possibly tell her that I sort of, kind of, might have possible itsy-bitsy feelings for her.

Ugh. Yeah, okay. There's nothing itsy-bitsy about my fucking feelings.

I like her.

I like her a lot.

Tenderly, I reach up and smooth her hair back from her face and then kiss her forehead. "It's okay to have feelings around me. Big feelings. Small feelings. Good, bad, or otherwise. I promise you're safe with me."

We're silent for a few minutes as I let her sit in her feelings because I know she needs that. I would need that if I were in her shoes. I kiss the top of her head again, noting the vanilla and coconut scent of her shampoo, and then I murmur, "I hope, for you, Corri, that when the sadness fades, you realize how much good you do for your patients. For those kids. For their parents and families. They're really lucky to have you. The hospital is lucky to have you."

"Thank you, Alan."

She's oddly quiet and not at all like herself tonight. Obviously she's been through the ringer today but something doesn't feel quite right about the way she's looking at me.

"What is it?"

Biting her bottom lip her eyes stray from mine and I can tell there's something she isn't telling me. "Corri, whatever it is you can tell me."

She closes her eyes briefly this time and takes a steadying breath then says, "Someone asked me out today."

"Asked you out?"

"Yeah."

"Like, on a date?"

"Yeah."

What?

Is she serious right now?

She wants to go out with another man?

She's literally sitting here with me right now and she's thinking about someone else?

Fuck. I guess she's within her rights.

We're not really a thing.

But fuck I kind of want to be a thing with her.

I'm attracted to her.

I like being around her.

I would love to see if there's something more between us.

But if she goes out with another man...

And then what if she...

Fuuuuuuck!

"Okay."

Okay?

That's all I have to say?

Okay?

I am so not okay about this.

"Is that what you want?" I shake my head not fully understanding. "Are you asking my permission or something?"

"No, I..." Her shoulders fall and she bows her head. "I guess I don't know what I want right now. I'm sorry. I shouldn't have said anything. This is the wrong day to even be talking about this."

I lift her chin with my finger. "It's okay. I'm glad you feel comfortable telling me anything at all. I want to be here for you."

As your boyfriend.

I want to be here for you as your boyfriend.

Because I like you.

Please for the love of Christ don't go out with someone else.

"You have to do what makes you happy, Corri. You deserve all the happiness in the world. So, if going out with this guy is what you want, you should do it."

Jesus fuck, what I wouldn't give to cut my own lips off right now to shut myself up.

"I...I don't know. I guess I need to think about it."

Yeah. Think about it.

Think about it for a long, long, looooong time.

Or tell that guy to fuck off because I'm right here.

"Alright. What can I do for you in the meantime?"

She wraps her arms around me in a hug again and asks meekly, "Can we watch some television?"

"Of course we can. We can do anything you want."

I'd do anything to be in your presence just a little longer.

"Wait, I don't get it," she says, gesturing to the television. "Cersei Lannister and Jaime Lannister are siblings, right?"

"Mhmm." I nod.

She gasps and then cringes in disgust. "But they're..."

"Yep."

"Ew."

"Right? I know!" I laugh. "But that's what makes this whole show interesting. Well," I say, bobbing my head, "that's not the only thing. I imagine incest was a pretty major thing back then especially when it came to blood lines but just wait until season three. Oooh, and season four." My eyes grow as a few amazing future scenes come to mind. "Fuuuck and season five. Honestly, there is so much drama that unfolds but I promise to try to answer any of your questions as we go."

I'll hope that we're still sitting together in the future as we watch the final season of *Game of Thrones*.

"Is there more Peter Dinklage? Because I think he's amazing at pretty much anything he does."

"Oooh yeah. There's a whole lot more of him. His character arc might be one of the best ones of the whole show."

"This was just what I needed tonight, Alan," she says with a sigh.

This is just what I needed too.

"The bloodshed isn't too much for you?"

"Like this? Sword fights and beheadings?" she asks, her brows lifting. "No way. I can get into this. The drama alone is fun to follow."

"Good. Shall we break open some snacks and watch the next episode?"

"Absolutely!"

Curled up on the couch, she's covered in the blanket I bought her and leaning on me as we watch another two episodes and then switch to something I've never seen that Corri is introducing me to. A fair trade since I introduced her to *Game of Thrones*. This show is some kind of story about a woman who walks through stones and ends up in a different century.

"Oooh the plot thickens! Her husband ends up being the villain in another time?" I ask. "So, does this mean she doesn't fall in love with him? And if that's the case, does that change her future marriage then? Oooh or does he like, take her as a wife in this past life even though she doesn't want it?"

Waiting for Corri to answer me with her knowing giggles, I glance down when she doesn't respond to me and find her out like a light.

"Corri?"

Her hand rests on my chest as she breathes evenly, not disturbed by the sounds of the television, nor the sound of my voice. I trail my hand down her hair, letting it slide between my fingers as she sleeps and I smile.

I smile because she finally let her body relax.

I smile because she needed a relaxing night and I was able to give it to her.

I smile because it's me here with her right now and not some other guy who would only be trying to get in her pants.

And I smile because there is a beautiful woman asleep on me and there is no other place I would rather be than holding her while she sleeps.

Because I actually care for her.

A lot.

Reaching for the remote, I turn the volume down a smidge and then slide down against the couch allowing her to rest her head on my chest rather than my shoulder. I pull her blanket over her shoulders and wrap my arm around her. I have zero problems lying here with her for however long she sleeps as long as she's comfortable.

And somewhere between sleep and awake, before my eyes close for the last time tonight, I whisper softly, "Please don't go out with him. Pick me."

CHAPTER SIXTEEN

CORRIGAN

U*gh, my neck.*
    Why does my body feel so sore?
And why is it so warm in here?

I can practically feel the sunlight heating my body which is only odd to me because I always close the blinds in my bedroom. But when my pillow moves up and down, I realize very quicky I'm not in my bedroom.

And I'm also not alone.

Opening my eyes, I'm shocked to see Bodhi Roche asleep underneath me. His arm rests on my back and his chest slowly rises and falls. My gaze moves to the television, which is still on. The annoying gray box that asks me if I'm still watching is waiting for a reply. I imagine it's been waiting for hours, but what do I know? I don't remember falling asleep but I clearly slept all night long.

And Bodhi stayed.

He didn't leave me.

I lift my head slightly and the movement causes Bodhi to stir, his eyes opening. His mouth turning up in a tired smile.

Alan!

Don't forget to call him Alan!

"Morning beautiful," he murmurs, licking his lips to moisten them. His gaze lifts to the sun coming in the windows. "Whoa. I think we slept much longer than anticipated."

I nod. "I think you might be right. I'm so sorry. I didn't realize I had fallen asleep."

Sitting up, his arm falls from my back but he lifts it to my hair, sweeping it from my face. "It's totally fine. I was kind of entranced by Claire and Jamie and Jack Randall and before I knew it, you were out."

"You could've told me to go to bed."

"And not get the pleasure of holding you while you slept?" He scoffs teasingly. "As if." His brows pinch momentarily as he looks around the living room. "Do we know what time it is?"

"Hot date today?"

I hate to admit I'd be crushed if he said yes.

I guess that answers my question on whether or not I should say yes to Sean.

I'll tell him no the moment I see him tomorrow.

"The only hot date I've ever been on was with you, Babe." He laughs and wipes his hand down his face, trying to rid himself of the sleepy expression.

How does he look so damn good this early in the morning?

"We've never been on a date," I tell him. "Not really."

"Hmm. Must've been in my dreams then."

Swooooon!

"The only date I have today is with the guys at work. We have a late morning meeting. Other than that, no. I have the rest of the day to get a solid workout in and maybe piddle around with a few other tasks."

I tap the screen on my phone sitting on the coffee table in front of us. "Well, rest assured it's only seven so you have plenty of time to get to your late-morning meeting."

His smile fades and his gaze meets mine. "I'd have no problem telling them to go fuck themselves if you need me."

Don't know what Dad would have to say about that.

I think I would rather Bodhi live to see another day.

"That's okay. Work meetings are important. And I'm actually having lunch with my dad today, so I should probably unpack a few boxes before I get myself ready to meet him. One of these days I might actually have a completely unpacked home."

"Don't be too hard on yourself. Life happens."

Placing my hand on his knee, I squeeze his leg slightly and say, "But thank you, Alan. Thank you so much for being here with me last night. Well..." I cock my head. "All night, actually. I think you had the right idea in not wanting me to be alone. I didn't realize I would need someone to help me through a tough day but I'm really glad it was you who knocked on my door. Layken is great and all, but you were much more comfortable."

"I was happy to do it. And I'd be happy to do it again any time. Besides," he says with a smirk, "I need to find out what happens if or when Claire goes back through the stones."

"True!" I chuckle softly. "And I need to know if Ned Stark gets set free."

"Then I guess we have a future date ahead of us at some point."

"I think you can count on it." I smile.

"Good. I'm glad."

Alan stands from the couch and offers me his hand. When I take it, he helps pull me from the couch and then folds me into his arms. His embrace is warm and soft, but his body is anything but. Warm, yes, but his arms are strong and his chest is solid. I bask for just a moment in the protectiveness of his embrace and the scent of his cologne still lingering on his clothes and try to memorize the feel of him until I can see him again.

I really like your hugs, Alan.

"I should head out. I'll need to shower and change before my meeting, but I hope you have a great lunch with your dad today," he says as his arms lift. He places a kiss on my forehead and then tilts my chin with his fingers and presses his lips to mine. His kiss isn't long but he sweeps his tongue lazily against mine and it's just enough contact to make my heart race and my body start to heat. When our mouths separate, I quickly cover mine with my hand.

"God, I'm so sorry. I probably have the worst morning breath."

He smiles. "No worse than mine and I don't mind one bit." He plants a kiss on my cheek and squeezes my hand before opening the door. "I'm sure we'll talk later."

"For sure." I nod. "Thank you again. You being here meant more than you know."

"Anything you need. Anytime, Corri. And I mean that sincerely."

And I know he does.

He gives me an understanding smile and nod and then waves goodbye.

I shut the door behind him and then lean up against it, replaying everything about last night that I can remember.

"What are we doing here?" I whisper to myself. "And why are you so outlandishly hot?"

Is this like...a thing?

Are we a thing?

Not a thing?

Are we just fuck buddies or...

Could we be more?

I don't even know if that would be a possibility.

And maybe he's not really interested.

The idea of going out with Sean when I could be spending my time with Bodhi doesn't sit well with me.

I would choose Bodhi in a heartbeat.

If only I could get the idea past my father.

I sigh against the door. "Whatever we are, whatever this is, I'm kind of here for it."

CHAPTER SEVENTEEN
BODHI

"I was watching a few tapes last night and I really think we can grab the advantage for tomorrow's game. Take a look at this." Oliver rewinds a few plays and then resumes the video he asked us to watch. This one in particular is part of Seattle's game last night against Detroit, but hell if I'm paying any attention whatsoever.

All I can think about is Corri possibly going out with another man.

And Corri kissing another man.

And Corri being touched by another man.

And Corri fucking an—

"STOP IT!"

I squeeze my eyes closed for a moment and try to shake the idea from my head. When I open my eyes again I realize the guys are all staring at me.

"Stop what?" Oliver asks.

"Fuck. Nothing. I'm sorry."

Oliver's brows furrow as his gaze moves from me to Ledger who shrugs helplessly and then he goes back to discussing the video.

"Their defense is loose with the puck so I think we could find ourselves a few opportunities to forecheck if we're smart about it."

August nods as we watch in the meeting room, his arms folded across his chest. "Alright."

Is he going to use tongue?

Is he going to have his hands on her the way I had my hands on her?

Is he going to taste her the way I've tasted her?

Is he going to get the pleasure of hearing her orga—

"FUUUUUCK!"

Oliver stops. "Dude, what the hell is going on?"

I bring my hand up to rub the back of my neck, my body tightening from the inside out. I'm so fucking hot I'm starting to sweat and my legs are restless.

I can't stop the worst-case scenarios from running through my mind.

I can't stop beating myself up for not just telling her how I feel.

For not begging her to just pick me instead.

"I can't fucking DO this right now!" I shout before I start pacing the floor.

I need to get rid of this anxious energy.

I need to skate.

I need to run.

I need to punch someone.

Or something.

Anything.

I need to fucking figure out what to do.

"Do what?" Ledger asks. "We're just talking about the game."

"Roche?" Harrison says my name softly, sensing my consternation. "Talk to us."

Treading back and forth in the corner of the room, I blurt, "She's going on a fucking date and I don't know what to fucking do about it!"

This is it, isn't it?

This is how I go crazy and end up in some kind of insane asylum.

Griffin catches my eye and asks, "Who is going on a date?"

"My girl."

His brows lift. "Your girl?"

"Okay THE girl. The girl. You know? The girl I've been... seeing."

"You mean the fuck-tutor? The sex lessons girl? That girl?"

"Yeah. Her name is...fuck, it doesn't even matter what her name is because she told me last night that some other guy asked her out and that's not sitting well with me." I push on my chest with the heel of my hand. "Because I think I like her and when she told me about this other guy I wanted to tell her to not to do it. I wanted to beg her to pick me instead."

Everyone nods, finally understanding.

"Are you guys in that kind of...you know, arrangement?" August asks me. "Did you agree not to see other people while she's, you know, helping you?"

I let out a long sigh. "No. Fuck! But I like her. I mean I really like her. And it's not just about the sex. I mean, the sex is..." I shake my head. "Well, what we've done so far, it's...it's out of this world and I want so much more of it with her. But also, she's kind and she's compassionate and she's trustworthy and she's funny and I like who I am when I'm around her."

"Sounds like you have a bit of a crush."

"Yeah, maybe I do, but none of that matters because some other guy asked her out and if she goes out with him, I could lose her. Not to mention the mere idea of some other guy with his hands on her makes me want to throw up or kill someone. Or both!"

"Alright, so if you like her, tell her," Barrett says with a shrug.

Finally, I plop down on the couch. "But what if she has me in the friend zone."

"A friend with benefits zone, you mean," Griffin corrects me.

"Yeah. Whatever. What if she doesn't see me as someone who could be good for her? What if she thinks that simply because I'm not as experienced in the bedroom as she is? What if this guy is a pro at using his dick for all the fucking things? What if he's God's gift to women and has the world's largest cock?"

Griffin and Ledger chuckle and wag their brows at each other. "I definitely want to meet that guy," Griffin says.

Ledger nods. "Right? I wonder how I measure up."

I raise my voice. "Would you guys please fucking help me? I'm going crazy here!"

Griffin nods. "I see that."

"Look, there's only so much you can do at this point," he says, sitting next to me. "But you do have options."

"What are they?"

"You can tell her how you feel and hope she sees you the same way, or you cannot tell her how you feel and watch her walk away."

"Ollenberg's right, Bodhi," August says. "That's basically the advice they gave me when I was in distress about Ella going on a date when I was crazy about her."

"So, what did you do?"

"Well, she went on the date and it was the most agonizing couple of hours."

Ledger rolls his eyes. "Tell me about it. You were beside yourself."

"I was. And then she came home."

"And?" I ask, waiting for the conclusion to his story.

"And lucky for me, she came home from a lousy date and was extremely upset so I saved the day by walking right up to her and kissing her." He shrugs. "Then I ate her out, gave her an immaculate orgasm, and the rest is history."

"Alright." I nod. "So, you're saying I should walk into her apartment tonight, eat her out until she screams, and stake my claim?"

The guys laugh. "Yeah. Something like that. Sometimes you've got to take what you want. Be bold. Put yourself out there. You're not afraid of players on the ice when you want the goal, are you?"

"Pft. Fuck no."

"Well, think of this girl as the goal. Now how are you going to score?"

"To Ella!" August says, raising his hot dog in the air. The team decided to grab lunch together at Harold's today. We let Ella pick the restaurant though we didn't tell her why.

She nearly spits out her food, covering her mouth with her hand. "What?"

"Well, we never really celebrated your one-year anniversary with the team. I know we're late but better late than never, right?" He leans over and kisses her. "Plus, you're my super-hot wife and I can celebrate you anytime I want."

"Amen to that," Griffin says, grinning as he raises his hotdog. "Plus, any opportunity to shove a wiener this large into my mouth is a good day. Cheers to the team's cutest mascot. You have done an exceptional job if I do say so myself."

"Wow. Thanks guys. I really appreciate the love," she says,

beaming at all of us. "There's not a better team in the league as far as I'm concerned and I've loved every minute of working with you guys."

"Every minute?" August's brow piques.

"Okay, maybe not every single minute. I could do without those minutes in the locker rooms because woof! I'm pretty convinced that nothing smells worse than a hot sweaty hockey team after a long practice or hard played game."

Harrison laughs. "You should smell our duffle bags."

"Oooh trust me. I don't even touch August's bag. He's in charge of cleaning it out and washing whatever is inside that smells like it laid down and died."

August gets a bunch of fist bumps from the guys as Ella shakes her head, laughing.

"Dude, what hotdog did you get?" Griffin asks me as I take a huge bite.

"Uh, pretty sure it's called a...what...the...fuck?"

"A what the fuck?" Griffin chuckles. "Do they really have a what the fuck hotdog on the menu?"

I don't answer him.

I don't answer him because my eyes are trained on the two people who just walked through the front door.

"Dude, Bodhi. You good?"

When I still don't say anything the guys turn their heads to see what I'm staring at, and Ledger waves his hand.

"Hey Coach! Fancy seeing you here. You guys want to join us?"

Join us?

Are you fucking kidding me?

Coach Hicks walks toward our table, his arm around the woman he's with.

The beautiful woman I've come to know quite well over the last month or so.

And suddenly I want to throw up.

Is she seeing him?

Is that the guy who asked her out?

Oh shit. Are they on a date right fucking now?

Oh my God! Did I...

With Coach's girlfriend?

Fucking Christ!

"Oh hey, Corrigan," Griffin says, smiling and waving at the girl I've only ever known as Corri.

Her name is Corrigan?

How does Griffin know her?

Her eyes find mine and then dart away just as fast when the rest of the team greets her like they've known her forever too.

"Hey guys," she says with a kind smile. You know, the kind of smile that tells me she knows everyone at this table and they know her and the joke is on me.

What in the actual fuck?

"Ella, Bodhi," Coach says, causing me to literally choke on my bite of hot dog. I start coughing loudly, until the bite dislodges and I can properly swallow. "You alright, son? You look like you've seen a ghost?"

"Yeah." I nod and then clear my throat before grabbing my water. "Yeah, Coach. I'm good."

"Well, as you two are the only ones at this table who don't know my daughter, allow me to introduce you." He wraps an arm around Corrigan again. "This is my daughter, Corrigan. Corrigan, this is Ella Blackstone, our new mascot, and Bodhi Roche. Bodhi is the newest player to our team this year."

HIS DAUGHTER?

CORRI IS HIS FUCKING DAUGHTER?

Fuck, I was so wrong.

I didn't tongue fuck Coach's girlfriend.

I tongue fucked his daughter!

Corri shakes hands with Ella and then holds her hand out to me and kindly says, "It's a pleasure to meet you Bodhi. I hear you're quite the player."

I stare at her silently.

I'M THE PLAYER?

ME?

Fucking hell, Princess, I'm pretty damn sure you're the one who played me.

Griffin clears his throat and nudges me with his elbow. "Dude, shake her hand. Be nice."

Acting on his words because I'm clearly not in my own body right now, I reach out my hand and wrap it around Corrigan's. Her soft warm skin the way I remember it from this morning.

This morning.

Because I was just with her this morning!

"Pleasure to meet you, Corrigan."

Fucking fuck.

I'm dead.

Like, dead, dead.

Coach is going to kill me.

My career is fucking over.

"Would you guys like to join us?" Ella asks them. "I hear you just got back from a few years in London? Welcome back to the States by the way."

"Thank you. Yes. I guess I missed this big guy too much to stay away too long," she says, hugging her dad.

Her dad, who is also our coach.

The coach who is going to chop off my dick and bury it under the ice when he finds out what I've done with his daughter.

How is this even happening right now?

How was I so stupid?

How did I fall for...

Wait...

Wait a minute.

Wait, wait, wait.

What if she's just as shocked as I am?

What if she really didn't know I played hockey?

If I'm new to the team and she's been overseas, maybe she really doesn't know me.

And so maybe she's equally shocked and upset that I lied to her about who I was.

Fuck.

I told her my name was Alan.

Now she knows I lied about that.

Now maybe she thinks I'm a lying douchebag.

Motherfucker, what am I supposed to do now?

"Thank you for the invitation," Coach says. "But we're actually getting our lunch to go so we can eat at the park. You guys enjoy though. We'll see you on the ice in the morning."

The guys all wave goodbye and Corrigan looks at me one more time, her face expressionless except for a friendly smile to everyone before she turns back toward the front counter with her father.

"What the fuck is wrong with you?" August asks, leaning across the table.

"Huh?"

"First of all, your face is white as fuck," Harrison says. "Are you feeling alright?"

"Huh?"

"And secondly, you were kind of a dick to Coach's daughter. She was just trying to shake your hand, man."

My body has gone completely still on the outside but on the inside, it feels like every organ in my body is summersaulting, banging into each other and then exploding on impact. I'm staring straight ahead but I'm not seeing anything. My hands feel clammy and beads of sweat are forming across my forehead.

"I-I-I...Uh..."

"Auggie he really doesn't look good," Ella whispers. "Maybe we should do something."

"No." I shake my head vigorously, wiping the sweat from my forehead with my napkin and then pushing away my food so I can hold my head in my hands.

"Roche, what's going on, man?" Griffin asks beside me. "Are you sick? Need to get out of here?"

Hell, yeah I want to get out of here.

Out of this restaurant.

Out of this town.

Out of this career.

Out of this life.

Fuck!

"I...I..." I shake my head and mumble, "I didn't know. I didn't know. I didn't know. I didn't know."

"What didn't you know?"

"Out with it Pickle Pants," Barrett demands. "We can't help you if you don't tell us what the problem is."

"She's the girl," I say softly.

Barrett's brows pinch together. "What?"

"Corri-Cor-Corrrrrigan."

Fuck why am I stuttering?

"What about her?"

I lift my eyes to meet Barrett's. "She's the...she's the girl."

God it's so fucking hot in here.

"What girl?" Ella asks.

Tugging at my shirt to try and cool myself down, I try to answer her. "The...you know, the..."

Shit.

I'm in so much trouble.

It only takes one more helplessly fucked glance at the guys for them to figure it out. Griffin's jaw drops and he stares at me in complete disbelief.

"Nooooo fucking way."

"Yes fucking way." I nod.

"SHE'S the girl?" Harrison whispers. "Corrigan Hicks?"

I sigh loudly because how the fuck am I going to get myself out of this mess? "She told me her name was C-Cor-Corri."

Barrett nods. "Yeah that's what everybody calls her. We've called her Corri for years."

"Duuuude." Griffin's eyes are bulging and his mouth has not yet closed shut. "You seriously...like, honestly, you didn't know?"

I shake my head as everyone else murmurs around the table.

"Know what?" Ella asks, completely clueless.

"I swear to God, I didn't even know he had a fucking daughter, man. What am I supposed to do now?"

"What's going on?" Ella asks again. August leans over and gives her a quick rundown and she gasps. "And his private tutor was Corrigan Hicks, Coach's daughter?"

Complete silence falls over the table as everyone takes in the news of how fucked up my life now is. God, what I wouldn't give for one of them, any one of them, to tell me that this isn't as bad as I fear it is. Not able to look any of them in the eye, I bring my elbow to the table and rest my forehead on the tips of my fingers.

"Why aren't they saying anything, Griffin?"

"Uh..." He chuckles. "I think they're all equally as flabbergasted as I am, bro."

August leans forward and quietly mumbles, "Bro, you

fingered her? That's what you told us when you first got together with her. You fingered Coach's daughter?"

Feeling queasy, I nod. "I did a whole lot more than that with her since then." Palming my forehead I murmur, "I'm so fucking fucked."

He pats me on the back. "Chin up, Roche. Don't be so hard on yourself...oops...I said hard on....which is something you got with the help of Corrigan. The coach's daughter."

I glance at Griffin, not at all amused. "Really?"

"I make jokes when I'm nervous, what can I say?" He shrugs. "It was nice knowing you?"

I slide down in my seat, begging the guys with my eyes to fucking help me out of this.

"What the hell am I going to do?"

Harrison sits up and leans across the table. "Okay, let's talk this out. So, it ended up being Corrigan who texted you all those nights ago?"

"Yeah." I nod. "She made spaghetti for her dad and now that I know who her dad is that all checks because the guy fucking loves pasta. I've heard him talking about Mario's on more than one occasion in the front office."

Ledger leans forward. "Alright so you two got to chatting via text. Did you not tell her your name?"

I shake my head. "No, I told her my name was Alan because why the hell would I tell a total stranger she's talking to Bodhi Roche, pro hockey player for the Anaheim Stars?" I shrug. "Alan is my middle name, so I went with it in hopes she wouldn't recognize me, and to my knowledge, she didn't."

August shakes his head too. "Yeah, I don't buy that for a second. Sorry. Not that I don't believe you. I do. It's Corrigan I don't believe."

"Yeah, I think I might agree with you," Oliver adds. "That girl lives and breathes hockey with her dad. She knows our stats better than we do. There's no way she didn't know who you were."

What. The. Fuck.

"Are you shitting me right now?"

"Afraid not, man. I'm sorry, but I just don't see a scenario where she doesn't recognize you. I mean, at least not when you met in person the first time. Did she give you any indication that she recognized you at all?"

Shaking my head, I answer roughly, "No. She's clearly a good fucking actress because she never gave me the impression that she knew who I was at all."

"Do you really think Corrigan is that manipulative though?" Ella slips a potato chip into her mouth. "You guys have always said she's such a cool girl. Funny. Razzes her dad. Great personality."

"She is a great person, yeah." Griffin nods. "Which is why this is all very weird."

"What if..." I sit up in my seat, trying like hell to put the pieces together. "What if she thinks I knew who she was this whole time but wasn't telling her that I knew? What if she thinks I used her for sex? What if she thinks I propositioned her? Coach will have my ass!"

"Did you?" Oliver asks. "Did you proposition her?"

"Uh..." My rolodex of memories spins in my brain. "Honestly I can't remember. I know I said something about sex lessons but it wasn't in the form of asking for them! It was an accidental text to begin with. I mean, I certainly didn't come out and ask Corrigan to fuck me. I was trying to come up with something to say to her and I kept deleting everything except that one time I accidentally hit send instead of delete, and then she answered me. Then the next thing I knew, she was writing me and saying we start tomorrow."

"So, you two have—"

"No." I bob my head. "I mean we've done other stuff. We were kind of starting off with other stuff first, you know?"

"Right. You did tell us about that."

"And you guys aren't a thing exactly because she said some other guy asked her out?" Barrett asks, taking the last bites of his hotdog.

I close my eyes and release a deep sigh. "Yeah."

"Tell us more," Harrison urges. "So, we know the whole picture and can help you."

"I spent last night at her place because she had a super shit day at work. A shit week actually. I didn't want her to be alone so I took her dinner and we watched television all night until she fell asleep on my lap."

"So, no sex last night?"

"What? No! That would've made me look like a fucking douche. She fell asleep on me so I stayed there."

"All night?" August asks.

"Yeah."

"While she slept on you?" Elle adds.

"Yeah."

She swoons. "That is so sweet of you, Bodhi."

"Is it?" I nearly shout. "Because I'm not sure Coach is going to think that way when he finds out."

"Shhhhh!" August raises his finger to his lips. "Bro, keep your voice down. People know us here."

"Sorry."

"Why does he have to find out?" Ella shrugs like this topic of conversation is the same kind we have when we're trying to decide what shoes we're going to wear tomorrow night at dinner.

"I..." My mouth hangs open. "I just assume he'll find out. Surely Corrigan is going to tell him."

"Mmmmm..." Oliver's eyes narrow as he shakes his head.

"Maybe not. It doesn't make her look any better to tell her dad that she's been messing around with one of his players."

Ella places her hand over mine on the table. "The question is, Bodhi, do you have feelings for her?"

Yeah.

I think I do.

That's what I want to say, but I feel like if I say them out loud, I'm damning myself to an eternity of hell from my coach. And that's if I'm lucky enough to stay on the team. And even if I do say them, who's to say Corrigan feels the same way? For all I know she's just in this to fuck a hockey player.

My chest tightens and my stomach churns at the thought.

"Yeah, he does," Ledger finally answers for me. "You can see it on his face. He looks the same way August used to look when we would talk about you." He nods at Ella. "Plus, he told us as much earlier today."

"What if I do? What would I do about it? I feel like I might be completely fucked at this point. And I don't even know if she feels the same way. Between this and that other guy I feel like this is a double whammy."

"You're going to have to talk to her," Barrett finally says. "The only way you'll be able to figure all this out is to know exactly how she feels too. And then you can take it from there."

"Bear's right." Ledger picks up his glass and takes a drink. "This can go a few ways. One, you tell her you have feelings for her and she tells you she feels the same and you navigate this relationship together. Two, you tell her how you feel and she doesn't feel the same at which point you apologize sincerely for any confusion between the two of you and walk away. Or three, she tells her dad and blames this all on you and you're utterly and completely fucked."

I bow my head, accepting my fate even though it scares the absolute shit out of me.

"You're right. I need to talk to her. If for no other reason than to clear the air and let her know I really had no idea who she was."

"You've got this, Roche." Oliver's reassuring glance gives me a tiny sliver of hope. "August and I will tell you, we've had to get through a few hard days to end up with the partners we now have."

"He's right," August says as he lays his arm around Ella's shoulders and kisses the side of her head. "Ella and I were best friends before we got together. We had to have those hard conversations."

Ella's face contorts and she turns toward August. "Uh, I don't recall it happening like that. If I remember correctly you fucking kissed me while I was crying over a horrible date and then told me I belonged to you."

"Yeah but it was romantic as hell, you have to admit." Ella blushes as she rolls her eyes, which makes August laugh. "Yeah, that's what I thought."

I push my chair from the table and stand up. "I've got to go."

"But what about your wiener?" Griffin shouts, holding up my basket of lunch.

"There's no way I can eat a wiener right now, Griff. You eat it. Eat my wiener. I'll catch you later."

"Hey wait!" Ella turns in her chair as I stop to see what she wants.

"What?"

"A word of advice?"

"Okay, yeah?"

"It's supposed to rain later and if it does, you make sure you kiss her in the rain."

I narrow my eyes. "What?"

"Do it! Trust me, Bodhi. It's super romantic and she'll love it."

"Uh...okay...is that all?"

"Yep. That's it." August nods and offers me a fist bump. "Go get her big guy."

I bump my fist with his and walk away but hear Ella mumble to him, "Oh my God, Auggie. Don't call him big guy. He's not a child. He's a man."

CHAPTER EIGHTEEN
CORRIGAN

*S*hit, shit, shit, shit, shit!
He's going to kill me!
How could I have been so stupid?
There's no way he'll believe that I didn't know who he was now.
The guys will tell him I know them all very well.
Fuck!

"Everything alright?" My dad eyes me from the across the picnic table as I pick at my food.

"Hmm? Oh yeah. It's fine. Just..." I shrug, looking for any reason to give him for not being extremely talkative. "A lot going on in my head. Yesterday was a really shitty day and I guess my mind isn't letting it go just yet."

Total lie.

Well...maybe not a total lie.

But it's believable, nonetheless.

"I can't imagine doing the job you do every single day, sweetheart. Especially with kids. It's always harder with kids."

"It is." I nod.

I really don't want to think too hard about yesterday when I have way bigger problems right now. Ever since Dad and I walked into Harold's for lunch and ran into the guys on the team—including Bodhi—my gut has been twisting and turning. I'll never be able to unsee the expression on Bodhi's face when he saw me with Dad. It was like I stabbed a dull knife into his chest and twisted it several times over. I wanted to apologize to him right then but there was no way I could do that with my dad standing next to me. And there was no way I was going to out Bodhi and the reason we've been together in the first place to his teammates. He's new to the team this year. I get how that probably feels being the odd guy out. He's trying to prove himself. The last thing I want to do is embarrass him in front of everyone. I considered sending him a quick text but this doesn't feel like the kind of thing I should just push away with an insincere text message.

I lied to him for weeks.

Alright, maybe I didn't lie but I omitted truths.

So did he, obviously, but I understand why.

I may not have known who I was talking to when we were just texting back and forth but the night we finally met, I knew exactly who he was. Any hockey fan would have recognized him and now that I think about it, he was damn lucky that nobody recognized him that night on the terrace.

I, on the other hand, knew everything about him.

I know so far this season Bodhi has scored twelve goals with five assists. I know he's only had a total of four penalty minutes. I know his time on the ice averages nineteen minutes total per game.

But he didn't know I knew that.

He didn't know I knew him at all.

My heart tumbles in my chest as a tear slips down my cheek and Dad is quick to notice before I can swipe it away.

"That bad, huh?"

"Yeah, Dad." I push at my food. "I'm really sorry, I guess I just don't feel much like eating today."

"Corri," he says softly before reaching his hand over to hold mine. "You don't ever have to apologize for your job and how it makes you feel. You're human. You spend your days helping and comforting tiny humans. Tiny humans with gigantic hearts. I would think it odd if none of what you do affected you. You are completely within your right to have feelings."

Dad and I have always been close. Especially when Mom was diagnosed with cancer and going downhill in the end. Dad and I relied heavily on each other. He knew I sort of understood some of the medical jargon and how to care for Mom so I was his safety net when it came to explaining it all, but he was my safety net as I watched my mom deteriorate right in front of my eyes. She wasn't just another patient to me. There was no way I could ever look at her that way and Dad knew it. I've always been able to talk to Dad. I could tell him just about anything. Hell, he was the one I called when I found out Leo had cheated on me. He was the one I cried to. He was the one who took the all-night flight to help me pack my things and then he was the one who flew home with me.

He would move Heaven and Earth to make me happy even if it means moving it all around for me. He was always good at putting out my personal fires before they spread into something wild but this time it's different.

This time I started a fire inside my dad's hockey team.

And I fear confessing to him about it would only fan the flames.

There was always one rule growing up around his hockey teams and it was to never get involved with one of them. When I was a young teenager I laughed at his stupid rule because duh, I was thirteen. At that time, he just didn't want me to be alone with them when he wasn't around. Was he overprotective?

Maybe. But he also knew the language and conversation that grown men were known to have in locker rooms and he wanted to shield me from that as best he could. It was harder once Mom died.

Once I hit eighteen he was adamant about not allowing his guys to charm me into anything. I guess in a way he was still trying to protect me, but I think really, he just didn't want anything to be awkward had I gotten involved with one of his players and things didn't work out.

I followed that rule easily over the years.

But now...

I had every opportunity to step back and say no, and I didn't.

I willingly walked into a physical relationship with Bodhi Roche.

I allowed myself to be wooed by his charm and his vulnerability.

I haven't been able to get him out of my mind.

I crave him when he's not around me and that scares me because I think I really like him. And not for his hockey playing or because he's a player on my dad's team, but for the raw, honest, compassionate man that I've come to know outside of the sport.

This whole thing, whatever it is between us, got very messy in a matter of seconds and now I have to somehow make this right.

"It's okay if you want to cut our lunch short," Dad says. "We're all allowed to have bad days every now and then. As long as you don't let it get you down too long. Better days are ahead." He squeezes my hand. "I promise."

I'm not so sure.

"Thanks Dad. Yeah I think I want to just head home and...I don't know."

Find Bodhi.

"Maybe I'll just unpack another box or decorate a little bit. Something to bring a little of this sunshine into my mind." I glance up at the cloudy sky. "Though it doesn't look as though we'll see too much sun today."

"It's California so you never know," he says with a soft chuckle. "May as well be productive while you can, right?" He winks and I try to give him a convincing smile even though my mind is racing, my body is sweating, and my heart is pounding against my chest.

I have to find Bodhi and talk this out with him somehow.

I refuse to go home until I find him.

But where do I even begin to look?

I wrap my lunch up in the to-go bag it came in and toss it in the trash next to our picnic table. "Hey thanks for introducing me to Bodhi and Ella. They seem cool."

Dad smiles. "Yeah. Ella's a sweetheart of a girl. She's a hard worker too. In fact, you should introduce her to Layken. I'm sure Layken could get her to show up at the hospital in costume for those kids."

"That's a great idea Dad. Did you say they're living in the same complex as some of the other team members?"

He nods. "Yeah. August, Ella, and Griffin are in the same building. And thank goodness a place opened up and I was able to get Bodhi in there too."

Yes!

I know where that is.

He has to be there.

And if he's not, I can wait him out.

I've got all day.

"Oh, that's good. I'm sure he appreciates that."

"He's a good kid. A little rough starting out. His head was a little bigger than the guys liked but they set him straight pretty fucking fast."

"I suppose so with the pickle pants stunt and all."

Dad chuckles softly, the twinkle in his eye telling me he cares for his team even when he has to be hard on them.

"Yeah. Fuck, that was a good one. They're still calling him that too." He grins.

"Well, I'm certain he'll be a great asset to the team. You don't pick just anyone when it comes to making offers to new players." I reach down to give my dad a hug where he's seated. "Thanks for the lunch Dad. And for giving me an excuse to get a little fresh air today. I needed it, but I'm exhausted."

"You're welcome. And if you need me..."

He doesn't even have to finish his statement. "I know Dad. I'll call you. I promise." I place a quick kiss on his cheek and then move to my car and slip inside before taking a huge steadying breath.

I need to find Bodhi.

Right. Fucking. Now.

I'VE BEEN SITTING OUTSIDE of Bodhi's building for almost an hour. The doorman said he's not home. For all I know he's lying to me thinking I'm some kind of crazed fan wanting to see where the famous Bodhi Roche lives. I even showed him my ID to prove I'm Coach Hick's daughter, but the man simply shook his head and apologized, explaining again that Bodhi wasn't home.

So here I am on a bench outside his building because security is tight here for their own benefit. In the time I've been sitting here, I've watched clouds roll in off the coast, and then I watched as the skies opened up and it began to rain.

It hasn't rained in weeks and now...it's pouring.

I guess I deserve this. I'm drenched and sitting here all alone on this bench because I can't make myself get up and leave. I need to talk to Bodhi. I need to make this right. Whatever I can do.

What if he's sitting somewhere all alone, sad and hurt because I lied to him?

What if he's mad at me, as he should be, and is purposely trying not to be found?

What if he felt so blindsided by me that he found someone else?

What if he hates me?

What if he tells my dad I used him?

Larger droplets of rain hit the top of my head as my phone dings in my pocket. There's a spark of adrenaline in my chest at the thought of getting a message from Bodhi but when I see Layken's name, my body deflates.

LAYKEN
Hey. You alright?

ME
No. Will explain later.

LAYKEN
Can I assume this is Bodhi Roche related?

ME
Yes. Why?

LAYKEN
Because he's standing outside our building drenched and looking for you. Are you not upstairs?

I shoot up from the bench and stare at Layken's message before rapidly texting her back.

> ME
>
> WHAT? No! I'm not upstairs! I'm sitting in front of HIS building...also drenched and waiting for him.

> LAYKEN
>
> LOL. Of course you are. If you guys aren't made for each other...

I start to head back to my car when my phone dings in my hand again.

> LAYKEN
>
> Bodhi says STAY THERE! He's coming to you.

I stop dead in my tracks. "Oh."

> ME
>
> Okay.

> LAYKEN
>
> I introduced myself. Hope that's okay. Also, I grilled him on what happened since he looked like a sad puppy dog and you are obviously feeling some sort of way as well. For what it's worth I think he has feelings for you. Get it girl!

> ME
>
> I hurt him, Layken. He knows I lied to him.

> LAYKEN
>
> Babe, that was inevitable and you know it. Just be honest with him. Tell him everything. I think he'll be understanding.

> ME
>
> That's all I can hope for.

LAYKEN

He drove out of here like a bat out of hell. I can't imagine he'll be long.

ME

Also, Sean asked me out.

LAYKEN

👀 Sean from Ortho?

ME

Yeah.

LAYKEN

Are you considering it?

ME

I don't know. Should I? At this point it would make things so much easier.

LAYKEN

Would it though?

ME

No.

LAYKEN

Let me help you make an easy decision. He fucked Tish for like three weeks, gave her the syph, and then blamed it all on her. Trust me. You want to stay far away from that one.

ME

How on earth did you hear that?

LAYKEN

Giiiirl, I have ears and I'm all over that building. #yourewelcome

ME

Thanks Lake.

LAYKEN

> Smooches babe. Good luck with Bodhi, whatever you decide.

Having nowhere to go to keep dry, and since I'm already soaked to the bone, I sit back down on the wet bench and pull my knees up to my chest while I wait for Bodhi to arrive. Rain drips down my forehead as I try to focus on the sounds of the water hitting the cement below me as well as the cars driving through puddles on the road.

I must be lost in thought because I don't hear a car pull up and I don't hear doors opening or closing but somehow Bodhi is here out of nowhere and is crouching down in front of me, his hands wrapping around the lower part of my legs.

"Corrigan..."

My breath catches when he says my name.

My actual name.

I lift my head and meet his gaze. "Bodhi."

Tears immediately stream down my face though who can tell what's rain and what's tears at this point. The moment I take a deep breath we both begin saying all the things on our minds. "I'm so sorry, Bodhi. I didn't mean t—"

"I'm sorry, Corrigan. I should've told you from the begi—"

"What? No." I shake my head, my eyes growing in size. "You don't owe me any—"

"I swear to God I wasn't using you," he pleads. "I swear I didn't know you were—"

"Using ME? No Bodhi, I was afraid you thought I was using *you* and I—"

"If I had just been honest from the—"

"But I should've told you I recogn—"

"You were just so damn nice to me and then—"

"You trusted me with your secret and I never wanted to—"

"You were all I thought about but—"

"I wanted to tell y—"

"I think I'm falling for you."

"But then I...wait..." I cock my head to the side. "What?"

He shakes his head with a confused chuckle. "Why are we still out here in this downpour?"

"Because..." I tilt my head slowly in the opposite direction, studying his face. "Because you said—"

"I'm falling for you?"

I nod silently.

He smiles. "Yeah. But I could be saying all this in the warmth of my apartment. I'm sorry I'm such a dick. I should've swooped you up and carried you inside and—"

"You're falling for me?"

He stands and reaches for my hand, helping me up off the bench. "Not really falling, I suppose," he mumbles. Our faces mere centimeters apart, he smooths back my wet hair hanging against my cheeks. "More like...fallen."

Fallen.

He's fallen for me.

He said that, right?

It wasn't the rain or some random wind?

He said he's fallen for me.

"But you barely know me Bodhi."

"Bullshit," he answers. "I know more about you than you think I do."

I shake my head in disbelief. "You're just...I don't know... infatuated. Because I'm the first girl you've—"

"The first girl I've ever wanted to get to know even more than I know her right now," he answers me with a piercing stare. "The first girl I've ever thought about for more than two minutes at a time. The first girl to make me feel things physically and emotionally that I've never felt before. Corrigan, if infatuation is the word you want to use, then okay, let's use it." He lifts his arms as he shrugs. "I'm infatuated with you."

"But—"

"You're a gorgeous woman Corri," he scoffs. "Way out of my league if I'm being honest, but yet you gave me a damn minute when I least expected it. You didn't pass me off like some sort of creep and you didn't laugh in my face when I was most vulnerable."

"But..." I shake my head. "We can't be together, Bodhi."

"The fuck we can't. Is this about that guy? The one who asked you out? Because fuck him! No, wait, wait...I don't mean fuck him-fuck him but *fuck* him." I pat my own chest and plead, "I'm right here Corrigan. Pick me. Date me."

"But my dad..."

He grabs my hands. "Your dad's not here, babe, and I don't care what he thinks. This isn't between you, me, and your dad. This is between you and me. That's it. Nobody else."

But how can this work realistically without my dad knowing about it?

When I don't respond, he continues. "The night we first met...you knew who I was. True or false?"

I nod slowly, a tear escaping down my cheek even though there's no way he can tell with this much rain falling on us. "True."

"So, you knew who I was and you didn't turn me away or make fun of me. You didn't scream at me and threaten some sort of lawsuit. You didn't fangirl and treat me like some sort of sex symbol. You didn't accuse me of lying. You continued to be who you are. The girl I started to fall for via text message." He smiles. "You were sweet and kind and funny and compassionate and most of all confident. You were everything I didn't know I needed but so fucking greatly appreciated and please don't go out with that guy, Corrigan. Let me take you out. Be with me. I can make you happy. Please let me try."

I don't even know what to say.

For the first time ever, I'm completely speechless.

My mouth hangs open and his gaze falls to my lips.

"I'm going to kiss you now, Corrigan. Right here in the pouring rain. Because Ella and the guys told me earlier that it was supposed to rain and if it did I needed to kiss you in a downpour because apparently it's fucking romantic and melts every girl's heart. So, this is your warning, alright? If you don't want me to kiss you, you need to tell me right now."

He watches me for only a moment and I'm so flabbergasted by his words I can't think of anything to say.

"One..."

"Two..."

He doesn't wait for three. Instead, he pushes his hands through my wet hair, palms my cheeks, and crashes his soft warm lips to mine. His kiss is firm but with a gentle pressure as his mouth guides mine open. His tongue dips fervently inside, tasting me with a moan-inducing lick. My hands move to his shirt, gripping the material and pulling him tightly against me as if he is my lifeline in an unsettled sea of emotions. Slowly and gently, he pulls away, his forehead connecting to mine as we stand in the rain together.

"Come upstairs with me," he murmurs.

"I'm soaked."

"Right." He smiles but his eyes are closed and then before I know it, he slips a hand underneath my legs and lifts me into his arms and carries me inside the building. When we reach the front security desk, he tosses his key to the man sitting there and says, "Tucker, will you park her for me?"

"Sure thing, Bodhi."

"Thanks."

Bodhi keeps walking toward the elevators but I watch Tucker smile at us as we pass by and I wave helplessly. He waves back with a friendly smile and then heads out to Bodhi's car. Once in the elevator Bodhi kisses my forehead and then murmurs again, "Come upstairs with me."

I let out a soft laugh. "I think I'm already on my way."

CHAPTER NINETEEN
CORRIGAN

He sets me down on my feet inside his palatial looking apartment, my eyes immediately trying to take in my surroundings. The entryway leads into an open living room with warm ivory walls and oversized windows adorned with white curtains. There's an ivory sectional in the middle of the room situated on a shaggy rug with flecks of white, gray, and blue. The large painting of the ocean on the wall opposite the television gives off a relaxing beach house vibe.

"Did you design this yourself?" I ask Bodhi as he unbuttons the front of my dress. When it falls open, he gently peels it off my wet shoulders and lets it drop with a thud to the ground.

"No." He merely shakes his head, his gaze never leaving mine even as my nervous eyes dart around the room. "It was like this when I got here."

"It's lovely."

"You're lovely."

"Bodhi," I whisper with a tremor to my voice.

"Step out of your shoes," he tells me as he does the same. Something about the raspy timber of his voice has me wanting to comply with anything he asks of me. He tears off his t-shirt and stands in front of me nearly naked but for a pair of soaking wet athletic shorts.

I slip off my sandals and push them to the side.

He reaches behind me and disconnects my bra with ease this time rather than getting frustrated and ripping it to shreds like the last time.

I lift a brow. "Have you been practicing Bodhi?"

He smiles but doesn't answer me at first. He pulls my bra straps away from my skin and then peels the wet garment off me, dropping it on my pile of clothes.

"Would you laugh at me if I said yes?"

"I might," I say with a mischievous grin. "But I might also be extremely impressed."

"I don't like to not be good at what I do." He crouches down, slipping two fingers between my body and the fabric of my panties and then shimmies them down my legs, kissing my thighs as he lifts each of my feet to remove them.

"Trust me, Bodhi," I breathe, "you're anything but bad at what you do."

He stands up straight, his gaze falling over my naked body, and shakes his head. "Jesus fucking Christ. Corrigan Hicks, you are..."

I smile bashfully, not because I'm not confident in my own skin, but because ten minutes ago there was so much raw vulnerability between us and...

"You don't hate me?"

His eyes meet mine, his brows furrowed. "Hate you? Why on earth would I hate you?"

"I lied to you, Bodhi." I try to fold my arms over my exposed chest, but he doesn't let me. He takes my hands and pulls them away from my body so I can't hide.

"You didn't lie to me," he answers, trailing the backs of his fingers down my cheek. "It's not like I stood in front of you and asked if you knew who I was."

"I know, but—"

"Shhh." He places a finger against my lips. "No buts." I keep his gaze as he pushes his gym shorts and boxer briefs down his legs and steps out of them.

Holy hell his naked body is...everything.

"No buts, Corri. For right now, it's just you and me."

"You want another lesson?" I ask meekly.

He shakes his head, letting his hand fall from my neck to my collarbone, to my chest and across to palm my breast. His thumb glides across my nipple, his touch causing it to harden and peak. "I want to figure this all out on my own. I want to explore you. Explore us. I want to find out for myself what makes you writhe beneath me. What makes you feverish. What heats you." He stares into my eyes like he's looking down deep into my soul. "What makes Corrigan Hicks so fucking wet I could literally drink her."

Well, those words for one.

"And then when I'm good and ready," he says as his lips graze the skin just behind my ear. "And when you're good and ready, I want to plunge inside you, feeling your body take my cock for the first time." His hands smooth down my hips to my ass and then he lifts one of my legs, hitching it around his waist so that I feel his stiff cock at my entrance.

I gasp at the surprising contact, my mouth falling open and my head falling back. He takes the opportunity to drag his tongue up the side of my neck sending chills over my body and goosebumps over my skin.

"I want to feel your warm wet pussy grip me as I thrust inside you. And I want to be staring into your mesmerizingly beautiful eyes when I make you come."

"Bodhi..." I sigh.

"Say yes, Corrigan," he pleads as he places his other hand under my ass and lifts me. I wrap my legs around his waist, as I always do, his hardened cock teasing me. He begins to take slow steps through the living room. Where he's heading I have no idea, having never been here before, but I can only assume we're going to his bedroom. "You're in my apartment, stunningly naked and in my arms and I'm dying to be with you so please say yes so I don't have to turn around and return you to your wet clothes."

I run my hand through his wet locks, loving the gentle confidence he seems to have right now. "I want those things too, Bodhi."

CHAPTER TWENTY

BODHI

Fuck, am I dreaming?
I'm dreaming.

I have to be.

How else would I be lucky enough to have a naked Corrigan Hicks in *my* home, in *my* arms, carrying her down the hallway to *my* bedroom as her hands play with my hair? How are her legs firmly wrapped around my waist while my cock springs up and down with every goddamn step I take? How is it her lips separate and so willingly connect with mine?

Heat courses through my veins as I enter my bedroom and lay her down on my bed. Her eyes meet mine, the blue in them sparkling back at me like sapphires as I hover over her, propping myself up with one arm. She reaches her hand up to my face, resting her palm against my cheek, and I lean into it, reveling in the feel of her touch. The touch that brings me peace and heats me at the very same time. Her other hand reaches up, palming my chest, and fuck if the feel of her fingers gliding over my skin doesn't make my dick even harder than it already was. She moves her hand from my chest, up to my shoulders and then into my hair, tugging on the dripping strands and bringing my face down to hers. And it's this moment, the wanton look in her eyes, that has me realizing she wants this just as much as I do.

"I want you, Corrigan."

"I want you too, Bodhi," she responds, her tongue dragging across her lips.

"I need you to understand something though." I shake my head and stare into her eyes, wishing she could see down deep into my soul. "This isn't just sex for me, Corri. This isn't like those other times. Although now that I think about it, I'm not sure those other times were what they were supposed to be either because I want you."

She smiles and softly chuckles. "I want you t—"

"No. I want...*you*, Corrigan," I try to explain. "I want this... this connection that you and I seem to have when we're together, but I want more and I want it with you."

Her eyes dart between mine and it's all I can do not to word-vomit all over her. "I love how our physical connection makes me feel. I love how you make me feel. Like I'm the most important person in the room at any given time. Like I'm important. Like I matter. Like I'm loved. So, this isn't just sex for me. If it was before, it's not anymore. Because I want *you*."

"Okay." She nods.

"Okay?"

"Mhmm."

Fucking Christ.

"You're okay being...mine?"

She smiles up at me, her doe-like eyes answering me before her voice does.

"I've been yours since the moment you replied to my text."

"Thank you, Jesus."

I bring my mouth to hers and part my lips, our tongues tangling, fingers gripping, voices moaning. I smooth my hand down the side of her body and back up, feathering my fingers along her skin, and then my palm connects with her breast.

Her eyes roll back as her mouth falls open. "Yesss."

I roll her hardened nipple between my thumb and middle finger and then lower my lips and suck it into my mouth. Her back arches and her body writhes beneath me as I flick my tongue over her while rolling the other between my fingers. Then I move to the other breast and suck that nipple into my mouth even harder.

"Oh God! Yes!"

Her response brings a smile to my face and a wave of pride through my chest.

"You're so goddamn beautiful Corrigan."

"I'm also goddamn wet, Bodhi," she says as I continue to play with her breasts.

"Is that so?" I ask, trailing my fingers between her legs, teasing her with a touch to her inner thighs. She squirms and opens her legs, allowing me full access.

"Yes. Please," she begs, but I'm not ready to give her what she wants just yet. I'm having too much fun exploring her whole body.

To placate her, I drag my finger through her arousal and—

"Fuuuucking hell, Corri."

I've never felt her so wet before.

"Oh God, yes! Again. Please!"

"What do you need?" I ask as I trail another finger through her warm arousal. "Tell me."

She bucks against my fingers, hoping to add to the pressure she so desperately seeks. "I need you to make me come, Bodhi."

She nearly cries when I pull my hand away from between her legs, but she watches anxiously as I suck my two fingers into my mouth, my eyes rolling back in my head as I savor the taste of her. "So fucking sweet."

I want to continue to tease her and make her crazy for me and then fuck her until neither of us can see straight but after one taste, I can't deny myself the delicacy that is Corrigan's sweet glistening pussy. Moving myself down her body so I can get a better position, I spread her legs with my hands and then flatten my tongue against her heated center, taking one long languid stroke.

"Oh...my...God," she gasps, lifting her pelvis off the mattress in search of more. "You're too fucking good at this. Please, Bodhi."

Her compliment revs my body and has me wanting to turn her over, spank her ass, and fuck her like they do in the pornos I've seen. But then a part of me wants to lie here all night long, between her legs, pleasuring her over and over again and proudly watching her fall apart at my touch. On my tongue. With my thrust. But then I'm also dying to be inside her, feeling her pussy take me, clench around me. Milk me.

"So many possibilities," I tell her. "Do you want to come like this, Corri? Should I devour you until you're screaming my name?

"Yes. Oh, God, yes."

Diving back in for more, I circle my tongue around her clit and slip two fingers inside her, curling them against her inner wall and adding just the right kind of pressure to make her crazy.

"Bodhi!" She pants. "Bodhi, please. God! Just like that. Don't stop!"

My dick is throbbing between my legs as I pick up the pace and add a bit more pressure. I have a feeling when it comes time to thrusting myself inside her I may not last as long as I want to but hell if I'm not going to make her feel like she's walking on fucking air. I lap at her clit a few more times and then suck it between my lips just as she comes undone.

"Yes! I'm...Oh God, I'm...Bodhi! I'm coming!"

The sound that comes from Corrigan's mouth is music to my ears. I lift my head to catch the look on her face as her body gives in and she comes apart. Reaching down between my legs, I fist my cock and tug at the base trying to relieve the throbbing ache as I watch her recover.

"I know you told me this before, but you're beautiful when you come."

She doesn't say anything but her sated smile is all I need to know she's with me.

Leaning over her, I pull open the drawer to my nightstand and pull out a condom, rip off the covering, and slide it over my cock as she watches.

"I'm on birth control, you know?"

I pause and meet her gaze. "I...I'm sorry, I didn't want to assume."

"It's okay," she says, shaking her head. "You're being responsible. I understand. I'm just letting you know. For now. For...later. I'm on birth control."

"Corrigan, I'm so fucking hard right now I fear I might blow all over you if I don't get myself inside you and I want to feel the inside of you more than I can explain."

"I'm all yours." She spreads her legs again for me as I hover over her, maneuvering between her knees. Gripping my cock, I line it up with her entrance.

"Ready?"

She nods. "Ready."

Slowly, I push the head of my cock inside her.

Motherfucker...

And then another inch.

Christ.

And another inch.

"God, it's so fucking good, Corri."

Breathe, Bodhi.

Breathe.

Fuck she feels incredible.

Breeeeeathe.

"Keep going. Fill me. Take me." Her words are my encouragement but so are her lips when I lean down and cover them with mine. She licks inside my mouth as I slide back a bit and then plunge inside her as deep as I can possibly go. Her mouth falls open in tandem with mine and we both moan.

"Fuuuck, you're so tight. You're squeezing the hell out of me."

"Oh, my God, Bodhi. I'm so full."

"I need to move, babe."

"Yes." She nods. "Please."

"You okay?"

"I'm perfect." She smiles and kisses me again. "You're perfect."

I lean back a bit on my knees and bring her legs up, her thighs pressed against her chest and thrust inside her again and again, watching our connection. It's a fucking turn-on watching my cock slide inside her.

"Fuck, you're stunning, Corrigan. You take me so perfectly."

Her bright blue eyes find mine and I refuse to look away as I pump into her over and over again. My legs start to tremble and I pick up my pace and chase my climax.

"Shit, Corrigan, I'm not going to last. I'm sorry."

I watch as she slides her hand between her legs and rubs her clit as I thrust into her.

"Don't apologize. Come with me, Bodhi."

My God, she's sexy as hell like this.

Finally letting go of my stare, her eyes roll back and her back arches causing her hips to pull down on my cock, squeezing it tight. A white-hot heat spreads across my body just before my balls tighten and my cock swells and then I'm coming inside her so furiously the room spins.

"Shit. Fuck! God!"

"Oooh fuck!" She brings her legs around my waist and locks me tightly against her as she moans loudly, her pussy pulsing around my cock as she comes a second time.

I try my best not to give her all my weight but she wraps her arms around me, cradling me to her chest, protecting me, soothing me, as we both catch our breath. She combs her fingers through my hair and whispers, "Suffice to say, you, Bodhi Alan Roche, are no longer a virgin."

She knows my middle name.

I should probably be very bothered by that but I'm not.

"That was..."

How do I even describe the moment we just had?

Amazing.

Exciting.

Delicious.

Better than I ever thought it would be.

Other worldly.

Earth shattering.

"Breathtakingly soul shattering."

"Soul shattering," she says, repeating my words. I lift my head a bit to see her face and she smiles at me. "Soul shattering is definitely what it was. How do you feel?"

Like the king of the goddamn world.

I pull off the condom and deposit it into the small trash can by the bed. Rolling myself over so that she's not bearing all my weight, I pull her into me. "I feel perfect. Tell me you'll stay. I don't want you to run off. Stay with me."

"Well, seeing as how my clothes are in a wet puddle on your living room floor, I can't exactly leave, now can I?"

Her comment makes me smile like a kid in a candy store.

"So, if those clothes would happen to get ripped up or burned or accidentally thrown out a window, you wouldn't ever be able to leave? How did I not think of this before?"

"I think Layken would come looking for me eventually." She giggles, and the sound of her relaxed voice makes something in my chest relax too. "She knows you live in this building somewhere."

"Right. Layken is your best friend."

"Yes."

"I met her earlier."

"So she told me."

"She knew who I was the moment she saw me."

Corrigan cringes slightly and then nods. "Yeah."

"She's known this whole time?"

She cringes again. "Yes."

"Can I ask you something?"

She closes one eye as if she's preparing for a painful blow. "Is it going to make me feel extremely guilty?"

"I just wondered what your best friend thinks of...you know, us?"

Corrigan opens her eye, her face softening before she smiles. "She told me I should have just come clean after the night we met, but she also gets why I didn't. She knew you had been very vulnerable with me and that you trusted me and she knew I didn't want to betray that trust." Her face contorts slightly as she watches me, the small lines of worry appearing on her forehead. "Does that upset you?"

I push a few of her curls behind her ear, playing with the ends of her hair between my fingers. "Not in the slightest."

"Can I ask you something now?"

"Anything."

"Do the guys on the team..." She swallows. "Do they know about me?"

"They do now." He huffs out a light chuckle. "I mean they knew I was talking to a girl and meeting with her, but they had no idea that girl was you until—"

"Until I walked into Harold's with my father."

I nod my head slowly. "Yeah. Sorry, but seeing you there threw me for a fucking loop and I didn't exactly react in the smoothest of ways. The guys gave me a hard time about it when you left and then I told them what was going on. They were..." I huff out a laugh. "About as shocked as I was and they had a feeling you knew most of the time. They agreed that you know a lot about hockey and probably know their stats better than they know themselves."

She covers her face with her hands. "They're probably right about that. Shit, I am so unbelievably sorry, Bodhi. I was just scared to tell you. I really was trying to protect your anonymity and your feelings."

"Don't apologize. The time for feeling sorry is over," I tell her, kissing her softly on the forehead. "Unless you have regrets about what we just did."

Her eyes grow large. "No! Never. Do you?"

"Are you kidding? I'm lying in my bed in my apartment after having the most incredible sexual experience I've ever had with the prettiest woman I've ever met. I don't regret a damn thing."

"So, the fact my father is your coach doesn't scare you?"

"Oh, it scares the living shit out of me." I laugh and pull her tighter against my chest. "But that's not going to stop me from wanting you. My feelings for you aren't going away just because of who your father is, Corri. I promise you that."

She wraps her arms around me in a tight embrace. "Good. Because I really, really like you, Bodhi."

"What do you think your dad would say?" I ask her. "If he knew?"

I feel her body deflate against me as she sighs. "I want to tell you that he knows I'm an adult and you're an adult and therefore he would let us do our own thing. I want to tell you he would be happy for me because he knows you're a good guy and I want to say he would be happy for you because he knows the kind of girl you would have supporting you and cheering for you and encouraging you..."

"Buuut?"

"But he always had this rule with me that I wasn't to fraternize with his players. I think it's always been more of a protective thing with me since I was a teenager. Then when my mom passed away he had this feeling...or more a fear, that I would fall for one of his players, because I was around so much, and it wouldn't work out and then I would never want to come around anymore. That he would essentially lose me too." She's silent for a minute and then adds, "It's crazy, I know."

I feather my fingers up and down her arm. "It's not crazy. It's understandable. You're all he has."

"Yeah. And he means well. He's always offered to give me whatever I want, but I want to prove to myself that I can make it in this world without the help of a rich dad."

"How about a rich boyfriend instead?" I grin and then wink at her, making her giggle.

"You know what I mean. And I don't want your money, Bodhi. I didn't do any of this for your money."

"I know." I lift her chin with my finger and kiss her lips. "You did it for my sexual prowess and exceptionally large cock."

That makes her laugh out loud. "Damn right, I did." She swings her leg over my hip, so I roll us both until I'm on my back and she is straddling me. "And if you didn't have either of those things, I'd kick you to the curb."

"Poor me. Then I'd be forced to stand along the street corner with a sign that reads *Adequate cock ready. Will fuck for food.*"

She snorts. "I can only imagine the number of women who would be lined up to share a ride."

I fold my hands around her ass, smiling up at her. "Well lucky for you, we'll never have to find out."

"So, what do we do now?"

"I could think of a few things." I wink and thrust my hips up a bit, my cock stiffening all over again at the feel of her warm pussy on top of me.

She giggles. "That's not what I meant silly. I meant what do we do about us? You know, when it comes to my father?"

"Well, maybe we just don't let him know yet."

She cocks her head. "You really think that's possible?"

"The guys aren't going to say a word. They stress all the time the importance of being a team and looking out for one another. Plus, they seem to like you, so I think they would be okay with it. They'd let us handle things on our own timeline."

She nods and I can tell she's mulling over the idea of keeping our relationship a secret from her dad. "He'd never hear it from me. I mean, it's not like I never come to games so my being there wouldn't be weird to him."

"And then when we both feel good about sitting down with him and telling him, we can do it together."

"Of course," she says. "I would never expect you to put any of that on yourself. We're a team. We do everything as a team. And that includes talking to my father. When the time is right."

"Then it's settled. We'll tell him when the time is right."

"Okay. Deal."

"You know what I think it's time for now?"

"What?"

I smirk and lift my hips once more. "Round two."

She laughs and then lowers her body to mine, her hardened nipples brushing against my chest. "You're incorrigible."

"And you love it."

CHAPTER TWENTY-ONE

CORRIGAN

"So, Connor, it looks like we have confirmation that we are looking at a dislocated shoulder," I tell the sweet young boy and his mother who is seated next to him on his bed. "The good news is at least we're not dealing with any kind of long-term fracture or tear." I explain to his mother, "The doctor plans to reset it and treat him for any residual pain along with a little bit of physical therapy but other than that, I don't imagine he'll have too many restrictions once everything is put back together and recovering. The doctor will be coming in in just a few minutes to talk you through everything and to reset Connor's shoulder."

"Thank you so much," Connor's mom says with an appreciative smile.

"You've must've been playing pretty hard, huh Connor?" I ask him. "I see you're a hockey fan." I nod to the Anaheim Stars t-shirt he's wearing. "You like the Stars?"

"Yeah. I want to be on their team when I grow up."

I lift my brows in surprise. "Ooh. Well, that's a big goal. What position do you want to play?"

"I want to be a Winger. Or maybe Center."

"I think you'll be great at whatever position you choose." I smile at the kid and lean down so I'm a little closer to him. "Can I tell you a secret?"

"Yeah."

"It just so happens that I know a few of the Anaheim Stars players."

One much more than the others.

Connor's eyes grow huge. "You do?"

"Mhmm. And I can't wait to tell them that I met you and that you're going to be on their team one day so they better keep working their butts off because when you're big and strong, you're going to come along and blow them all off the ice."

Connor laughs as I'm paged to the nurse's station.

"Oh, that's me. If you guys will excuse me, the doctor should only be another minute or two."

Connor's mother thanks me again and then I hustle out to the nurse's desk to see where I'm needed.

"They need you in Oncology," Brenda, one of the charge nurses, tells me when I check in.

"What?" My brows pinch together. "What for?"

"No idea." She shrugs. "They just called down and asked for you specifically."

"Huh. Okay. I'll head up. Thanks."

Not knowing anyone on the cancer wing, I scurry up a few floors and am buzzed through a few locked doors just before I run into a beaming Layken.

"Lake? What the hell? Did you page me?"

She nods her head excitedly and loops her arm through mine. "Yes and I'm sorry if I interrupted anything but I thought you might want to see this."

She walks me down a hallway toward the end of the wing.

"See what?"

"Last room on the left."

We stop outside a large room that is primarily used for gatherings or meetings between certain patients and family members or friends, but today, is filled with smiling children, three Anaheim Stars hockey players, and one very loved team mascot. There's a small net on one end of the room and several different colored plush balls for each of the kids piled on the opposite side. Lumin helps one of the kids from her seat and hands the young girl her very special light-up hockey stick. The one she carries on the ice at all Anaheim home games. She helps the girl line up her plush ball and use the stick to shoot it across the floor where none other than Bodhi Roche stands by to watch as each ball enters the net.

I watch with an elated smile on my face as Bodhi raises his hands and announces to the room, "She shoots! She scoooooores! High fives for Chelsea!"

Layken leans over and murmurs in my ear, "I just thought you might want to see your guy in action. He's really great with the kids."

"I didn't even know they were coming today. Bodhi didn't mention it."

"They met with me about the Children's Art Auction next month and even helped some of the kids with some artwork earlier. Bodhi was already in for helping out, but he asked the others to join in too and they all said yes. The whole team is coming this year, and every year after if Bodhi has anything to say about it, but these guys were available today so after we met in my office they agreed to stop by and say hi to the kids."

"Bodhi did all this?"

"Mhmm." I glance at Layken and notice she's giving me a happy side-eye. "He's a pretty good guy and I'm going to have to approve of whatever relationship you two have got going on because I can't find a reason not to."

"Yeah," I sigh as I watch him through the window. "He is a pretty good guy."

"So does that mean you guys are...you know."

I nod slowly. "I think so, yeah. We both agreed it's what we want so we're giving it a go and we'll see what happens."

"What about your dad?"

"We're not telling him just yet. When we're both ready we'll sit him down."

"Please let me be a fly on the wall when that day comes." She snickers beside me and I bump her with my hip.

"You'll be among the first to know for sure."

Layken gestures to the net and plush balls being used by the kids. "Ella said they had this stuff in storage to use with kids when they're at the arena so she asked if she could bring it along and the team said yes."

I smile nostalgically at the net where Bodhi stands. "That net was mine when I was a kid. Can you believe that?"

"No way."

I nod. "Yep. Mom didn't want to get rid of it when I outgrew it and Dad suggested saving it for things just like this."

"Well then I guess I should be thanking you. These kids seem to love it."

I watch quietly as Bodhi teases the hair on the head of one kid and makes him laugh with his silly plush ball tricks and then he stands and shakes hands with the kid's parents.

Harrison Meers wheels the next kid over to where he'll shoot his ball across the room and August Blackstone crouches down to allow the boy to choose what color ball he wants. When he points to the green ball, August sets it down in front of his wheelchair and Harrison helps him line up his stick. Together they shove the stick against the ball and watch as the ball rolls into the net. The families in the room applaud as once again, Bodhi raises his arms and says, "Another excellent scoooooore! You guys are good at this!"

I can't help but smile warmly as I look on from outside the room because Bodhi Roche is every bit the good guy I thought he was. And that knowledge further confirms the decisions I made the night we met. That the decision not to tell him I knew who he was because somewhere inside the professional hockey player was a normal young guy who needed a little guidance and encouragement, was the right decision.

A few minutes later Bodhi happens to look up and sees me standing with Layken near the doorway.

"Hey!" His beaming smile is enough to melt all my insides. But I melt even more when he leans down and kisses my cheek.

"Hey yourself."

"What are you doing here?"

"I work here, silly. If anyone should be asking that question round here, it's me."

"I was going to stop down and see you on my way out," he tells me. "Looks like Layken beat me to it."

I wiggle my brows. "She's super sly that way. That's why I keep her around."

"Huh." Layken sighs. "And here I thought it was my taste for Chinese and my sparkling personality."

I nudge Layken's shoulder with my own. "That too babe."

She laughs. "Bodhi here is going to make sure our children's art auction is the biggest hit yet."

"Oh yeah?" I cock my head. "That's a pretty big promise."

"Lucky for you, I know a few people with heavy pockets."

"Lucky for them," I say. gesturing to the kids still laughing inside with Lumin and August. "Not for me."

"Don't worry Diary Girl," he says with a wink. "I'll make sure you're feeling lucky too. I promise."

Layken's brows shoot up and she gives me an amused

glance. "Oooh listen to this guy, Corrigan. I do believe you found yourself an ooey gooey cinnamon roll."

"Cinnamon roll?" Bodhi lifts a brow. "Is that code for something?"

"Yeah." I reach out and pat Bodhi's chest with my hand a few times. "It's the super nice guys who are really good at doing things for other people. The guy who cares more about his girl than he does himself."

"Yeah." Layken nods. "Like the guy who carries his girl's bags when they're out shopping."

"Or the one who takes his girl to a bookstore on a date because what could be better than buying her one of the books on her TBR."

"Oooh yes!" Layken claps her hands as Bodhi cocks his head.

"TBR? What is TBR?"

"To Be Read," Layken answers. "Every girl has one."

He looks at me. "Do you have one?"

"Pshhh." Layken waves her hand dismissively. "Bodhi, my man, she's got one a mile long. She has TBRs for her TBRs.

"That's only because this hospital takes up all my free time and I don't get the time to relax and read. And when I do, it's your book."

"Your book?" Bodhi turns to Layken. "You have a book?"

"She *wrote* a book," I tell him. "And it's badass."

"Really? You wrote a whole book?"

Layken nods. "It's almost done. But yes."

"Wow. That is pretty badass. Congrats. When will I get to read it?"

Layken's cheeks turn bright pink. "Uh, that's a great big never."

"What?" Bodhi smiles. "And why not? Is it one of those spicy kinds of books?"

"Yes. And I do not need my friends judging me for my steamy bedroom scenes thinking the way my characters act is the way I act."

"Friends, huh?" He rubs his chin between his thumb and forefinger. "So, we're friends now? Like, officially?"

Layken turns with a smile and we follow along as we start to head out of the oncology department.

I suppose I do need to get back to work.

"Mr. Roche, I was officially your friend the very night I found out about you." She turns again and points a finger at Bodhi. "But if you do anything to fuck over my best friend, I can guarantee you I will quickly become your worst enemy. Do I make myself clear?"

"Crystal." He smiles. "I promise I won't let you down."

"Good." She puts her arm around him. "Now, what can you tell me about Griffin Ollenberg?"

"I'M REALLY glad I got to see you, Bodhi. That was a nice surprise."

He squeezes my hand in his. "Ditto. I didn't expect to see you at the door. I knew you were probably busy downstairs so I didn't want to bother you."

"It's kind of a slow day today so bother away. The only patient I had was a kid who dislocated his shoulder playing hockey."

"Ooh," Bodhi cringes. "That hurts like a bitch as an adult. I feel bad for the kid."

"Yeah. I should've looked to see if he was still here and

asked if I could introduce you. He even told me he wants to be an Anaheim Star one day."

"Wouldn't be this kid coming out, would it?"

He lifts his chin, gesturing to a woman pushing her son in a wheelchair outside the hospital doors.

"Oh my gosh, yes! Connor!" I smile at the kid who immediately sees right past me to the man standing beside me. "How's your shoulder, Bud? Did you get it all popped back into place?"

"Uh huh," he says, staring open mouthed at Bodhi.

"That's great! Make sure you take extra special care of it and don't push yourself too hard, alright?"

"Uh huh."

"Oh, and look who I just happened to find standing out here waiting for you to come outside?" I pass a wink to Bodhi who smiles in response. "Do you know Bodhi Roche?"

"Umm, yes! I know all about you! You were killer when you played in Boston and now you're on our team!"

"That's right." Bodhi nods. "I heard you had a bit of a rough go today, huh?"

"Yeah." Connor shrugs like it's no big deal. "Simon Kinney checked me into the glass and then knocked me over and I dislocated my shoulder. But the doctor popped it back into place and it doesn't hurt so much anymore."

"That's good to hear. But make sure you take care of it at home, alright? Do all the things your doctor told you to do so you can get back on the ice in no time."

"I will. And one day I want to be an Anaheim Star."

"I have no doubt you will be Connor. How old are you?"

"I'm nine."

"Well, you know the Stars hold a hockey camp every season that many of us help out with." He glances up at Connor's mom. "If you look on our website, you can register him around this time next year. The camp starts in January."

Connor gasps. "Can I Mom? Please?"

His mother smiles and pats his good shoulder. "Well, let's see how well you do with this shoulder recovery and then pray you don't suffer any more major injuries and then I think we could definitely look into it."

"Yes!" Connor pumps his fist. "I can't wait!"

"Good!" Bodhi offers Connor a fist bump. "Then until next year, Connor. I hope to see you around so we can play a little hockey together. How does that sound?"

"That would be amazing!"

"One last thing." Bodhi reaches behind his head and pulls at the fabric of his jersey until it comes up and over his head. He pulls a black marker from his pocket and signs his name across the number on the back and hands it to a shocked and elated Connor. "Here ya go. Consider it something to inspire you to keep up the great work and get better so we can get you back on that ice."

"Wow!" Connor exclaims. "Thank you so much."

"My pleasure."

"Wow! High five, Connor!" I lift my hand for Connor to give me a high five and then lean down to murmur, "I don't even have a Bodhi Roche jersey. I'm kind of jealous."

Connor shrugs innocently and whispers back, "Maybe if you ask him for one, he'll give you one too."

I chuckle. "You're probably right. I'll have to consider that."

CHAPTER TWENTY-TWO
BODHI

"This calls for a celebration."

I hand a glass of iced tea to Corrigan as we stand in the middle of her living room and then raise my own glass. "To finally getting rid of all your boxes."

"It only took about three months." She laughs and then glances around the room. "But everything looks great. I finally have a place to call my own and it fits me perfectly."

I wrap an arm around her waist and kiss her neck. "Just in time to scrap it all and move in with me."

"What?" She squeals and pushes away from me playfully. "Be serious."

"Who says I'm not serious?"

"Bodhi! I can't move in with you."

I kiss her temple. "You can if you want to. It's not like I don't have the room, but I understand. You need your own space and I respect that."

"I need my own space." She nods. "Not that I don't want to be with you because I do."

"No need to explain. I promise, I get it."

"Thank you though for helping me all day. I really didn't expect it to take so long to empty a few boxes."

A few boxes?

A few?

"Corri..." I cock my head, trying not to smile too wildly. "You had twenty-four boxes to unpack. That's kind of your entire apartment. You've been living out of boxes for months."

"Yeah, well..." She kisses my cheek and gives me an equally cheeky smile. "Now I'm not thanks to you and you're supreme helpfulness." She slides her hands down my chest and like a poor sad maiden asks, "How will I ever repay you?"

I throw my head back in laughter. "I'm sure I can think of something." I spank her ass as I move to the curtains waiting on the couch to be hung. "Let's hang all your curtains so we can call this place done and really celebrate."

"You mean by closing all said curtains and running around this apartment naked?"

I stop and turn, wagging my brows at her suggestion. "I like the way you think, Hicks. You will definitely not hear me complain."

CORRIGAN

I miss you already.

ME

I miss you too. Just got on the plane.

CORRIGAN

Are you sitting near my dad?

ME

Nope. He's at the front. I'm in the back.

CORRIGAN

Good. Then I can send you nudes and he won't see them.

ME

Send away, babe. But if you make me hard on this plane, the guys will never let me live it down.

CORRIGAN

Challenge accepted. *Picture from the waist down with fingers on clit* You mean like this?

ME

Fuuuck me. Yes, like that.

CORRIGAN

I would fuck you...if you were here. But you're not and now I'm forced to play with myself until you get back.

ME

How do you think my cock feels? My fist isn't nearly as good as your sweet mouth.

CORRIGAN

Guess we'll need a phone date or two while you're away, huh?

ME

If by a phone date or two you mean one every single night until you're back in my arms? Then yes.

CORRIGAN

I think that can be arranged.

"I THINK I can steal the puck from their D-men," Oliver continues, gesturing to the screen in front of us. "But my wingers on either side would have to be in their spots and ready for a blind pass. I won't know which way to go until it happens and I sure as hell am not taking my eyes off the puck to see if you're there."

"No problem," Ledger adds. "You know we've got your back."

"Yep." August nods. "And depending on how they're breaking out, we can always change our alignment to interfere with their passing."

Oliver nods. "Yeah. I feel pretty good about overcoming their defense. Plus, Seattle's got a lot of younger players now. Not as experienced as in years past."

"That McClacken is still an asshole," Griffin reminds us with a mumble.

Oliver scoffs as his nostrils flare. "Oh, he's more than an asshole. I want to beat the living shit out of him every time we face off."

I huff out a laugh at the mention of Jared McClacken, causing the rest of the guys to turn their heads.

"What's funny about that?" Oliver asks me. "You know he abused my sister for years."

Wait...what?

"He what?"

"Yeah." Oliver says, grabbing his water bottle and taking a quick drink. "He verbally and mentally abused her for years and then he hit her one day out of nowhere."

"But...isn't she married to Milo Landric now?"

He nods. "Yeah. She left Jared and fled to Chicago. She stayed with Milo as a favor while she hid from Jared."

"Why didn't she just come here to be with you?"

"Because I didn't know," he says, irritated. "She never told me. She didn't want anything to fucking damage my career, as if I would've ever chosen hockey over my sister, but still. Had I known at the time, I would've grabbed her and brought her here to stay with me in a heartbeat. She didn't tell me until she was already in love with Milo. She even changed her name from Charlene Magallan to Charlee Mags so Milo never knew she was related to me."

"How did Milo find out then? I mean, he clearly knows now."

"Because of Jared fucking McClacken." He shakes his head. "Ran into Milo and Charlee together in the tunnels before their game several years ago. Outed her right then. But Milo didn't miss a beat about it, thank God. He stood up for her. Fought for her. Beat the shit out of Jared right there on the ice."

I snap my fingers. "That's right! I heard about that game! Milo Landric is famous for that fight."

"Doesn't get much better than Milo Landric. He's a stand-up guy," Harrison says.

I shake my head in utter disbelief. "Man, I'm sorry to hear about your sister, Oliver. That really is terrible and I'm glad she got out. But listen. Where McClacken is concerned, he's a grade-A douchebag and not worth the breath it takes to mention his name. And quite frankly, he's not that great a player anymore."

Barrett laughs and hitches his thumb gesturing to me. "Listen to this kid."

"What?" I shrug. "I mean it. The guy spends more time swinging fists than he does playing hockey. Statistically speaking, over his last ten games, he's spent more time in the penalty box than he has on the ice."

"I actually read somewhere that it's rumored he has a drinking problem," Griffin states.

"Wouldn't surprise me given the way he plays now," I tell them. "Why he's even still with the team is beyond me."

Harrison laughs. "Well, we don't want him so it's good that he's still under contract with Seattle."

Oliver snarls. "The day Jared McClacken becomes an Anaheim Star is the day I walk out of here forever."

"That's not happening. I'm just saying that McClacken is the least of our worries. If he comes in strong, just say something to piss him off and he'll earn himself the penalty and we'll have the power play. Easy peasy."

Oliver switches off the big screen on the wall. "Well, at least we should be able pull a win as long as we play smart and don't lose our heads. Jared might not be the strongest player, but he's headstrong and he knows how and when to pick a fight. As much as I'd like to be the one to kill that guy with my own bare hands, I respect this team. And we all need to get through the game without a shit ton of penalties and no league fines or bad press."

"Agreed," Griffin says with a nod.

The rest of us nod with him. "Yep. Agreed."

"Good. Now I'm starving. Let's eat."

CORRIGAN

That was an awesome assist you had out there tonight.

ME

Thank you babe. Felt pretty good to pull one over on McClacken. That guy is such a douche.

CORRIGAN

I can't believe you didn't deck the shit out of him.

ME

I wanted to, but we talked about him earlier this morning and Oliver made it very clear he wanted us all to skate a clean game with no penalties. Besides, if any deserves to beat the shit out of McClacken, it's Oliver Magallan.

CORRIGAN

McClacken spent more time in the sin bin tonight than he did on the ice. He's such an idiot. And why Oliver Magallan?

ME

You don't know about McClacken and Magallan's sister?

CORRIGAN

Should I?

ME

I didn't until this morning. Long story but apparently McClacken and Oliver's sister were together before she married Milo Landric.

CORRIGAN

Red Tails Landric?

ME

Yeah. The guy abused her and she left him while he was on an away stretch.

CORRIGAN

WTF? I had a feeling the guy was a real life douche.

ME

Yeah.

CORRIGAN

Well, I'm glad you guys kicked their asses tonight.

ME

It's what we do. 😊 We kick ass and take names. What about you? How was your day?

CORRIGAN

Layken and I did a little Christmas shopping and had lunch at Hopeless Ramen-Tic. I have to take you there sometime. Seriously sooo good.

ME

If I'm going to spend my time slurping something, I'd rather slurp you.

CORRIGAN

Hmm, you'd have to get me wet enough to be able to slurp anything...

ME

And you think I can't make that happen?

CORRIGAN

I never said that...

ME

I guess we'll see.

CORRIGAN

Oh?

ME

Just wait...

CORRIGAN

Wait for what?

ME

You'll see

CORRIGAN

Secrets secrets are no fun...

ME

They are when they will make you come!

THIS IS the longest away stretch of the season so far. We're two weeks out from Christmas and I'm missing Corrigan like crazy. We've texted back and forth and I call her every night but she's working an overnight shift tonight so I can't bother her. We're not even slated to get back to town until late on the twenty-third. The guys have more than noticed a slight change in my demeanor and have been giving me a hard time about missing her for the last three days. I'm about to give up for the night and just go to sleep when my phone dings on the nightstand. Assuming it's Corrigan, I reach to pick it up and roll my eyes when I see Griffin's name appear.

GRIFFIN

Hey Roche! What are you getting Corrigan for Christmas?

ME

I have no idea yet. Why? You got a suggestion?

LEDGER

How about a pair of cute pickle pants to match yours? 😏

GRIFFIN

I can make that happen! They're just one click away!

ME

I don't think she would appreciate a pair of pickle pants the way I do.

HARRISON

How about a ruler to slap your ass during your uh...lessons. #naughtynun

LEDGER

LOL! Oooh or a sexy student costume so it doesn't feel like you're fucking your teacher.

ME

So, I'd be fucking a kid instead? No thank you! 🤮

AUGUST

Nah you don't need any of that. Just give her good tongue lashing and she'll be a happy woman.

GRIFFIN

Good idea. Maybe snap a picture of your balls for her while you're apart.

BEAR

Dip them in glitter first.

ME

Glitter? Why?

BEAR

#decktheballs

ME

I'm pretty sure it's actually deck the halls...

BEAR

bitch slaps Bodhi Not today!

OLIVER

LOL! Yeah. Show your fucking Christmas spirit dumbass.

ME

By decking my balls in glitter?

HARRISON

Don't you think a pic of your sparkly balls would make your girl smile?

AUGUST

Ella says ABSOFUCKINLUTELY!

ME

She would definitely laugh, that's for sure.

HARRISON

Then do the thing and take the pic.

GRIFFIN

And then PUH-LEASE send that pic to us!

BEAR

Uh...I don't think I really need to see Bodhi's glitter balls.

OLIVER

Pretty nuts eh, Bear? Hehe! Pretty nuts. See what I did there?

BEAR

SMH

AUGUST

BAHAHAHAHA I see what you did there. Ella just busted a gut at that one.

ME

Hey, you're the one who told me to do it, Bear, so you're getting a private showing.

BEAR

Then Griffin better deck his balls too so we can have a competition.

AUGUST

Oooh a sparkly balls competition.

OLIVER

This is Scarlett and I say if Bodhi and Griffin are dipping their balls in glitter, then so is Oliver.

AUGUST

This is ELLA and YAAAASSSSSS!!!! Sparkly balls competition!!! And then me and Scarlett and Corrigan get to be the judges!!

BODHI

Christ. What have I gotten myself into?

GRIFFIN

I'm in if you are, Roche.

ME

Googles how to get glitter via Instacart

AUGUST

Ella rubs hands together This is going to be so good. Also, I now hate you all.

ME

Ho, Ho, Ho motherfuckers.

CHAPTER TWENTY-THREE

CORRIGAN

ME

What is this, Bodhi?

BODHI

What is what?

ME

The big box that was just delivered to my door with overnight shipping from Indianapolis.

BODHI

You haven't opened it yet?

ME

No. I wrote you first. Should I wait until tonight to open it with you?

BODHI

Fuck no. I want you to open it now. You'll need it for tonight…

"Oh God, what could that mean," I mumble to myself after reading his text. Grabbing a pair of scissors from the kitchen drawer, I cut open the box and immediately smile at the scent wafting into my nose.

This box smells like him.

Or rather the contents of the box.

Folded neatly inside is Bodhi's jersey. The number thirty-seven staring at me when I pull back the tissue paper. I pull the jersey out of the box and bring it to my nose, inhaling his scent and committing it to my memory all over again.

Fuck have I missed him.

Something small tumbles to the ground and rolls across the floor. I bend to pick it up and realizing what it is, I smile to myself and then reach for my phone to text my gracious gift giver.

ME

And just what do you want me to do with this?

BODHI

I want you to fucking wear it, Babe.

Quickly slipping off my clothes, I pull his jersey over my naked body and then sit on one of my dining room chairs with my legs spread wide open.

ME

Happy to oblige Mr. Roche... 😏

BODHI

Fuuuuuuck. Corrigan. I don't have time to get you off at the moment. I'm about to get dressed for tonight's game.

ME

This is what you wanted, isn't it?

BODHI

This is exactly what I want...after the game. You in my jersey and nothing else.

ME

And as for the vibrator that came with it...?

BODHI

Hmm. How'd that get in there?

ME

If you're not careful, you're going to turn me on.

BODHI

Good. I want you wet and wanting when I call you later.

I sit on the couch with one leg bent so my foot rests on the couch cushion and one hand is posed between my legs and then I set the three second delay to snap a picture.

ME

Good luck tonight, Bodhi.

BODHI

Do you know how hard it is to put a jock strap on when your dick is hard?

"HEY STRANGER."

"Whoa," he says with an appreciative smile on his face as he leans back against his hotel headboard. He smooths his hand down his face and shakes his head slightly as he takes in my body. Draped only in his hockey jersey, I'm positioned on my side giving him a view of my bare hip and part of my torso. "You are stunning."

Knowing Bodhi would be calling tonight for a little intimate fun, I grabbed a charcuterie board from the kitchen and set my phone on top of it attached to a small ring light tripod. That way I could be hands free and he could get an up-close experience.

"I've been draped in you all night long and I don't think I'm showering until you get back into town because I don't want to lose this scent."

"You look fucking amazing in my jersey. August told me there's nothing like seeing your girl in your jersey but I didn't believe him. And I was fucking wrong. Don't ever take that off."

"If I never take it off, you won't be able to see my whole body when you make me come."

"All I need to see is that pussy babe. That's the show I want tonight. The rest is right here," he says, pointing to his temple, "in my mind. Do me a favor and spread those beautiful legs for me."

I do as he asks and roll over, propping myself up on my back and spreading my legs giving him the perfect view of my pussy.

"Fuuuck that's hot."

"What do you want me to do now Boss?"

"I want you to slide your hand up my jersey and wrap it around your breast just like I would. Play with those nipples. Feel how soft your skin is. You know how much I love touching your soft skin."

I do as he says, my mouth falling open when I fold my hand over my breast and give it a light squeeze. "Bodhi..."

"I'm right here with you, Babe. Your hand is my hand. Lift that jersey for a minute so I can peek at those beautiful nipples...yeah, just like that. If I were there right now, I'd have those babies in my mouth, sucking them in and flicking them with my tongue."

"Your tongue on my nipples drives me wild."

"I know it does. And just seeing them right now is making my cock hard as fuck."

"What now, Bodhi? Tell me what to do."

"Slide your hand between your legs and touch yourself the way I do. Trail your finger slowly through that pussy, let's see how wet you are."

I reach down and drag my finger through my arousal, moaning when I realize I'm much wetter than I expected I'd be. I hold my finger up to the camera for him to see.

"Bodhi...oh, my God look how wet I am."

"That's right you are. Suck that finger into your mouth, Corri. Taste what I can do to you even from half a country away."

When I suck my finger into my mouth I see Bodhi's head fall back against the headboard and his eyes close momentarily. "Fuuucking hell, Corri."

"Are you touching yourself?" I ask him.

"My hand is your hand, Babe. As far as I'm concerned, you're touching me right now. Feels good, doesn't it? Tease yourself with me."

"Move your camera so I can see."

He angles his camera so I can get a good view of him fisting his cock, tugging it at the base and pulling his hand up and over his shaft.

"Oh God, Bodhi. Yes."

"Tease that clit, Corri. Make it good and wet. Spread that arousal every-fucking-where. I want you dripping."

I bite my bottom lip to keep from moaning but the sensation is too much. My breathing quickens and my head falls back as I let out a moan.

"Shiiit Bodhi. It's too good. It's like you're right here with me."

"I will be in a minute, Baby. You have that vibrator next to you?"

"Yes."

"Stick it inside you and click the button for the pulse setting."

"Bodhi..." I shake my head ,the overwhelming need to finish myself off growing ever present. "I don't think I—"

"Yes you can. I'm not done with you, Babe. Let's go. We're doing this together."

With a shaky hand, I push the vibrator inside me as far as it'll go and then hit the pulse button on the remote.

My mouth falls open and I gasp loudly. "OH FUCK! BODHI!"

"That's it. Good Girl, Corri. Relax and feel that pulse. Look at me. Pretend it's me pulsing inside you."

He pumps his cock with his hand a few more times and Christ it is a turn on like I've never experienced before. The two of us getting ourselves off together though we're far apart is wildly intimate and not like anything I've ever done before. The irony is not lost on me that although I've been so many firsts for Bodhi, this experience is a first for me.

"If I were with you right now, Bodhi, I'd have that beautiful cock in my mouth."

"And I'd be watching you gag every time I hit the back of your throat because you are a fucking super star. Hell, even thinking about it right now just made me harder. God, I love when you suck me off."

"Bodhiiiiii, I'm not going to last." I try to steady my breathing but the sensations are too much. "I need to come!"

"Not yet, Babe. Don't you stop touching that clit. Get it good and wet and then we'll race to the finish line together, alright?"

I nod furiously as I continue to rub my finger over my clit. "Oh, my GOD!"

"Look at me, Corri." Bodhi tugs at his cock harder, faster, his hand moving up and down his thick shaft. The muscles in his arm straining with every stroke. "Fuck you feel so good. Look what you do to me."

"I want you, Bodhi."

"You have me, Corri. Fuck, you've got me by the balls. All you want and more. Shit." He squeezes his eyes closed. "I'm going to come. Come with me."

"Yes! Yes! I'm right there."

"God, fuck!" He grunts as his teeth roll over his bottom lip and his neck strains.

I allow myself to focus on the pulsing vibrator smacking into my G-spot over and over again and then tap at my clit, rubbing the swollen mound frantically before my climax takes over and I'm squeezing my legs together as I come fast and hard. Words don't even escape my mouth this time and I feel like I'm having an out of body experience.

Finally, I gasp a huge breath, not realizing I had been holding it as I came, and release a loud, "Oooh fuuuuuuuck."

"Corrigan..." My name is a pleasured whisper from his lips and even in my state of blissful satisfaction, I register the deep and soft timbre of his voice and know without a shadow of a doubt that this man means more to me than I ever thought possible.

"That was..." he says.

"Yeah."

"Is it always like this?" he asks.

"With you? For me? Every single time," I confess. "But this? Getting ourselves off together like this? That was a first for me."

His eyes find mine and I watch as his lips turn up into a proud smile. "Is that so?"

"It absolutely is."

"I gave you a first?"

"You've given me several firsts, Bodhi Roche."
You were my first virgin.
You were my first student.
You're the first man I've envisioned a future with.
The first man I've ever truly loved.

MY PHONE DINGS as I'm placing Christmas cookies on a tray to take to work tomorrow. Layken and I have been busting ass all day baking every cookie known to man. I'm pretty sure we baked no less than twenty-five dozen cookies from sun up to sun down. I'm exhausted but it smells delightful in my apartment so I'm in no way in a sour mood. Plus, we've had wine. Copious amounts of wine.

"I bet it's just Bodhi. Will you check that for me?" I ask her as I step to the sink to wash my hands.

"Yep. Oh, not Bodhi. It's Ella."

"Ella Blackstone?"

"Yeah."

I'm reaching for the soap when she squeals. "OH, MY GOD! WHAT AM I LOOKING AT?"

"What?"

"Corri!" She bursts out laughing. "Are these? Oh fuck, what is this?"

"I don't know. What is it?" I ask, rinsing my hands and grabbing for a towel. I glance to my left where Layken is standing with my phone, her eyes narrowed and her head cocked to the side. She's studying way too hard. "Oh Lord, this has to be good if you're speechless."

"I think it's..."

She hands me the phone and I glance at the picture that reads DECK THE BALLS NUMBER 1 in a red bold font above a square picture of a set of glittery balls topped with an animated bow.

"Holy shit. What did they do?"

Layken snickers and points to the pictures behind this one. "Look! There are more of them!"

"Oh my God! What is this?"

"Wait, wait," Layken says, moving her finger over the screen. "Scroll up. Maybe I missed an explanation."

Sure enough, a text from Ella was sent before she sent the group of seven pictures. The text chat is between three of us, but I'm not sure who the other number belongs to.

Glad it's clearly not my dad!

ELLA

Corrigan, welcome to the Anaheim WAGs (I learned about WAGs from the Chicago Red Tails wives and girlfriends...also, we totally need jackets). As one of the newest of the WAGs, Scarlett and I thought you deserved to be a judge with us for the first, hopefully annual, DECK THE BALLS team competition (please don't be grossed out or offended and pretty please don't tell your dad! This is just silly fun and all started with Bodhi...I'll tell ya later!) YOU are about to receive a set of seven anonymous pictures. Each one a set of balls belonging to our gloriously sexy Anaheim players creatively decorated in holiday glitter. It is your job to assess each picture and respond with your top three winners. Happy Holidays! (And we should totally hang when the team gets back!)

SCARLETT

OMG why do I feel like this is going to be epic?

ELLA

LOL because it is! Here you go!

Layken giggles. "Oh my God! We're actually looking at the balls of some of the country's biggest hockey stars!"

"Yeah but we can't tell whose is whose." I shrug.

"That's okay!" She nudges my shoulder. "It'll be fun to guess. I wonder which ones are Griffin's! Let's go sit down and study this a little closer."

Scrolling through each picture, Layken and I scream in laughter. The first picture was a set of balls covered in a spattering of red and green glitter titled MERRY DICKMAS. Another set of balls is decorated in red and silver glitter resembling a candy cane or a piece of peppermint candy. The words IT'S NOT GOING TO LICK ITSELF written at the bottom. Another all in green with the words HE'S A MEAN ONE written across the middle.

"Oooh this one shows creativity!" Layken says, pointing at the picture of balls covered in red glitter with white glitter around the bottom so it looks like a Santa hat. The words

HE KNOWS IF YOU'VE BEEN BAD OR GOOD scrolled across the top.

"You're definitely right there. Someone took a hot minute to make that look good. Doesn't look like Bodhi's balls though so I bet they're not his."

The next one is all gold and resembles a bell, and unsurprisingly reads JINGLE MY BELL and the next is completely red with the words WILL YOU RIDE MY SLAY TONIGHT.

Layken cackles. "Nice play on words with that one."

The last one makes us laugh so damn hard we both lose our breaths. With the words NAUGHTY GIRLS GET NOTHING BUT COAL, the last set of balls is decked in black glitter and very much resembles the shiniest piece of coal we have ever seen.

"Oh shit! That one might be the winner!"

SCARLETT

OMG! These are TESTI-TACULAR! LOL!!

ELLA

Right? I can't even figure out which pair belongs to August! Does that make me a bad wife?

SCARLETT

Nah. They're all covered so it's hard to tell. Though I think the Will You Ride My Slay Tonight might belong to Oliver. His right side hangs a little lower than his left 😉

ME

The things I didn't know I would learn tonight... LMAO!

SCARLETT

Teehee! Sorry! I guess I'm a bit of an over-sharer. Or I'm just comfortable enough among like-minded women to not care. 😊

ELLA

So, do you all have a favorite? Because I snorted at the black shiny piece of coal.

ME

I have to admit, I laughed a little extra hard at that one too. Definite creative points.

SCARLETT

Yep. I can definitely give props to the shiny black ball. Corrigan, does that naughty girl ornament belong to you?

ME

GIF of Elmo shrugging I mean, I can hope, right? Cause I wouldn't mind being naughty and playing with that a little but also if those balls belong to one of your men, then just pretend I said absolutely nothing.

SCARLETT

LOL deal!

ELLA

I knew I liked you!

CHAPTER TWENTY-FOUR
BODHI

ME

Tonight's the night! I finally get to come home to you!

CORRIGAN

Will your balls be donned in glitter?

ME

LOL hell no! That shit was itchy as hell.

CORRIGAN

But oooh so enjoyable! I hope Griffin is proud of himself.

ME

Are you kidding? He hasn't let us live it down that he has the best balls on the whole fucking team.

CORRIGAN

Well for what it's worth, I thought your balls were stellar. And although they may not lick themselves, I would be happy to lick them anytime.

ME

I might just have to take you up on that. 😊

CORRIGAN

I hope you do. 🩶

ME

Can I ask you a favor?

CORRIGAN

Of course!

ME

It's kind of a big one...and I'd understand if you say no.

CORRIGAN

Bodhi if it's important to you, it's important to me. What can I do for you?

ME

Will you sleep at my place tonight?

CORRIGAN

Umm...I don't have a key...

ME

I'll have one waiting for you at security when you get there. They already have your name and I've already told them you get free passage to my place any time you want even if I'm not there.

CORRIGAN

You know I would never just invade your space when you're not there, right?

ME

I understand, but tonight I really want you to do this. For me. I'm not above begging.

CORRIGAN

Is there a reason?

ME

Yes. I haven't seen you or touched you or smelled you in over two weeks and it's killing me. We won't be getting in until after tonight's game so when I do get in, I want to be able to walk into my bedroom and find you curled up in my bed. I want to be able to wrap my arms around you and pull you into my chest and hold you against me while we sleep. I just...I want you in my space tonight.

CORRIGAN

Well, when you put it that way... 🩶 You know I have to work Christmas Eve...

ME

That's okay. I'll drive you in if you'd like. I'll even stop and get you that holiday latte you like so much. I promise I'll try my best not to wake you. I just want to know my girl will be in my bed when I get home.

CORRIGAN

Your girl will happily sleep in your bed tonight. 😊 Can I tell you something?

ME

Of course.

CORRIGAN

I kind of like it when you call me your girl, Bodhi.

ME

I like that I get to call you my girl. I won't ever take that for granted.

CORRIGAN

🩶 Good luck tonight. I'll be watching.

ME

Thanks babe. I'll see you soon.

"Move aside, gentlemen, the world's best balls are coming through!"

Most of us groan and throw Griffin the bird as he struts through the locker room in nothing but a pair of pajama pants with Christmas balls all over them.

"I know, I know," he says with a bow. "You can stare at my balls all you want. I'll even do a little"—he thrusts his hips a few times for general effect—"schwing a ding dong action just for you to get the full effect."

"Trust me," Bear says straight-faced, "we get enough of your balls on a daily basis."

He wags his brows as only Griffin can. "Yeah but only the naughty girls get to play with these balls."

"Alright asshat. Catch." Oliver tosses Griffin a jock strap. "Go sack up and then let's prepare to kick some ass tonight so we can get home. I'm ready to be home so I can fuck my wife in my own bed."

"Hey at least your wife has been able to accompany you on this away stretch," I whine. "This has been the longest two weeks of my life."

Ledger laughs. "Says the guy who wasn't having any sex at all up until a few months ago."

"That's right Ledge. I drank the Kool-Aid and I like the fucking Kool-Aid..." I yank on Ledger's t-shirt and pull him close to me so our faces are mere inches apart. "And I neeeeeed the fucking Kool-Aid."

"Sorry man," Ledger says, holding up his hands. "I can't help you there."

"You know what you should have done, Bodhi?" Harrison asks, pulling on his uniform.

"What?"

"You should've sprinkled your balls with blue glitter and

titled it *I'll Have a Blue Christmas Without You*." He laughs. "Hashtag blue balls."

"Fuck!" I laugh. "You're right. I might have won had I done that."

"Nooope!" Griffin drops his pants and pulls on his jock strap right there in the middle of the damn locker room for all of us to witness. "Nobody has better balls than me, I'm afraid. Sorry, Pickle Pants."

"You know what? It's fine, Ollenberg. You can have the best balls, because pickles are big and round, juicy and delicious. So, I'm happy to have the pickle in my pants while you carry around those tiny crystal rocks in your sack."

"Roche!" Coach calls through the locker room.

"Yeah, Coach?" My butt puckers and all heads turn toward me when he calls my name. For a moment I fear the absolute worst.

Did she tell her dad about us?

What did she say exactly?

Does he hate me now?

What's he going to do?

Can he kick me off the team?

What's my agent going to say if I get kicked off?

What are the guys going to say?

What am I going to tell Corrigan?

Will he tell me I can't see her again?

Will I abide by his rule?

I can't stay away from her.

I'm in love with her.

Whoa...

I really just had that thought...

I'm in love with Corrigan.

Fuck, what if her dad ruins everything?

What can I say to him to make this right?

"YOU, Bodhi Roche, were on fucking fire tonight!" Coach Hicks beams at me and offers me a double high five followed by a proud parent pat on the back. "You've come a long way, kid. Finally turning your talents into something that benefits your entire team."

Oooh thank Christ.

I really thought I was a dead man for a minute there.

My shoulders fall in relief as do the shoulders of everyone else in the room collectively.

Coach is right though. Old me would have kept the puck in my possession multiple times tonight and tried to score for myself. And most likely I would've failed. But instead, I saw the opportunities when they arose and was able to pass the puck to my teammates who were in a better position to score and they did.

Just call me Captain Assist.

"Thank you, Coach. That means a lot."

He pats me on the back one more time and then points at me as he walks backward out of the room. "MVP, son. You were tonight's MVP."

The guys stare at me while I watch Coach leave the room and when he does, I practically fall to the bench and hold my head in my hand.

"Dude," Ledger murmurs next to me. "You totally looked like you knew you were walking to your death."

"I totally thought that's what was about to happen."

"Same." Griffin nods. "When that man shouts my asshole puckers tighter than a snare drum."

"So, I take your sudden fear to mean he still doesn't know about you and his daughter?" Harrison asks.

I shake my head. "We decided to wait to tell him when we're good and ready."

Oliver takes a seat on the bench in front of his changing cubby. "And you think he won't take the news well when you deliver it?"

"She's not so sure, yet. He's always had this rule with her about not fraternizing with the players and she's always respected that. So, I agreed that we didn't have to tell him right away. I want her to be as comfortable and happy about it as possible. I'm not going to push her."

"Good. That's good."

"Yeah I guess, but it also sucks because I want to be with her. Like, publicly. I want to show her off and make her feel like a beloved queen when we're out. I don't want to have to sneak around or hide our relationship just because one man might not be happy about it."

"Yeah." Harrison frowns. "But that one man is her world. He's her everything. Especially after her mom passed away."

"I'm in love with her, you guys." I lift my head, glancing around the group to see their shocked expressions at my confession.

"Whoa." Ledger says, his brows raised. "I guess I didn't realize you guys were that serious."

"Yeah it's serious. At least it is for me. And I think it is for her but we haven't exactly talked about it. That night she told me she was asked out on a date by another man almost wrecked me. I hated every minute of wondering if she was going to say yes. Or if she even wanted to. I knew then that she was someone special to me."

August claps my shoulder. "Look at our Pickle Pants all grown up with real man feelings."

The guys chuckle and I toss my sweat-soaked shirt at August. "Fuck you, Blackstone."

"Look, everything you do is a choice, right? So, you can choose not to tell Coach about you guys and continue the charade for a little while longer or choose to simply sit down like mature adults and tell him how you feel."

"Do you think I should tell him face to face? Like in his office when we get back?"

A collective "No" is said around the room as everyone shakes their heads.

"It'll be way too late to spring something like that on him tonight," August tells me. "Go home to your girl. Enjoy your night and then in the coming days maybe talk to Corrigan and see how she feels."

Get home to my girl.

That sounds like an excellent plan.

It's a little after midnight when I finally walk through my door. I toe off my shoes and step through my living room, inhaling a deep breath. Already I can smell that Corrigan has been in this room. The lingering scent of her perfume tickles my senses and leaves me feeling excitedly content. I want to run down the hall and whisk her into my arms, but I know it's late given she has to work tomorrow so instead I smile knowing she's here with me and move through my nightly routine before joining her in my bedroom.

The room is dark except for a sliver of moonlight shimmering through the window. It's just enough to highlight her shape snuggled beneath the covers. Padding over to the side of the bed, I unbutton my dress shirt and pull my arms from the sleeves before draping it over the chair in the corner of the room. Then I unbuckle my belt and slip out of my pants as quietly as possible. I tear off my socks and then pull back the covers slipping in right behind Corrigan, her body facing away from me. She moves ever so slightly when I fold my arm over her torso and pull her against my chest. I slip my other hand around her body so I can hold her in my arms and that's when I discover—

Hooooly shit...

She's naked.

It may be late and it's been a long ass day, but feeling her body against mine makes me instantly hard.

How the hell am I supposed to fall asleep like this?

She never sleeps naked.

She did this on purpose.

Lowering my mouth to her neck, I kiss her smooth skin and then inhale a deep breath, reveling in the beachy scent of her shampoo that I've come to love as uniquely Corrigan.

"Fuck, I've missed you," I whisper before kissing her neck a second time. I trail my fingers lightly across her abdomen just underneath her breast with my right hand, and with my left I reach around to cup her other breast in my palm.

Motherfucker her body feels amazing in my hands.

Soft and warm.

Mine to touch.

Mine to pleasure.

Mine to love.

"Mine," I whisper.

I intend to fall asleep just like this, my hands cocooning her breasts, my dick as hard as stone, until her soft and sleepy voice answers, "Yours."

I lift my head slightly from my pillow. "You're awake?"

She giggles ever so softly. "Well, it's kind of hard to sleep when a man has his hands wrapped around my tits."

Her reasoning makes me smile, unapologetic as it may be. "I couldn't help myself, Corr. They feel so fucking good in my hands. And I needed to hold you. I swear to God I can fall asleep like this and my dick will settle down eventually. He just missed you as much as I did."

Like she's the angel of my dreams, she lazily drapes her right leg over my hip, leaning back against me. "Well, I missed you both and I need you inside me. Slow and lazy so I can feel every part of you sliding against every nerve inside of me."

I take the spreading of her legs as an open invitation for my fingers to explore and swipe a couple through her soaking slit.

"Christ, baby, you feel amazing."

She moans softly, wiggling her ass tighter against me and I waste no time positioning my cock at her entrance. Both of her breasts in my hands once again, I push inside her, groaning at the tight, warm, and deliciously wet sensation before leisurely pulling out so I can repeat the movement again.

"This isn't going to take long, Babe. I've got two weeks of pent-up sexual frustration inside me. Your sweet cunt is no match for my fist, I'm afraid."

"Then use me, Bodhi. Fill me. Make me overflow. Drown my body in your cum."

"If I do this, you know I may very well be dripping down your legs for days."

Okay I realize I'm no super sex God but shit...two weeks of not feeling the inside of Corrigan Hicks is two weeks too long.

"Give it your best shot, Mr. Roche. It'll be the greatest Christmas gift I've ever received."

"God, I missed you so fucking much."

"I missed you too."

Come they told me, pa rump pa pum pum...

CHAPTER TWENTY-FIVE

CORRIGAN

"Girl! You look absolutely fabulous!" I gawk at Layken when she meets me in the entrance of the ballroom where tonight's Pacific Children's Hospital Annual Art Auction is taking place. "And you really knocked it out of the park with this entire set up! Look at this place!"

She wrings her hands and bites her bottom lip. "Do you really think so?"

I scoff out a laugh. "Are you kidding? Of course I think so! You've talked a lot about your vision for this event and look around the room, girlfriend. It's exactly as you had pictured it."

The ballroom is decorated in white cloth covered tables with white table settings. The centerpieces of paper flowers in vases were made by the children from area school districts wanting to give back in some way for this event. They bring the perfect amount of color to the room. White twinkle lights hang from the center chandelier across the width of the entire room. Around the perimeter of the massive space are more easels than I can quickly count displaying a variety of artwork created by the children who enter Pacific Children's Hospital and stay for longer than three days' time. The amount of cheerful color surrounding this room creates an overwhelmingly happy and positive aesthetic for tonight's guests.

"It's simply beautiful and fun in here, Lake. You can't look around this room and not smile."

She wraps her arms around me in a gigantic hug. "Thank you Corr. You always know just what I need to hear."

"Of course. You're my best friend. You know that. I'm always going to be here for you. And I'm here for you tonight. Anything you need." I squeeze her tightly, smiling as I feel her inhale a deep breath and release it slowly. Sometimes I know she just needs a steadying hug to settle her nerves.

Anxiety is a bitch.

"You feeling alright? I know how much nerves can get you sometimes."

"Yeah. I think I'm okay." She shrugs. "I just don't want to disappoint anyone, you know?"

"What? How in the hell could you possibly disappoint anyone? Look around. Look at all you've done."

"Yeah. I know it's good. And I feel good about it. Sometimes I just get up in my own head, you know? I'm someone who is good at many things but great at nothing and therefore, somewhere in the dark parts of my brain, I fear I'm a disappointment."

"Well, we'll see how great at nothing you are when you help Pacific Children's Hospital raise millions of dollars tonight."

Layken grabs my arm, gasping. "Oh my God! Which reminds me! I haven't even told you the best part about tonight!"

"You mean the part about the Stars helping out?"

She looks beyond me and claps her hands giddily. "Not just the Stars! So, a couple months ago I looked at the season schedule and saw who the Stars were playing next and sent their team an invitation to join us for this event alongside the Stars and...well..." She turns me around so I have a view of the main entrance where camera flashes are going off like a fireworks display as photographers and paparazzi shout to a large group of gentlemen followed closely by a group of women.

My jaw drops. "Oh, my God! Layken! Is that...is that Dex Foster?" I gasp, bringing a hand to my chest. "And Hawken Malone?"

"Yes!" She squeals. "And Milo Landric, and Colby Nelson, and Quinton Shay, and Zeke Miller!"

I spin around, unable to hide my enthusiastic smile. "You invited the Chicago Red Tails to the auction?"

Her head nods furiously. "Uh huh! And they accepted! Can you even believe it?"

"I..." I shake my head in disbelief. "No. I actually can't believe it!"

"Your dad was a tremendous help! Turns out he and Coach Denovah were old college buddies so he made a few calls and helped me make it happen. I figured with two professional hockey teams here, along with all the guests on the list with very deep pockets, we would certainly make a killing for the hospital tonight."

"Layken Hobbs, you are a freaking genius!"

The both of us stand by watching, emphatic smiles on our faces, as the men from the Chicago Red Tails enter the room already intermingled with our beloved Anaheim Stars. Milo Landric and Oliver Magallan shake hands in what looks like a secret handshake and head for the bar followed closely by Scarlett and Milo's wife, Charlee, who is also Oliver's sister. Colby Nelson, Harrison Meers, Dex Foster, and Griffin Ollenberg pose for a picture taken by Carissa Nelson, Colby's wife. Zeke Miller and Barrett Cunningham are like old-time bros with what looks like an old fashioned already in their hands. The last group though, that's the group I watch the longest. Hawken Malone, Ledger Dayne, Quinton Shay, August Blackstone, and Bodhi are all laughing over something Ledger must have said as they enter the room.

"Holy hell, Corrigan," Layken murmurs next to me. "Your man looks like a fucking snack, no?"

Bodhi is dressed head to toe in black, his dress pants fitting his form perfectly as they hug his sculpted legs. With his suit jacket covering the top, I feel confident that nobody in this room except for me and his teammates know what a fine specimen his ass is. His black button-down shirt giving his outfit a sexy monochromatic vibe underneath his jacket, the only color on his body tonight is his tie. Designed by children with several handprints and squiggly lines all over it in different colors of the rainbow, his outfit is the perfect background to showcase the colorful piece.

My jaw hanging so low I wouldn't be surprised if drool is dripping down my chin, I nod. "Not just a snack, Lake. A full four course meal."

She giggles and nudges my elbow. "Well don't look now but that four course meal just spotted you and is coming this way."

Somehow her words finally translate in my brain and I shake my head, pulling myself from whatever trance I had myself in.

"Corrigan," he says when he finally approaches. "Layken."

"Hi Bodhi," Layken says with a smile and a wink. "Thank you for coming tonight." She reaches out and gives Bodhi a gentle hug, careful not to get her makeup on his jacket or mess up her own gown and hair.

His gaze falls to me as Layken steps back and then his arms are around me and he's whispering, "You look fucking stunning tonight."

My cheeks heat at his compliment. "You don't look so bad yourself, stranger."

"Please tell me I get to peel you out of this dress later because it's all I'm going to be thinking about all night long."

"I guess we'll see if you play your cards right."

He pulls back and I smile mischievously.

"Layken, I'll just go ahead and buy all the art so we can call this night over," he tells her while still staring at me.

Layken laughs out loud and pats Bodhi on his shoulder. "Oh Bodhi. I'm afraid your salary can't quite cover the amount of money I hope to make tonight on its own. I therefore have no choice but to run the event as planned."

"Ah, I see Mr. Roche has already found a few ladies to try to flirt with, huh?" The voice I hear behind me is a voice I could never not recognize as I turn around and spot my father joining our group conversation.

"Dad!"

He wraps his arm around me. I know he thinks it's a loving gesture but I also know it's a protective one since Bodhi is standing here talking to two single women.

I've got to sit him down and talk to him about me and Bodhi.

Soon.

"You know me, Coach." Bodhi chuckles and shows off his charming smile. "How could I not tell these ladies how beautiful they look tonight?"

"It's true," Dad agrees with a friendly nod. "You do both look exquisite this evening." He wags his finger at Bodhi. "But I would encourage you to stay away from this guy. He's nothing but young trouble."

"Aww come on, Dad. He can't be that bad, right?"

Seriously.

Come on, Dad.

Bodhi is a perfect gentleman.

What makes you see anything but?

"Yeah, I can't be that bad, right?" Bodhi repeats my words, causing my dad to laugh. "Pretty sure you were calling me MVP not too long ago."

"Uh huh. Right. Like we haven't read all about your reputation in Boston." He laughs like he's teasing but he steps forward and wraps an arm around Bodhi's shoulder. "Come on, Roche. Let's go get a drink and get far away from my daughter."

What the hell, Dad?

I'm not a child.

Bodhi doesn't even have the chance to say goodbye before he's turned away from me and walking with my dad across the room to the bar and I'm forced to stand here and watch.

"Ouch," Layken murmurs nudging me. "You okay?"

No.

I'm not okay.

I'd love nothing more than to be on Bodhi's arm tonight.

"Yeah. I'll be fine. It's my fault anyway."

"What do you mean?"

"I'm the one who didn't want to tell Dad about our relationship just yet."

"Maybe do me a favor and don't tell him tonight." Layken cringes in that please-don't-be-mad-at-me kind of way but I laugh at her suggestion.

"You do not need to worry about that. The last thing I want to do is embarrass him or upset him when he's in public." I squeeze her hand reassuringly. "I promise. We'll both be on our best behavior tonight. You know that. I'll just talk to him next week during our lunch date."

"Now there's a good idea. Order him a footlong wiener to shove in his mouth and then tell him you're getting all the big dick energy from Bodhi Roche."

If I had a drink in my mouth right now, I'd be spitting it all over myself. "Oh fuck, Layken!" I laugh. "This is why I love you so much."

The dinner portion of the night is just about over as the wait staff hurries around the ballroom clearing plates and simultaneously refilling cups of coffee or glasses of wine as they pass out dessert. I'm stuck at a dinner table with my father, Coach Denovah and his wife, as well as the general managers for the Stars and Red Tails. Layken was beside me for much of dinner but now she has responsibilities. Events like these means schmoozing the board and showing off all the fancy details.

Needless to say, the tables to my right, where the players are all seated together, seems much more fun. I'm trying my best not to constantly turn my head to look their way or to draw attention to my obsession with Bodhi. My phone tucked inside my dress pocket—because who goes anywhere anymore without a dress with pockets—vibrates and I reach for it to check my incoming text.

BODHI
I miss you.

ME
I miss you too. I promise you're having much more fun than I am right now.

BODHI
That dress on you... 🐱

ME
Oh, this old thing?

BODHI

I've done nothing but think about all the ways I'd like to pleasure you while you're wearing it... and then not wearing it.

ME

Oh? Let's hear them.

BODHI

With a plunging neckline like that, I would definitely have easy access to those gorgeously round tits.

ME

And?

BODHI

You chose a ballgown type of dress and not a skintight number. Why? Would it have anything to do with how high up that slit goes? The ease of which I could steal a quick touch. How long would it take for me to reach the luxurious spot between your thighs?

ME

Guess that depends on how fast you are...

BODHI

I'd give anything to have my fingers inside that sweet pussy for just ten seconds. If only you were sitting next to me right now. I'd do it right under the table and everyone around us would be none the wiser.

ME

My face is flushing.

BODHI

I see that.

"Corrigan, are you alright?" My father touches my arm as it rests on the table but I flinch at the contact, having gotten a little too carried away with Bodhi's texts. Storing my phone back inside the pocket of my gown, I push back from the table and stand.

"Yes. I'm perfectly fine." I laugh nervously, patting my cheeks. "I think just a little too much wine. It makes my face flush. I think I'll just run to the restroom quickly before the auction starts." I glance around the table and pass everyone a friendly smile. "Can I bring anyone anything upon my return? Another drink? More dessert?"

Everyone shakes their heads so I excuse myself and move toward the restrooms. When I open the bathroom door, I'm practically assaulted by none other than Ella, Scarlett, and all the Red Tails WAGs.

"Corrigan!" Ella smiles and claps her hands. She rushes over to me and claps her hands on my shoulders. "Oh, my gosh, your cheeks are pretty pink. Are you okay?"

Blushing again, I nod and head right for the sink where I sprinkle a little water on my face. "Yeah uh..." A nervous laugh escapes me again. "Was just texting with Bodhi."

Scarlett pulls a cloth towel from the sink—because this hotel is fancy—for me to blot my face. "Oh man. Let me tell you, that guy is so smitten by you. He's done nothing but talk about you all night."

"Oooh so this is the lovely girl of Bodhi's dreams, huh?" Carissa Nelson asks, taking me in with a smirk. She offers me her hand and introduces herself even though I already know who she is. "I'm Carissa Nelson, Colby's wife. And Scarlett is right. Bodhi has been talking about his girl," she says using quote fingers, "all evening."

"It's a pleasure to meet you, Carissa. I'm Corrigan Hicks."

"Hicks?" she repeats.

"Remember Carissa?" Charlee Landric nudges her. "Corrigan is the one I told you about. She's Coach Hicks' daughter."

"Oooh right!" Carissa exclaims. "Shit, I'm so sorry. My brain has been so foggy lately."

"Pregnancy brain, am I right?" Tatum Foster laughs as Rory Malone steps out of the bathroom stall looking nearly ready to pop. "Can one hundred percent commiserate. Pregnancy brain is a thing."

"Hi Corrigan, I'm Kinsley Shay. Quinton's wife. Pleasure to meet you."

"Likewise."

"So Bodhi Roche, huh?"

"Yeah." I nod. "Isn't he the sweetest?"

"You tell us!" She laughs. "Because we've always heard that he's a bit of a player and a kind of self-proclaimed superstar on the ice. Kudos to you for changing the kid."

"Oh, he's totally not the guy you all probably heard about. Trust me, I heard the same. All those articles and vlogs about the amount of women he's had or the shit he does on the ice is totally not true. Well, I mean the way he plays may have been true. I wouldn't really know. I was overseas working for several years so I didn't know a ton about him until my dad hired him."

"So, is that how you met then? Through your dad?"

I shake my head adamantly and Ella giggles. "You guys, her dad doesn't even know they're together."

There's a collective gasp in the bathroom and all eyes are on me.

"Scandalous!" Tatum sings. "Oh, my God girl we need all the tea!"

"Well, we met via text when I accidentally sent a text to my dad but hit the wrong number."

"Seriously?" Rory asks.

"Yep. Their numbers are literally one digit off from each other and I had texted my dad over some left-over spaghetti and he answered my text. We didn't even know who we were each talking to for weeks."

Scarlett nudges me. "Keep going, tell them the good part."

"Well...we sort of bonded over talking about food and then started talking about different aspects of our lives and then..." I close my eyes for a moment, trying to decide if I should say the next part or not.

Charlee raises her hand. "For the record, I know exactly what you're going to say because Oliver and Milo were kind of giggling about it a few weeks ago over Christmas."

"Oh, this ought to be good," another woman says with her hand on her hip. She waves and says, "Hi I'm Ada by the way. Zeke Miller's wife."

"Oh hi. Nice to meet you. Anyway, uh, so sort of out of nowhere Bodhi asked if I knew if sex lessons were a thing."

"Pbfbft!" Carissa laughs. "Oh shit! He seriously asked you that?"

"Yeah." I nod.

"As in, he had never had sex?"

"Correct."

"Wait...Bodhi Roche is a virgin?" Rory's eyes nearly bulge right out of her face.

"Well, not anymore," I proclaim with a smile and a wink "My BFF out there, tonight's hostess, her name is Layken, she was with me when I received that text. So, she grabbed my phone out of my hands and replied to him telling him I didn't know but that I would fuck for food...aaaand the rest is history." I shrug like we're talking about brands of tampons and not the peculiar way in which my relationship with Bodhi Roche turned into several nights of lessons on how to fuck.

Ella claps her hands proudly. "Is this woman not the absolute queen when it comes to catching the perfect guy? A virgin she got to mold into the lover of her dreams and a nice guy to boot. I can one-hundred percent vouch for his personality. And the way he cares for Corrigan?" She shakes her head. "Swoon worthy."

"Wow, girl. You are one lucky woman." Tatum winks. "Way to work your voodoo magic."

This time I give them a teasing shrug. "I mean a girl's got to do what a girl's got to do, am I right?"

CHAPTER TWENTY-SIX
BODHI

"If ever you're going to have a chance, it's now, bro," Griffin leans over and whispers to me knowing full well that Corrigan just got up from her table and went to the restroom. All the ladies from our table went as well so I can only imagine the gossip going on in there.

Why do they always travel in packs?

What I wouldn't give to be a fly on the wall.

Or maybe I'd rather not.

"You think?"

Griffin nods. "Fuck yeah. Coach hasn't moved at all. He's busy talking to Denovah. You're good."

Dex Foster leans over from the other side me. "Why does it matter if your coach sees you kissin' on a girl?"

"Because dumbass," Griffin says, rolling his eyes and smirking. "His girl is Coach Hicks' daughter."

Dex's eyes grow huge and his mouth opens. "No shit! Seriously? You're fucking the coach's daughter?"

"Who's fucking the coach's daughter?" Hawken Malone asks, having overheard Dex who gestures to me.

"This little shit right here." He laughs. "Scandalous,

wouldn't you say, Malone?" He turns back to me. "You know, actually, you and Malone here should talk about how secret relationships don't work because chances are the person you're trying to hide from already knows you're fucking."

I whip my head in his direction. "There's no way Coach knows. We're never around each other when he's around."

Griffin points to me. "Maybe he does know and that's why he was so excited to name you MVP back in New Orleans!"

Possible?

No fucking way.

But is it?

I shake my head and glance over to where Coach Hicks is still seated. "I really don't think so. I think if he knew, I'd know. He'd never let me get away with it. Even when we got here tonight, he steered me away from Corrigan and accused me of flirting with her."

Dex cocks his head. "Were you?"

"Fuck yeah, I was. She looks hot. How could I not?"

He pats my back. "That'a boy."

Griffin chuckles. "So, I was just telling him that now is his chance to grab Corrigan when she comes out of the bathroom and steal a kiss or a boob graze or a fuckin' nipple twist while her dad is still having dessert. The bathrooms are out of the way. Pull her over to the side of that alcove. Nobody is going to see you with those curtains over there."

Dex laughs. "Always the nipple twist dude. Go for the fuckin' nipple twist. Maybe even a pussy grab if you can manage it. She'll be eating out of your hand all night, I promise you."

I take a deep breath and glance once more at Coach's table.

They're deep in conversation.

It's now or never.

Be bold Bodhi.

Just one kiss.

One touch.

Pushing back from my chair, I lay my napkin on my seat. "Gentlemen, if you'll excuse me. I have a girl to find."

"Yeah you do!" Griffin gives me a fist bump. "Go get 'em tiger."

Looping my way around the other tables in the room, I move toward the back where the restrooms are and find the perfect spot to wait for Corrigan. I can hear giggling in the bathroom so I send her a text to let her know I'm out here and then shove my phone back in my pocket.

ME

Ten seconds. I'm outside the bathroom.

The moment the bathroom doors open and several women step out laughing together, I find Corrigan's purple gown and grab her hand, pulling her around to the alcove on the other side of the bathroom wall.

She squeals slightly at my tug but giggles when I spin her around so her back is against the wall and then press my lips firmly against hers. Her plump soft lips move right with mine and then she lets out a soft moan as we taste each other, forgetting the world around us for just a moment.

Christ she makes me feel every fucking thing.

Her mouth alone brings me a sense of calm mixed with a sense of euphoria.

Her touch makes me brave but allows me to be vulnerable.

She's perfection and magnificence rolled into one.

And I want her like I've never wanted anything in my life.

"One...two...three..." she whispers. "Better get everything you want before your ten seconds tick away."

Guiding her lips open with the press of my tongue, I dip

inside her mouth as I trail my hand up the slit of her dress, reaching for the warm softness of her pussy.

"Fucking hell, Corr. You're soaking wet."

Her head falls back against the wall and she gasps. "Shit! Bodhi! You make me this way."

Trailing my tongue up the side of her neck, I nibble her earlobe and then whisper, "Kiss me again so I can swallow the orgasm I'm about to give you."

She brings her head back down and crashes her lips to mine as I trail my fingers through her arousal.

And then suddenly I'm torn away from her. Corrigan cries out as my body is shoved hard into the wall beside her, a strong unyielding hand around my throat.

"Just what the fuck do you think you're doing to my daughter?" Coach Hicks' breath is hot and smells of whiskey as he pins me against the wall.

Caught off guard, I hold up my hands. "I...Coach, I—"

"Daddy stop it! Let go of him!"

"Stay out of this Corrigan."

"No, YOU stay out of this, Dad! What the hell are you doing?"

With one hand still around my neck, he points a chastising finger at Corri. "I told you years ago to stay away from my players, Corrigan. And never in a million years did I ever think you would defy me." Rage flows through him like an electric current. "You are my daughter! You are supposed to be class and sophistication. If you think you're going to find yourself an easy hook up by flaunting yourself around my guys, you can think again. You're better than that, Corrigan." He shakes his head. "It's bad enough I had to find you like this, hiding in a corner with your legs open, but to find you whoring yourself out to this—"

WHAM!

My fist flies into Coach's stomach simultaneously with Corrigan's hand on his face.

Whoa!

What just happened?

Did she?

Fuck.

She did.

She hit him.

My eyes grow huge when it registers in my brain what we've both done, worried that we've just caused a huge scene at a very public event. But Corrigan doesn't give two shits. She lifts her chin and stares at her father in complete defiance. There's a tightness in her eyes I've never seen before.

This girl means business.

"You can say I am many things, Father," she spits out angrily, her voice trembling. "You can say I'm a fuck-up and you can say I'm a disappointment, but don't you EVER call me a whore again or so help me God it'll be the last time you ever see me."

"Corrigan—"

"I LOVE HIM, Dad," she seethes. "I LOVE HIM. And NOTHING you do or say right now is going to change that so I suggest you get your fucking hands off Bodhi right now before I make a scene and embarrass the living hell out of you for assaulting one of your very own players at a fucking public children's charity for Christ's sake."

Coach Hicks' demeanor changes when he sees how pissed off Corrigan really is. His hold around my throat weakens and then he finally lets go but reaches for her. Hastily I put myself between Coach and Corrigan.

"Don't you fucking touch her."

He stares me down as if he thinks I'll step aside for him, but I merely chuckle in his face.

"If you want to hit me, Coach, hit me. But if it's the last thing I do, I'll fight for Corrigan's honor. I'd fight for her every fucking day even if it means putting my own career at risk because I love her too. And I'll be damned if you're going to keep me from loving her the way she fucking deserves."

He opens his mouth to speak but Corrigan shakes her head. "Not another word, Dad. You're done here." She gestures to the ballroom doors on the left-hand side of the room. "Get your shit and get out."

"Corri, I didn't mean—"

"Get. Out," she says, her face emotionless. "Or I'll have security remove you."

The moment he walks away I turn to Corrigan who is now shaking, tears falling down her cheeks. I cup her face in my hands and smooth away her tears with my thumbs. "Shit, Corri, I'm sorry. I'm sorry. I'm so fucking sorry. Are you alright? Did he hurt you when he grabbed me?"

She shakes her head. "No. I'm fine. I've just...that was..." Her hands reach for my face and her brows raise as her glistening eyes meet mine. "Oh, God. Wait, are *you* alright?"

"Babe, I'm fine." I pull her face to mine and kiss her lips, her tear-stricken cheeks, and then her forehead before wrapping my arms around her and pulling her into a hug. "I'm just sorry that happened. I never intended for him to—"

"No, no, it's okay." She shakes her head, sniffling. "I mean I knew he might be upset but I never thought he would act like..." She steps back, squeezing her eyes closed, frustrated as she desperately wipes at her tears. "God, I'm so sorry, Bodhi. I've made this all a terrible mess for you."

"Hey." I hold her face and lean down until she opens her eyes and meets my gaze again. "I can handle myself, okay? I'm a big boy and I'm just as much a part of this as you are. I love you, Corrigan. And nothing your father says to me is going to change that. I can handle whatever he throws at me."

"But your career..."

"He can't do anything to me for loving his daughter. You're not part of the contract."

She sniffles again. "You really love me?"

Her question melts away any residual anger toward Coach Hicks and loosens the tightness in my chest. My shoulders fall and my lips turn up into a sincere smile as I nod. "Corrigan, I'm so in love with you I don't know what to do with myself most of the time."

Her glassy blue eyes stare back at me. "Really?"

"Really. I love everything about you." I smooth a few loose tendrils of her hair back from her face. "I love you for your sense of humor. I love the way you take such care of your patients. I love that you're compassionate and helpful. I love that you allow me to be vulnerable around you but then you let me take over and be my possessive self when we're together. I love that you make me feel so many emotions all at once. I love that you're the one who showed me how passionate and sensual and emotional and carnal and fun sex can be with the right partner. I love that I can lose track of time so easily with you. And I love that I feel amazing around you whether we're cuddled up on the couch watching shows about people walking through stones or ones where sons kill their fathers while he's taking a shit. I love hanging curtains with you."

That makes her smile and laugh a little.

Her smile is my favorite thing.

"I love you so damn much, Corrigan. I'd do anything for you."

"I love you too," she says, the gentle touch of her hands on my chest bringing me a sense of strength, but at the same time peace and calm.

"Oh, my God, Corrigan. Are you alright?" We turn to see Layken hurrying toward us. Seeing Corrigan's tears, her eyes widen as she asks, "What the hell happened?"

"I'm so sorry Lake," Corrigan cries a little more. "My father found us and he attacked Bodhi and I tried not to make a scene and I'm so fucking sorry but I told him he had to get the hell out and—"

"Whoa, whoa, whoa," she says, throwing her arms around Corrigan's neck and pulling her in for a hug. "He's gone, okay? I watched him leave myself and he looked pretty sick and somehow I just knew something was wrong when I couldn't find the two of you anywhere." I watch Layken's eyes close and hear her whisper, "Just breathe with me for a second, okay? He's gone. He left."

Having a front row seat to witness the love between Corrigan and Layken, I smile appreciating the bond these two ladies have with each other. There's nothing in the world like a best friend and they're both lucky to have one. Layken opens her eyes and raises her brows, giving me a glance as if to silently ask *"Are you okay?"*

I nod and she blinks slowly back at me, squeezing her best friend a little tighter. When she pulls away from Corrigan she brings her hands to Corrigan's shoulder and says, "You know I think you may have found yourself a Mister Perfect."

Corrigan smiles and lets out a little laugh. "I think you may be right."

Damn right she is.

CHAPTER TWENTY-SEVEN

BODHI

"To Bodhi." Dex lifts his beer as we're situated around a few tables in the back of Jay's Bar following tonight's event. Thank God Oliver Magallan has it in good with the owners here. They never turn us away when we need a back room to hang out in while having a few beers. Even tonight when we have two teams squeezed into the space. "For living to tell the tale about almost dying at the hands of his coach."

There's a collective laugh around the room as glasses and bottles are lifted and everyone chants, "Here, here!"

Corrigan leans over and kisses my cheek and then her hand grasps mine resting on her thigh.

"We don't call him Pickle Pants for nothing," Griffin tells the group. "He's a slippery lil' sucker." He raises his arms. "But hey! At least it's out now, huh? No more secrets!"

I steal a glance at Corrigan, letting her call the shots since it's her dad we're talking about. As much as I'm willing to go to bat for her, I also will never be the reason she has a strained relationship with her father. Even after tonight, I know I need to make sure she talks to him, if not for his sake, then for hers.

She nods and then happily announces, "No more secrets. I'm dating Bodhi Roche!"

Several of the WAGs with us tonight clap and call out, "YAAAS GIRL!"

"GET IT GIRL!"

"THAT'S RIGHT!"

"WOOOT!"

"Well, I think I can speak for us all," Harrison says, "when I say we are glad you're here, Corrigan, and welcome you officially to the Anaheim family. I don't think you'll be going anywhere aaaaany time soon if Pickle Pants has anything to say about it."

There's a collective agreement around the tables and then Ella, Scarlett, and Corrigan do this little secret handshake finger wiggle thing that I've never seen before but apparently it's a thing.

Corri laughs and I can't help but smile. I love seeing her happy.

Fuck, I just love her.

"Thank you, Harrison," she says with a nod. "I'm very happy to be here."

August leans forward, looking down the table at me. "So, what's this going to do for tomorrow's game?"

"Nothing at all." Milo shakes his head and shrugs his shoulders. "We're still going to kick your asses just as planned."

August spits out his beer in laughter. "Oh really? It's like that?"

Milo and Hawken both nod. "Yep."

"Care to make a wager on those big balls, Landric?" We all look down the table to the opposite end to find Barrett watching Milo with one brow raised.

"What have you got in mind, Cunningham?"

Bear rubs his chin between his thumb and forefinger. "The

losing team has to wear winning team's jersey and have a picture taken for all of social media to see."

"Oooh." Carrissa's eyes bulge and her smile widens. "This guy is a heavy hitter. I like it."

"I'll add to that wager," Milo says with a nod. "The losing team also must make a team donation of a collective 1 million to the charity of the winning team's choice."

Barrett slams his hand down on the table. "Done!"

Milo and Barrett shake hands as the rest of us raise our glasses in agreement.

"Hey Carissa," Ella says with a smirk on her face and twinkle in her eye. "Remind me to tell you about a really fun competition your guys can have. Just for you wives of course."

Rory laughs. "And maybe we should tell you about the competition we made these asshats have while in Key West at the end of last season."

Tatum roars with laughter. "Oh, my God, best day of my life."

"Wait." Dex's brows furrow. "I thought the day you met me and we...you know...I thought that was the best day of your life."

She pats his face endearingly, saying, "You're right, honey. Totally right." But then she turns back to me Ella and shakes her head, whispering, "Not even close."

CORRIGAN

It's just after dawn when I enter Dad's house with two glasses of coffee and a couple pastries from his favorite bakery around the corner. I'm not in the kitchen more than ten minutes gathering plates and napkins for us both before Dad walks in and sees me sitting at the table.

"Corrigan? When did you get here?"

"Few minutes ago," I tell him. "I brought coffee and pastries from Louise's Bakery. The kind you like." I gesture to the seat next to me. "Sit."

I see the trepidation in his eyes. He can't tell if he's about to be ripped a new ass crack or if I'm here to make nice. I suppose up until a few minutes ago, even I wasn't sure.

I'm still not.

But I have to say what needs to be said.

I watch Dad while he sits and reaches for the coffee I brought him and then I take a sip of mine as he sips his.

"Mmm. Thank you for this."

"You're welcome."

I hold back a moment, hoping that maybe Dad will start this much needed conversation but he doesn't. So, in his place, I simply state, "I love him, Dad."

And then I wait.

He bows his head and takes another slow sip of his coffee, turning my words over in his head before he responds. "Tell me everything."

"What would you like to know?"

Finally, his eyes meet mine. "For starters, I'd like to know how you met."

Reaching for the box of pastries, I tell him, "Actually that was all your fault."

"My fault?"

"I sent you a text message months ago about leaving left-over spaghetti for you in the fridge. Remember that?"

"Vaguely."

"Well, the text you got was actually my second attempt. My first attempt never got to you because I sent it to the wrong number."

His brows furrow. "Okay..."

"And then that wrong number answered me. And we texted

back and forth about food." I rip a piece of the orange cranberry scone I picked for myself off and toss it into my mouth. "We talked back and forth via text for days having no idea who each other was."

"You never told him your name? He never told you his?"

"I told him my name was Corri." I shrug. "Everybody calls me Corri. You call me Corri. Plus, it meant I wasn't giving my full name...you know, in case he was a creeper."

Dad actually chuckles at that comment. "Smart girl."

"Dad, I didn't know Bodhi was Bodhi until the night we decided to meet for the first time. He told me his name was Alan, which is his—"

"Middle name," he says, nodding.

"Yeah. The night we met, he gave me zero indication that he knew who I was, and why would he? I spent the last few years in London so he wouldn't know who I am."

"But you knew who he was."

I cock my head. "Dad, am I your daughter or am I your daughter? Of course, I knew who he was immediately. I could've rattled his stats off to him faster than he probably could've told me himself."

"That's the truth." He laughs again and I breathe a little easier hoping that maybe I'm getting somewhere with him. Maybe I'm lightening the tension.

"This is where it gets...I don't know, awkward," I warn him.

Dad's face goes still. "Did he hurt you? Did he say something to you?"

"No, no, no. Nothing like that Dad, but in our conversations he was very vulnerable and I was a safe space for him. He trusted me and I wasn't about to betray his trust just because I recognized him. So, I kept the secret to myself. He had no idea for weeks that he was falling for his coach's daughter."

"When did he figure it out? When did you tell him?"

"I didn't tell him," I murmur, bowing my head. "We walked into Harold's together that day, remember? And the team was there?"

Dad's jaw drops. "Corrigan Hicks. Are you telling me he saw us together that day and that's the first time he learned about who you were?"

I nod slowly. "I'm not proud of it, Dad. I should've told him. I know I should've told him. I took that responsibility and I apologized profusely because I felt horrible."

"So, you didn't really lose a patient that day? You were just upset about lying to Bodhi?"

"Oh, no, I really did lose a patient. All this hit at the same time and it was a hot mess and I was a dumpster fire but," I add, raising my head to meet Dad's gaze, "he stuck by me through all of it. He held me while I cried my eyes out over that little boy, Dad. He sat on the couch all night long because I fell asleep with my head on his chest. He helped me unpack my apartment so it wouldn't be a mess if you stopped over." I reach over and lay my hand over his. "He loves me, Dad. He cares about me and I care about him."

I sit up a little taller having gotten that all off my chest. "I love you, Dad. I do, but I'm an adult now and I'm very good at making my own decisions. I'm responsible and I'm a good judge of character." I bob my head. "Except for Leo, of course, because you taught me those traits. And so, I'm here this morning to tell you that I love Bodhi Roche. And we're together now. And we're serious. And you don't have to love that I'm with him. It's okay if you don't. But you do have to respect my decisions as an adult, because I'm not your little girl anymore."

Tears well up in his eyes and his nose crinkles the way it does when he's trying not to cry, but then he whispers, "Corri you will always be my little girl."

"I suppose that's true." I give him a soft smile.

"I'm sorry I gave you such a hard time last night," he finally says. "And I'm sorry I insinuated you were a...a..."

I raise my brows. "A whore?"

"Yeah. That." He cringes shamefully. "I guess I didn't exactly have the best night last night. But seeing someone attached to my little girl like that was..." He shakes his head. "I wasn't ready for it."

"Well, for what it's worth, I'm sorry we threw you for a loop, but I'm happy Dad. Bodhi makes me really happy."

He finally reaches for his favorite double chocolate chip muffin from the box of pastries and takes a bite. "He treats you well? Because if that little shit ever does something to hurt you..."

Relaxing a bit more now, I smile at my dad. "If he ever hurts me, you'll be the first to know...er..." I cock my head and cringe slightly. "Okay second to know."

We both look at each other and in tandem shrug and say, "Layken."

CHAPTER TWENTY-EIGHT
BODHI

"So, you're doing it?" Griffin asks, whispering as much as he can with both of us riding exercise bikes.

"Yeah."

"Today?"

"Yep."

"Before or after the game?"

"Before."

He blows out a breath. "Do you think that's a good idea?"

"Why wouldn't it be?"

"What are we whispering about over here, gentlemen?" Ledger tosses his towel and water bottle on the floor and swings his leg over the bike on the opposite side of me.

Griffin gestures to me in the mirror in front of us. "He's doing it today."

Ledger glances at me. "You are?"

I nod confidently. "I am."

"Before or after the game?"

"Before."

He cringes. "Oooh, do you think that's a good idea?"

"What's a good idea?" Harrison grills, having pulled his earbuds from his ears.

Griffin tilts his head, nodding toward me. "Roche is doing it."

Harrison's brows shoot up. "Today?"

"Yeah," Ledger answers.

"Wait..." He brings his hands to his hips and cocks his head. "Before or after the game?"

"Uh...before?" I pose it as a question this time because now that I've told Griffin and Ledger, their responses have me wondering if I'm making a horrible mistake.

Harrison shakes his head, doubtful. "You sure that's a good idea, man?"

"I don't know. I figured it's the best option."

"Hey guys!" Ella walks into the gym along side August. "What's the word?"

In tandem, Griffin, Ledger, and Harrison all say, "Bodhi's doing it."

Ella stops and gives her husband a knowing glance before she asks, "Today?"

"Yeah."

Ella moves toward one of the treadmills while August takes the last bike in the row. "Uh, dude, you sure that's a good idea?"

"Why wouldn't it be a good time?"

"What's not a good time?" Oliver asks, emerging from the bathroom. "Because I just took the biggest shit of my life and let me tell you, a good time was had by all."

"You're a sick fuck, Magallan," Ledger says, laughing.

Oliver grins, accepting Ledger's label but winks at him regardless. "But I have a good time."

"Oliver, Bodhi says he's doing it. Today."

"Today?"

I nod.

"You're sure?"

"I'm sure."

"Before or after the game?"

"After."

Everyone's heads turn toward me with looks of confusion on their faces.

"Dude," August frowns. "That's not what you just sa—"

"I know it's not what I just said but each and every one of you seem to think before the game is a bad idea so I changed my answer." I turn my body while continuing to peddle. "Where the fuck is Bear?"

Oliver shrugs. "Goalie warmup. Why?"

I shake my head. "No reason."

"So, if you do it after the game, and we lose..."

"We're not going to lose, Ollenberg," I scoff, passing Griffin a scornful look.

"I'm just saying if that were to happen, Coach will be in a pissy mood and that's not going to do you any favors."

Ugh. Obviously.

"But if I do it before the game?"

"I mean..." Ledger's head bobs back and forth. "The guy's in game mode. He's going over plays and all the regular gameday shit. Is he going to have time for this?"

"Yeah," Harrison adds. "Do you think before is a good time?"

A little irritated if not overwhelmed by all their concern for my timing I throw my arms up and shout, "Is there ever a good time to tell a man you've been fucking his daughter privately for months and now you want to date her publicly?"

"ROCHE!" a stern voice calls from the gym door.

The very wide-open door.

Fuuuuuuuuuck meeeeeeeee.

I'm dead.

He heard me, right?

He had to have heard me.

All the averted eyes in the room tells me yes, yes he heard every word.

"Coach?"

His nostrils flare and his jaw clenches and then I watch as he takes a steadying breath before he demands, "My Office. Now."

"Sure thing, Coach."

Oh fuck.

Shit.

Hell.

I might be a dead man.

Yep. That's me.

Dead man walking.

I spring off the bike careful not to smash my nutsack though it's all but shriveled up and died at the moment anyway. Then I reach for my water bottle and towel, wiping the sweat off my face. Everyone's heads begin to rise as the guys and Ella all stare at me.

I square my shoulders and take a deep breath and tell them, "Well, I guess it's happening now."

"It was nice knowing you, Pickle Pants," Harrison says.

"Thanks, Meers."

Before I even make it to the door, Ella's on me, wrapping her arms around my neck and giving me a huge hug. "You can do hard things, Bodhi Roche. Lumin believes in you."

'Thanks Ella."

"You're doing this for Corrigan." She pulls back and looks me in the eye. "Because you love her."

"I do love her."

She swats my ass. "Then get in there and do what you have to do."

I move silently down the hall inwardly pepping myself up because Ella is right. I'm doing this for Corrigan.

I'm doing this for us.

When I reach Coach's office, I don't even bother knocking. He's sitting at his desk so I step inside the door and wait for his instruction.

"Sit."

Yep. That's all he says.

So, I move around to the other side of his desk and take a seat in one of the two chairs settled there.

Do I wait for him to start?

Or do I just take the bull by the horns?

He's just staring at me.

Why isn't he saying anything?

I should say something.

Okay. I'll go.

"Look, Coach, I think we—"

"I owe you an apology Roche," he finally says, interrupting me.

I'm sorry...what now?

"Oh. Uh..."

I'm not really sure what to say here.

He wipes his hand down his face and then leans back into his big comfy office chair. "My daughter...she's uh..." He fidgets with a pen in his hand, obsessively clicking it in and out.

Click click.

Click click.

Click click.

"Coach?"

"She loves you, Roche. Corrigan." He finally raises his gaze to look me in the eye. "She loves you."

"Sir..."

"Do you love her?"

His question actually throws me off guard. Never in a gazillion years did I think I would ever find myself sitting with Coach Hicks talking about love.

"I love her more than anything, Sir."

His brow lifts. "More than hockey?"

"Without a shadow of a doubt. If being with your daughter means ending my hockey career, I'll go clean out my locker right fucking now."

"Well, let's not go that far, son."

"I'm not your son."

Shit.

I squeeze my eyes closed in response to my own dickishness.

"I'm sorry, Sir. I didn't mean to be an asshole."

"It's alright." He eyes me. "But you do realize if there's a future with my daughter, you could end up being my son-in-law one day?"

"Yes, Sir. I understand." I lift my head. "But you should understand that my father passed away several years ago and uh...we were really close. He didn't get to see me make it into the league. He gave me everything, so the term son is...well, it's..."

"I get it," he says. "I'm sorry he didn't get to see you move up. I'm sure he would've been damn proud to see all you've accomplished. You've come a long way."

Fuck, why is he being so nice?

"Thank you, Coach."

"So, back to my daughter." He leans forward, propping his elbows up on his desk. "Your reputation with women precedes you. How do I know you're going to be faithful to her and treat her how she deserves to be treated? Because I'll be honest. I'm not a fan of the things I've heard out of Boston."

My cheeks heat and I shake my head in disbelief that I'm about to say these next words to my coach but fuck it.

Here goes nothing.

"Would it help if I told you none of those rumors have any truth to them whatsoever and that I was virgin before I met your daughter?"

I don't think I've ever seen a man look both like he's about to throw up but also fall over in shock. His jaw wide open, his brows pinch, and he cocks his head.

"Come again?"

Deep breath.

"I was a virgin, Sir. Before I met Corrigan."

"A fucking virgin?"

"Yes, Sir."

He bursts into laughter so hard and loud I fear he may end up losing his breath and dying of a heart attack right in front of my eyes.

"Oh fuck, Corrigan must've had a field day with you!" He laughs. "A fucking virgin!"

If you only knew.

Wiping tears from his eyes and finally calming down he says, "Well, damn Roche. I certainly hope she was gentle with you, because if she's anything like her mother was..."

I shake my head trying not to cringe too hard. "Some things I don't need to know, Sir. It's probably best we don't discuss it."

"Fuck no, we're not discussing it. There are some aspects of a daughter's life her father does not need to know and this is one of them." He shakes the thoughts from his head and continues. "Oh fuck...a virgin. That's..." he shakes his head again. "That's something. But listen, as I said when you came in here, I owe you an apology. My actions the other night were misguided, unprofessional, and a bit irrational."

A bit?

"I'm sorry too, Sir," I tell him. "I shouldn't have even had her there in the first place."

"Nah," he waves me off, "Between you and me, I did the same thing with her mother on more than one occasion. But maybe don't tell Corrigan that." He winks and I finally allow myself to laugh.

Just a little bit.

"Deal."

"So, what's the plan for you two. Have you talked about it?"

"Uh, no. Not really. Honestly, because of all the time I spent focusing on hockey, I've never really been in a relationship before. So, I'd really like to date her."

"Date her?" His brows lift. "Isn't that what you two have been doing for a while now?"

If by dating you mean...fucking.

A lot of fucking.

Then yes.

"We never went out anywhere publicly because we didn't want to risk being recognized and having you find out before we could talk to you about it. She didn't want you to find out the way you did, obviously. Regardless though, Corrigan deserves to be taken out on fancy dates and fun dates and I want to be able to show her off in public as my girl."

The corner of his mouth tips up just enough that I know he doesn't mind the idea of that at all.

"You know the last guy she was with was a fucking twat. That's what they say over there in England. They call them twats."

"Right." I nod, stifling my laugh. "She told me about him. But I promise you I have no intention of hurting Corrigan, Sir. I'm in love with her and if I have my way, she'll be wearing my number for the rest of her hockey loving life."

He nods, his eyes studying me for several seconds before he finally says, "Well, alright then."

"Okay?"

"Not that you need my blessing," he says. "Because my blessing doesn't mean shit, but for what it's worth, if my daughter has to fall in love with someone, I can appreciate the fact she's fallen for you. You're a good man, Bodhi. And I can see that you're good for her. Thank you for being in her corner."

Wow.

This is not at all how I expected this conversation to go.

"Uh, yeah. Of course. Anything she needs."

Coach stands and holds out his hand. "Good luck to you, Roche. My daughter can be a feisty one. She's headstrong for sure."

Returning his handshake, I add, "She's also compassionate, kind, funny as hell, and has great taste in food."

I follow him as we head for the door of his office and he pats me on the back. "Mario's?"

My eyes grow at the mention of our favorite Italian restaurant, the subject of which was our first textual encounter and I nod. "Mario's."

Once Coach is down the hall and out of earshot, I sprint to the locker room where the guys are getting dressed for tonight's game against the Chicago Red Tails.

I push open the door and all heads turn, expectant faces watching me to decipher how our conversation went.

Am I a dead man?

Or do I live to see another day?

Taking the deepest fucking breath I think I've ever taken, I blow it out and crumble against the set of lockers next to me. "We're good. I survived."

I imagine a collective unclenching of everyone's assholes happens around the room. Shoulders relax and smiles abound as the guys each give me their congratulations and pats on the back

"So, what are you going to do now?" Griffin asks me. "Is there a plan?"

Beaming back at him I nod. "Yeah. Actually, I do have a bit of a plan. I just need to find Ella first."

"I just left her in her dressing room," August tells me. "She's getting into costume."

"Perfect!"

I watch from my spot on the bench as Oliver faces off against Milo Landric to start the game. Landric wins and passes to Malone but Ollenberg's on his tail as Malone moves the puck down the ice. There's Blackstone taking it back and passing to Dayne. He goes for the setup and passes back to Magallan who tries to make it in but, no! Zeke Miller doesn't allow it.

Ledger comes off his shift and I hit the ice running in his place as Meers takes the puck away from Shay. He sends the puck to Landric who tries to sidestep Ollenberg who is relentless in his block, but I cut inside and steal that little rubber fucker from right under Landric's nose. With Foster and Nelson hot on my ass, I set up the play beautifully for Blackstone but he doesn't hit the target.

Fuck!

I swing around the net to take possession back, sending the puck over to Magallan who shouts, "Yours, Roche! Here comes the assist!" He tosses to Blackstone who sets up one of the offensive plays we talked about when studying the tapes and then I spot my opening.

Yes!

Positioning myself between Foster and Nelson, I drive them back until I know I'm close enough, spin around the net like a rebounded play, and push the puck inside. The sirens go off and the net lights up and the home crowd is on their feet.

"LET'S GOOOOO!"

"FUCK YEAH!"

"THAT'A BOY PICKLE PANTS!"

The guys all crowd around me, giving me hugs and high fives, slapping my helmet and spanking my ass, but all I care about is the beautiful woman I see standing two rows behind the bench. The woman wearing my jersey with my number on her back. The woman cheering for me so loudly I can practically hear her voice over the entire arena. The woman I can't wait to take home tonight.

The woman I can't wait to sink myself into.

The love of my life.

My Corrigan.

CHAPTER TWENTY-NINE

CORRIGAN

"Holy shit this game is action packed!" Layken says next to me as we watch the end of the second period. Thanks to the amazing comradery between the Stars and the Red Tails, this game has been free of any major fights and really, only a handful of penalties. When the bell rings for the end of the period, both teams leave the ice.

"What's that?" I ask her as I watch Bodhi skate off the ice.

Man, does he look good in that uniform or what?

Before the game I got a text from Bodhi explaining that he had an interesting conversation with my father. For a moment I worried that perhaps this was going to be a tense night until he told me he had my dad laughing so hard he cried. That coupled with the fact that my dad gave me a huge hug when he saw Layken and me in our usual spots behind the bench told me whatever they talked about, we were going to be perfectly fine.

"Uh huh...I get it." Layken laughs. "You can't keep your eyes off your little sex toy down there."

"Can you blame me though?" I ask with a lovesick sigh. "He's just so fucking hot in that uniform."

"Tell me about it." I turn my head to catch her eye but she's watching someone on the ice too, which makes me smile.

We're up four to three at the end of the second period. Layken and I take part in the usual chants and cheers with the rest of the crowd, watching Lumin, the shooting star, do her thing not too far from where we're seated and then before I know it, she's coming this way.

"Hey Lumin! Lookin' good out there babe!" I shout when she gets close enough. She brings her yellow furry hands to her chest and then makes a heart shape with her fingers and then pretends to sprinkle me with her stardust magic.

"Aww, thank you!"

But she doesn't stop there.

She wraps her hand around mine and escorts me out of the seat.

"Where are we going, Lumin?"

She doesn't answer me of course but I feel Ella squeeze my hand so I completely trust her as she brings me down to the ice. The guard opens a section of the wall so I can be on the ice where Lumin hands me off to Remi Redtail. She follows us to the center of the ice and when I look back at her, now that we're out of earshot from anyone, I hear Remi say, "Trust me, Corri. You got this."

Remi Redtail gives me a hug and a high five and then begins to chase Lumin around the ice—much to the crowd's entertainment. Lumin outskates Remi by a mile and he falls to his stomach chasing after her. The crowd cheers for Lumin who twirls happily and shakes her sparkly wand.

A moment later we're joined by Zeke Miller, goalie for the Red Tails who heads straight to the net and a member of Anaheim's front office activities team. Her name is Marlee. With a microphone in one hand and a hockey stick in the other,

Marlee hands the stick to me and then explains to the crowd what they're about to see.

"Alright whoooooo's ready for a little half rink hockey?"

While the crowd cheers, I happen to look down at the stick in my hands, a message written in gold sharpie along the black tape reads

Don't miss. It's for the kids. I believe in you - Bodhi.

"What in the world?" I mumble but shake my head in amusement.

"With us tonight we have none other than Miss Corrigan Hicks! For those of you who might not be familiar, she is the daughter of our favorite Anaheim Stars head coach, let's give it up for Corrigan!"

The crowd cheers again and I take a moment to give them a wave and a smile as Marlee continues.

"Corrigan has no idea what we're doing here tonight or why we pulled her out to the ice, so allow me to explain. Last night, the Anaheim Stars, together with the Chicago Red Tails, helped raise over eight million dollars for the Pacific Children's Hospital. The Anaheim Stars family gives our sincere thank you to the Red Tails for their help and generosity in raising these much needed and very important funds. But the members of the Red Tails team decided eight million dollars is not enough and they'd like to challenge Corrigan here to raise a little more.

What the...?

Marlee turns to me. "So, Corrigan, you have one puck and you have a stick in your hands." She gestures to the net where Zeke Miller stands. "If you can shoot the puck from right here and get it into the net, the Chicago Red Tails have agreed to pay a combined one million dollars out of their own pockets to bring your total to nine million dollars raised."

"Whaaaaat?"

My jaw drops and I cover my mouth with my hands in complete shock.

"That's crazy!"

"Do you think you're up for the challenge?"

Remi waves his feathers to get the crowd to cheer and Lumin claps her hands excitely, twirling on my behalf.

I nod to Marlee. "Hell yeah, I'll give it a try!"

Lumin and Remi lead the crowd in a slow clap for me as I position myself behind the puck and steady my stick in my hands. Glancing down once more at Bodhi's sweet handwritten message on the stick tape, I rear back my arms and slap the stick to the ice shoving the puck forward. The crowd is on their feet cheering as we watch the puck slide across the ice in anticipation. Zeke hunkers down ready to block the shot but knowing this is for the money, I don't see why he would ever block my shot.

My shot that is actually heading straight ahead!

My shot that is now only a few feet from the net!

Don't stop!

Don't stop!

Don't stop!

Zeke spreads his legs at the last minute and the puck slides right through and into the net!

"HOLY SHIT!"

The crowd goes wild and tears of gratitude fill my eyes and spill down my cheeks. Lumin gives me a huge hug and then leads me down to the goalie to say my thank you to Zeke Miller. Except when Zeke takes his helmet off, it's not Zeke at all.

"Bodhi?"

He beams back at me and skates forward, scooping me up in

his arms and spinning me with his arms wrapped tightly around my body.

"Congratulations, babe! I knew you could do it!"

"This is so crazy! Nine million dollars!"

"Fuckin' right. It's for a great cause. How could we say no?"

"I know you did this, Bodhi Roche."

He shrugs, still smiling at me. "I'd do anything for you, Corrigan. I love you so fucking much."

"I love you too."

"I have something for you."

"For me?"

"Yeah. Maybe Lumin can help me out."

What?

I turn and find Lumin holding a flat square box in her hands wrapped in a yellow bow.

"Bodhi! What is this?"

"Open it babe."

I pull open the lid of the box and inside is a beautiful shining gold necklace with an elegant star diamond pendant.

"It's not a ring," Bodhi explains. "But it's still my commitment to you. Because before I ask you to marry me, and believe me, I will absofuckinglutley ask you to marry me one day, I want to date you."

God, I can't wipe this giddy smile off my face.

"You want to date me?"

He nods. "Hell, yeah I do. I want to take you out on the town. I want to eat at Mario's with you. I want to take you to that ramen place, and to Harold's for all the hot dogs. I want to travel with you and spend days and nights with you and treat you like the precious queen that you are. So, will you say yes? Will you date me?"

I shake my head in disbelief. "Bodhi Roche, it would make

me the happiest woman on the planet to date you! Yes! Of course!"

He wraps me in a hug again, lifting me up and pressing his lips to mine. "Now lift the velvet backing from the box."

"Wait, what?"

"You heard me," he laughs. "Lift it out."

Lumin still holding onto the box, I carefully lift the backing out of the gift box and find a folded piece of paper. I pull the paper from the box and unfold it and squeal when I see what it is.

"HOLY FUCKING SHIT!"

"Wait, wait, wait, ladies and gentlemen, I do believe we might have another amazing announcement," Marlee states into the microphone. Bodhi skates me over to her where I show her the handwritten check for another million dollars for the Pacific Children's Hospital from the pockets of the Anaheim Stars.

It's ANOTHER MILLION DOLLARS FROM OUR STAAAAAARS!" I shout to the crowd who erupts in excitement. Once the announcement is made, both teams make their way onto the ice to start the last period of the game, but not before they all swing by to give me their congratulations and I my thank yous to all of them. Bodhi takes me off the ice and into the tunnel along with Remi, Lumin, and Marlee.

"Holy shit! I did not expect any of this! How did you make this happen?" I ask Bodhi.

He merely shrugs like it was easier than stepping into his underwear. "Nothing is impossible when you're in love."

"You got all these guys to donate more of their own money?"

"Hell yeah. I wasn't going to let you go with eight million when I knew we could make it an even ten."

"How?"

"Because I'm the boy who lived."

My brows furrow. "You're Harry Potter?"

He laughs. "No. I'm the boy who lived...to tell the tale of how I won over the coach. The coach who also happens to be your father."

I throw my head back in laughter.

"Oh, my God! I love you so much, you crazy goof!"

"And I love you." He kisses me again and then gestures to the Red Tails uniform he's wearing and says, "I need to get out of this fucking red piece of shit. It makes me itchy. And then we're going to win this game and then we're going out to celebrate and I'm going to kiss the fuck out of you in front of all the press and tell the whole world that you belong to me."

"I can't wait." I kiss his cheek and then smack his ass, not that he can feel it with all the padding he's wearing. "Go get 'em Roche. Show them how it's done."

Want to know what happens right after the Stars win their game?
Visit my website to subscribe to my newsletter!

Want a sneak peek of the next book in the Anaheim Stars Series? Read on for an excerpt of What If I See You!

WHAT IF I SEE YOU EXCERPT

GRIFFIN

"Flip the wiener, Ollenberg!"

"I'm doing it, Blackstone! I'm doing—"

"No, you're not! You're fucking it up!" He gripes, flustered and frustrated. "Hurry up before they flip their cock! Fucking flip the goddamn wiener already and make it stick this time!"

"Do you not see my eyes are closed?" I shout back, my adrenaline soaring to levels similar to when I'm about to score a goal. I slap my hands across the table trying to locate my wiener. "Help me find my wiener guys, because I can't see for shit right now!"

"Got that right," Ella laughs. She claps her hands. "Scarlett is the queen of the cock! You get it girl! Wrap your hand around that girthy cock and flip the hell out of it!"

"Yeah," Corrigan adds, snickering. "Double fist it so it doesn't slip from your grasp and then you flip that cock like your life depends on it!"

Finally, my hand connects with the rubber wiener I flipped a few seconds ago and I grip it in my hands.

"Yes Griff! You've got it." Harrison is so the better teammate when it comes to game night. Always supportive. Never a dick like the rest of us. "Now flip it! Flip it good!"

I toss the wiener lightly up in the air and hear the recognizable sound of the suction cup bottom hitting the tabletop. It's followed by pats on the back and cheers from my teammates.

"FUCK YES! You did it, Ollenberg!" Bodhi exclaims.

"Knew you would get it done, man," Ledger says, clapping for me.

"Finally." Barrett rolls his eyes but smirks at the same time. "A man should know how to stick his wiener by now, Ollenberg."

"That was an impressive wiener grip," Ella tells me with a conceding nod.

I shrug my shoulders. "It's nothing really. I've been practicing for this my whole life."

She laughs. "Gripping your wiener or flipping it?"

"Don't let him full you, babe," August says, wrapping an arm around his wife. "Griffin's hand rarely leaves his wiener. The fact he let it slip a few times there was a rarity in itself."

"No kidding," I laugh with my friend and shake out my hand. "I was beginning to think someone pranked me by rubbing lube all over that wiener before I even touched it."

Scarlett nudges Ella and murmurs, "Good idea. We better remember that for next time."

I lean forward. "You're not invited next time, Dayne."

"What?" Ledger steps out from the kitchen with two beers in his hand. One for himself and one he's holding out to me. "What the fuck for? I brought you a beer and everything?"

"Sorry, Ledge. I was talking to your cousin over here."

"Yeah, your friend is a sorry loser, Ledger," Scarlett winks at me. She knows I know she's kidding but at least she lets me hate on her for a few minutes anyway."

One of the cellphones piled up on the coffee table in front of us dings bringing our attention to the center of the room.

"Whose is it?" I ask.

"Mine, I think," Corrigan says.

"Better answer it in case it's daddy dearest." We all laugh but I'm pretty damn sure there are seven buttholes in this room that just puckered at the thought of Corrigan's dad, who just happens to be our coach, showing up at our hangout. Don't get me wrong. We love the guy, but that doesn't mean we want to be playing Cock verse Wiener, or realistically named Chicken Vs Hotdog, with him. Especially Bodhi. He's a brave guy for sticking up for his love for the coach's daughter. Things may have started out super weird for the two of them but watching them together these past several weeks has been fun. Corrigan is great and she fits in with Scarlett and Ella and of course all of us so well.

Okay, okay, maybe I'm just a tiny bit jealous, but who wouldn't be? Oliver and August and even Pickle-pants himself, Bodhi, have found partners who make them deliriously happy. It's cute and gives me the warm fuzzies even if I do want to throw up in my mouth sometimes watching them all lovey-dovey together.

"Oh nooooo!" Corrigan's brows pull together as she reads the message on her phone.

"Who is it, babe?" Bodhi asks, his hands around her waist.

"It's Layken. She lost her job."

"Wait," I scowl. "What? Layken from the hospital?" I've worked with her a few times. As the Development Coordinator for Pacific Children's charity foundation, she introduced herself to us several years ago when she took on the job and Coach got involved playing Santa for the kids during the holidays. We've always helped wherever and whenever we could and just a few months ago we helped out with her Children's Art Auction. It was a huge fundraiser for the hospital. The largest they've had to date.

Corrigan nods her head. "Yeah. She says when the hospital got bought out two weeks ago, she had a feeling in her gut that she wouldn't get to stay because the guy from University Hospital has seniority over her."

"Brandon Jeffries?" Harrison asks but Corrigan shrugs and shakes her head.

"I don't know him. Is that his name?"

Harrison nods. "Yeah. The guy's about five years too late for retirement if you ask me. He hasn't done shit when it comes to community involvement in his fundraising for years. He merely writes to the celebrity agents and encourages them to have their clients make year-end donations. Tax write-off for them and a financial win for the hospital."

"Ugh, so there goes any fun for the kids who are actually stuck inside the walls of the hospital." Ella frowns.

"And there goes my best friend's job," Corrigan mumbles.

"Where is she now?" Bodhi asks her.

"Heading home, I guess." Her thumbs trace across her phone as she texts her friend and then it dings again.

"Nah. Tell her to come here," I tell Corrigan. "She shouldn't be alone when the world just shit on her."

Corrigan turns to me, her eyes hopeful. "Are you sure? I don't want her to be alone either."

"Of course." I shrug. "We're just hanging out. Maybe it'll help distract her from a shit end of her day. And besides," I say raising the bottle in my hand. "I've got alcohol. Just tell her to check in at the security desk and give her name. I'll call down there and make sure they know to let her in. What's her last name again?"

"Hobbs. Layken Hobbs. Thank you so much, Griffin. You're the best."

She sends a few more texts to her friend and then sets her phone back on the coffee table. "She's on her way. Thanks again, Griffin. I really appreciate it."

"Don't mention it. How do they say it? *Mi Casa es moo Casa.*"

Corrigan laughs. "Yeah something like that."

"You know he's just inviting her here to flirt with her and eventually get into her pants right?" Ledger snickers from across the room.

I flip him off. "What the hell are you talking about Dayne?"

"Poor vulnerable woman meets flirty aloof hockey guy who promises a night to wash away all her hurt and anger. Come on. It's not like you haven't played that card before."

Standing to reach for my phone I bring a hand to my chest. "Who me? Come on, Ledge. I may be a helpless flirt much of the time, but I would never do that. She's Corri's best friend and she's had a shitty day. Any friend of hers is a friend of ours."

I don't miss the corner of Corrigan's mouth lifting and wonder what she might be thinking but push away the thought. "Plus, it's not like she doesn't know us. Surely we can help lift her spirits a little for the rest of the evening. I'm just trying to be nice."

"I think it's very nice of you Griffin. She'll appreciate it very much."

I raise my brows and cock my head at Ledger. "See?"

Fifteen minutes later, there's a knock at my door. I get up to answer it and Corrigan comes with me ready to offer a welcoming hug to her best friend. I turn the knob and open my door and in tandem, Corrigan and I drop our jaws and stare at the crying wet mess of a woman standing before us.

Sometimes when it comes to women I think I'm Superman. I can get a woman to laugh or smile so easily thanks to my positive and fun-loving personality. But if there's a kryptonite to my Superman, it's a woman in tears. I'm too empathetic of a person to see anyone cry, let alone a woman. I don't like to hurt people because I know what it feels like to be hurt by someone so anytime I see a woman crying I feel for them immediately and try to do anything to make them feel better.

But this?

Layken Hobbs standing in my doorway, the front of her literally soaking wet and splashed with mud, dripping from her hair, her face and her body.

Yeah. I don't know how to fix this.

"Oh no! Layken! What the hell happened?" Corrigan is pulling her inside while I shut the door.

"Are you hurt?" I ask her sincerely concerned. Everyone already seated around the living room turns to see what's going on.

"No. I'm fine," Layken squeaks, trying to reign in her tears but failing miserably. "I mean my ego is obliterated and my tits are a soggy mess but what's another sprinkle on top of my shit sundae anyway?"

Well, that's a way of putting it.

Also, I'm not looking at her soggy tits.

Rephrase: I'm trying very hard not to look at her soggy tits.

But she said soggy tits and now I really, really, REALLY, need to look at them.

Just a quick peek.

Won't hurt anyone, right?

Okay. Yep. They're a hot mess.

Wet. Muddy. Well defined under her sopping blouse.

Probably very pretty when not covered in mud.

Actually, even splashed with mud they're pretty.

Wait. No.

She's crying.

Not funny, Griffin.

Okay all done looking at the soggy tits.

See?

Didn't hurt anyone.

"What happened to you?"

"I parked around the corner and was walking down the sidewalk and out of nowhere this asshole driver got a little too close to the sidewalk," she starts and then cocks her head bobbing it this way and that. "Or now that I think about it, he probably did it on purpose because he's a pecker pinching wiener beater, drove right through a huge puddle on the road and it soaked me from head to toe."

Pecker pinching wiener beater...

She said that like it's a nickname she uses every day.

A girl after my own heart.

"Oh Lake, I'm so sorry," Corrigan tells her. "Let's get you cleaned up." She turns to me. "Do you have anything she can change into?"

"No," Layken shakes her head. "That's o—"

"Of course, I do. I've got a closet full of comfy pants and sweatshirts." He gestures to his bedroom. "If you don't care that they're not the most fashionable, I'll grab you a few things. And feel free to use my shower if you want to wash off. We can wash and dry your clothes while you're here if you want."

"That's so kind of you, Griffin." She sniffles and my chest tightens.

"It's nothing. Give me two minutes and I'll have you all set up and ready to go."

I leave her Layken with Corrigan and run back to my bedroom quickly picking up any random dirty clothes on the floor and tossing them into my hamper and then I double check my bed to make sure it's completely made and looks nice. Not that I'm trying to impress anyone, but I certainly don't want to come across like a slob or someone who doesn't care. Once the room looks presentable, I throw open my closet and look through everything I have that could possibly fit Layken's body without sliding off of her completely. Obviously, everything I have will be too big for her, but I find a pair of pajama pants with a tie on the front so she can adjust them and then I grab a t-shirt and one of my hockey sweatshirts so she can choose whatever she wants.

I lay the clothes out on my bed and then step into my bathroom to make sure it's presentable too. I pull out a couple clean towels and place them in the warmer for her and then meet them both back out in the living room where Layken is wiping her face with a paper towel.

"I've laid out a few things on my bed and there are towels in the towel warmer for you if you want to jump in the shower. I can show you where everything is if you want."

Layken glances at me, her honey-brown eyes the shape of saucers. Her gaze reminds me of a sad lost puppy dog and I swear to God if she asks for a fucking pony right now I'll do all I can to get one for her. "Are you sure you're okay with that?"

"Absolutely." I smile at her and nod. "My house is your house. Whatever I can get for you so you're comfortable."

Her voice is soft and meek. A change from the woman I've known to be peppy, confident and witty on any regular day. "Thank you. Griffin."

"You're welcome." She follows me back down the hall silently except for the random sniffling, and for the first time ever, I'm struggling to come up with something to say.

For the love of Christ, say something, Griffin.
Anything.
Put the girl out of her misery.
"Maybe when you're done you can flip the cock."
What the fuck?
Mother fucking hell, Griffin!
Anything but that!

Cringing, I turn to see her staring at me, one brow raised. I shake my head and palm my forehead laughing nervously.

"Shit. I'm sorry. That came out all wrong."

She chuckles. "You think?"

She chuckled.

I heard it.

She's had a shit day but there, right there.

I made her laugh.

"I'm sorry. We we're...it was a...this game...earlier...I forgot you weren't here and have no idea what I'm talking about."

"I'm sorry, I don't. But cock flipping sounds...interesting."

"I'm really sorry to hear about your job."

"Thanks," she says with a shrug before she pushes back her shoulders. "I know at some point I'll get to my when-one-door-closes-another-one-opens phase, but for now, it's just been a super fucking terrible day and I just need to wallow."

"You have my full permission to wallow all you want. I'll even give you a beer if you want when you're done."

"Got anything stronger than a beer?"

"Vodka? Tequila? Bourbon?"

"Vodka would be perfect."

"Vodka it is. Towels are in that dryer right there," I tell her gesturing to the heated box next to the shower. Feel free to use anything in here. I hope you don't mind the pajama pants." I gesture to the ones I have on. "It's kind of my thing."

"I'm aware. And it's perfectly fine. Thank you again, Griffin. I really appreciate your kindness."

"Of course. Anytime. If there's anything else you need, just ask."

I rejoin the group in the living room making small talk and head to the kitchen to pour Layken a drink. "Corrigan, what does Layken like in her vodka?"

"Cranberry juice if you have it?"

I swing open the door to the fridge and smile when I spy a bottle of cranberry juice inside. "Yep. Got it."

Several minutes later, Layken steps out into the living room, and my chest tightens all over again. Wearing a pair of light blue pajama pants with cinnamon rolls all over them that she's rolled at the bottom and my hockey sweatshirt that is four sizes too big on her, she's the cutest thing I think I've ever seen. Her wet blonde hair hangs down past her shoulders and she's wearing a pair of black rimmed glasses that she didn't have on before.

She must wear contacts.

Christ, she's adorable in my clothes.

She wears those pajama pants like they were made for her.

Watching her from the kitchen, suddenly she's not Layken Hobbs, Corrigan's best friend anymore.

She's Layken Hobbs, the cutest most beautiful woman I've ever seen in my entire fucking life.

What If I See You releases March 20, 2025, and is available for preorder!

OTHER BOOKS BY SUSAN RENEE
ALL BOOKS ARE AVAILABLE IN KINDLE UNLIMITED

The Anaheim Stars Series

What if We Do: Jilted Bride

What if I Told You: Childhood Friends to Lovers

What if I Knew You: Coach's daughter

What If I See You: Accidental Marriage (March 2025)

The Red Tails Hockey Series

Off Your Game Angry Meet Cute

Unfair Game Strangers/Roommates to lovers

Beyond the Game One Night Stand/Surprise Pregnancy

Forbidden Game Teammate/Best Friend's Sister

Saving the Game Fake Relatonship

Bonus Game Single Dad/Nanny

The Bardstown Series

(Prequel) I LOVED YOU THEN: Second Chance at love

I LIKE ME BETTER: Enemies to Lovers/workplace

YOU ARE THE REASON: Second Chance

BEAUTIFUL CRAZY: Friends to Lovers

TAKE YOU HOME: Boss's Daughter

The Camel Club Series

Smooch: One Night Stand/Strangers to Lovers

KEEP IN TOUCH WITH ME!

Click to join Susan Renee's Newsletter!

Join Susan's Sweet-Tarts Facebook Reader Group!

ABOUT THE AUTHOR

International bestselling author, Susan Renee, wants to live in a world where paint doesn't smell, book boyfriends are real, and everything is covered in glitter. An indie romance author, Susan has written about everything from tacos to tow-trucks, loves writing romantic comedies but also enjoys creating an emotional angsty story from time to time. She lives in Ohio with her husband, kids, three dogs and a cat. Susan holds a Bachelor and Masters Degree in Music Education and a self-awarded Doctorate in Sass and Sarcasm. She enjoys laughing at memes, speaking in GIFs and spending an entire day jumping down the TikTok rabbit hole. When she's not writing or playing the role of Mom, her favorite activity is doing the Care Bear stare with her closest friends.

Made in the USA
Columbia, SC
24 February 2025

54352178R00178